THE KENSEI

R0061551719

01/2012

W9-AMO-053

PALM BEACH COUNTY
LIBRARY SYSTEM
3650 Summit Boulevard
West Palm Beach, FL 33406-4198

Also by Jon F. Merz

The Fixer
The Invoker
The Destructor
The Syndicate

THE KENSEI

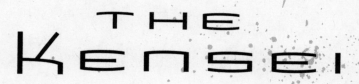

A Lawson Vampire Novel

JON F. MERZ

St. Martin's Griffin ❧ New York

This is a work of fiction. All of the characters, organizations, and events portrayed in this novel are either products of the author's imagination or are used fictitiously.

THE KENSEI. Copyright © 2011 by Jon F. Merz. All rights reserved. Printed in the United States of America. For information, address St. Martin's Press, 175 Fifth Avenue, New York, N.Y. 10010.

www.stmartins.com

Library of Congress Cataloging-in-Publication Data

Merz, Jon F.
   The Kensei : a Lawson vampire novel / Jon F. Merz.
      p. cm.
   ISBN 978-0-312-66223-3
   1. Vampires—Fiction.   2. Yakuza—Fiction.   3. Japan—Fiction.
I. Title.
   PS3613.E7885K46 2011
   813'.6—dc22

                                                2010037786

First Edition: January 2011

10 9 8 7 6 5 4 3 2 1

For all the Lawson fans
who have waited for his resurrection
with patience, good cheer, and everlasting friendship

THE KENSEI

CHAPTER ONE

"Welcome to Japan, Mr. Lawson."

No accent. There never was. And despite the fact there's no *l* sound in his native tongue, the immigration official pronounced my name like he'd been born to say it.

I took my passport back, bowed once, and thanked him before moving down the escalator to the baggage claim area. It rode smooth. They oiled them twice a day here. Below me I spotted two teams of sweepers pushing their brooms along the floors. I could eat off that floor if I wanted.

I didn't. After the fourteen-hour flight from Boston, followed by an impromptu extended layover in Manila that damn near killed me, all I wanted was my hotel. And a long, hot shower.

The thing that always impressed me about Japan was how utterly professional and polite it was. Didn't matter what the job was. Everyone took an obvious amount of pride in their work. I had a flashback to the kid who took my burger order back at Logan Airport like I'd asked him to contort into a pretzel and then beat off an elephant in his spare time.

But Boston was thousands of miles and a hundred nightmares away from where I stood now. I got through the baggage claim with no problems. Just another gaijin—Westerner—come to town to do some business and eat some noodles. Maybe take in the nightclub scene in Rappongi or set the schoolgirls on the subway giggling in their white tube socks and short skirts.

That was what they saw anyway. For me, this trip was different.

As I walked, the sheer weight of everything that had transpired in my life the past few months seemed to catch up with me. I was beat to shit. My body felt tired. My head swam with too many thoughts about conspiracies and people who would like nothing better than to see my body being used as food by a community of ravenous earthworms.

And my spirit?

That was about as down in the dumps as you could get.

I needed redemption in a big way.

I'd come to Japan looking for that. Over the years I'd found that the best way to elevate my spirit was to get involved in some physical training. The problem was I didn't always have access to the kind of training I longed for.

But here, I could have it. Tucked just north of Tokyo in a dingy little town called Noda-shi—a place that stunk like the soy sauce they brewed at the town factory—there lived a wisp of a man who could kill easier than he blinked. What he taught was about more than just killing, however. Any damned fool could do that, as I'd managed to prove so often before.

He could teach me so much more.

I caught the Keisei Limited Express train. The gleaming Keisei Skyliner sat on the next track and that ran direct to Ueno Station about twenty minutes faster and ten bucks more expensive than my train. Money wasn't an issue. But accessibility was. The Limited made a few extra stops. I always prefer having the luxury of jumping out on a platform if the need suddenly arose, as it often did in my godforsaken life.

I ducked inside the train and collapsed onto the heated seats. A pair of young twenty-something Japanese lovers with their hair colored to a bright reddish brown—what they called *chappatsu* because it resembled a dark tea color—was already fast asleep across the aisle. That's the way it worked over here. Heated seats knocked you out. I tried to fight it when I first came here years back. Now I welcomed the heat creeping up my spine like some kundalini yoga experience. God knows I could use a lot more sleep than I'd been getting lately.

My eyelids dipped on reflex, but I took a moment to study the couple. Japanese youth seemed almost too anxious to rid themselves of their natural looks. Girls dyed their hair as soon as they could. They got surgery to make their eyes look rounder and more Western. The boys spoke hip-hopese in a vain attempt to sound like they grew up in Compton rather than Shinjuku. They wore bright pink billowing parachute pants and spun on their heads at improvised break dancing sessions set up on the street. I heard more old-school rap in Japan than anywhere else in the world. Not necessarily a bad thing if you happened to appreciate the lyrical stylings of A Tribe Called Quest like I did.

Disdain between the generations existed, but only if you looked for it. On the surface, Japanese society would never tolerate open ridicule. It just didn't work that way. Face was everything over here. You didn't do anything to embarrass another person unless you'd had copious amounts of alcohol. Liquor gave you a bit of a safety buffer zone for your behavior.

Not the easiest way to live.

I could have used a buffer zone myself.

But not from anything in particular. Maybe just life.

Overhead, the conductor's voice came on. We'd be moving out of the station shortly. I found myself switching over to Japanese fairly easily. I spoke over a dozen languages and could have mastered more if I cared enough to learn them. They didn't pose much difficulty for my race. We could pretty much move around the world without trouble. It came in handy sometimes, even more for those of my race who held the job I did.

The doors chimed and started to close, but at the last second a man shoved his way on to the train car. His hair was cut extremely short. Crisp. His features were thin and narrow, but he had a lot of strength packed into his wiry frame. I could see his sternocleido-mastoid neck muscles standing out in sharp relief, the razor edge of his jawline, and the way his eyes instantly swept over the entire train car like some futuristic cyborg.

Then there were his shoes. Thin-soled rubber slip-ons.

Designed to make very little noise.

He also stood, despite there being no one else but me and the couple in the car.

And as much as I fought it, my alarm instincts started shouting at me.

A killer.

I sighed. I didn't want to deal with this right now. Not for a long time, in fact. I just wanted to relax.

I shifted in my seat and stretched my right leg out a bit to better position myself. When he came at me, I'd have to go for a kick to his knee to slow him down. I wasn't packing any weapons aside from what I could do with my bare hands. Usually, that was enough.

Then again, lately it seemed like I needed to start hauling suit-case nukes with me to take care of my ever-increasing fan club.

He didn't look at me. In fact, my movement didn't draw so much as a blink from him.

He was good.

I used my peripheral vision to take in the rest of his details. He held the pole with his left hand but kept his fingers loose and re-laxed so he could better shift with the fluctuations in the train's movements. He kept his knees bent and loose as well.

Swell.

Judging from the way he rode the train, the guy knew martial arts.

That in and of itself wasn't necessarily something unique. A lot of people in Japan studied something. Martial arts was a throwback to the warrior culture that had thrived here for centuries. The trick nowadays was reading enough about the person in question to be able to decode what type of martial art they studied.

A lot of office lackeys—the *sararimen*—took kendo. After hours spent slaving away in the corporate machinery, they put on padded armor and took turns shouting and whacking the snot out of each other with bamboo swords called *shinai*. It wasn't even close to being like real sword fighting, *kenjutsu*. But it was still considered a martial art.

Other people took aikido. In the United States, those people are easy to spot. They're usually New Age types who think that the guy who started aikido, Morihei Ueshiba, is some kind of saintly figure. In reality, the guy was a fruitcake. And like their founder, most aikidoka are fruitcakes, too. They're the ones who constantly espouse being gentle to all creatures. Go into any health food or organic store in the United States and I guarantee at least 20 percent of the clientele study aikido. And while they're being all super-duper nice and as enlightened as their tofu-laden brains will allow, someone is usually knifing the ever-loving crap out of them.

In Japan, those people are tougher to pin down. Over here there are a bunch of branches of aikido and some produce fairly good fighters. The Yoshinkan aikido guys are among the toughest.

I didn't think the guy on the train fell into either of those categories.

That left a whole bunch of other systems ranging from types of Okinawan karate to some real esoteric arts like koppojutsu and older styles of jujutsu.

That would make this guy a lot more dangerous than I felt

comfortable dealing with at the moment, considering I was supposed to be on vacation.

My best bet seemed to be to pretend I was sleeping. Lure him in. Just another stupid gaijin asleep on the train.

It was the Lawson come-hither stare. And I didn't even have to shave my legs.

I yawned again and then closed my eyes almost all the way. Over the years, I'd worked hard on perfecting the appearance of having them closed when in fact I had a sliver of space with which to see.

It worked.

He let go of the pole and started moving slowly toward me. He kept his knees low and bent, shifting in time to the train's motion so I wouldn't sense anything out of the natural rhythm.

He was good.

I saw a slim stiletto blade appear in his hand. Where the hell had that come from?

I'd heard a report a year back that this was the new way killers worked over here. They'd get close enough to stab right into the heart. A quick couple of thrusts and their victims bled out so fast they never had a chance to fight for their lives.

It took a lot of skill to get that close—to shut down the distance and get into the kill zone—without tripping any alarms on their victims.

Unfortunately for this guy, he'd picked the wrong guy to fuck with.

Worse, his knife blade wasn't going to do all that much damage to me.

His world was about to go badly wrong.

Something tickled my subconscious and I made sense of it pretty quick: if this guy was here to kill me, why hadn't he been properly briefed? Anyone who wanted me dead would know they'd have to use a wooden blade or bullet. Curse of being born a vampire instead of a human.

Maybe he just wanted my wallet.

No.

He was a professional hitter. I'd been around enough assassins to know what the good ones looked like. This guy was no street urchin.

Someone had put him onto me.

But why?

My Control, Niles, the guy who got my assignments from the Council and passed them down to me, had worked hard to keep this trip off the books. No one back home even knew I was gone. And if the Council had found out, they'd probably be relieved, given the love-hate nature of our relationship.

Niles had promised he'd run interference for the ten days I was overseas. And so far—apart from him diverting me for a quick and dirty operation in the Philippines—he'd been true to his word.

He'd seen me off at Boston's Logan Airport. "Relax, Lawson. Anything comes up, me and Arthur can handle it."

I'd seen Niles handle himself well enough back when we dealt with the crazy half-vampire–half-lycanthrope assassin, Shiva, who'd come into Boston to take out the head of the Council.

And Arthur was top-drawer stuff. A grizzled ex-Fixer from London long since supposedly retired, he handled security at the Council building on Boston's Beacon Hill. The way he wielded a pump-action shotgun, there wasn't much he couldn't take on by himself.

If things really got bad, they could always pull Wirek into the mix. As an Elder charged with preserving the ancient rites and rituals of the vampire race, Wirek had been trained in an obscure old martial art specializing in the use of a three-foot staff. He'd been indispensable in Nepal a few years back.

It felt pretty good knowing I had friends like them to take up the slack while I scored some rest for a change.

But now this.

I fought back the surge of anger at having to deal with this so soon into my vacation. Emotion was lethal in combat. I had to stay calm. This guy would smell any change.

I could feel the adrenaline dripping into my bloodstream. My heart rate kicked up some. My legs muscles spasmed a bit. I breathed deep down into my belly and fought to get control.

Despite it all, when the killer moved, I was completely surprised. Because he didn't go for me.

He went for the young kid across the aisle asleep with his girlfriend.

I responded automatically as the killer lunged. I came alive and out of my seat, aiming a kick at the underside of his knife arm.

His skill became apparent fast. Without any visible stutter, he shifted targets to handle my sudden involvement.

Dammit. Once again, I'd gotten myself into a situation that didn't concern me.

But even as the killer lunged at me, I knew that wasn't entirely true. There was no way I was going to let a murder happen in front of me on a train in Japan. Cripes, the police would haul my ass in for nonstop questioning if I'd let this guy complete his assignment.

I pivoted and chopped down on his wrist with a sword hand strike. He grunted but held onto the knife. Damn. I must be getting soft. My strikes usually knock blades out of attacker's hands.

He turned and cursed at me under his breath. *"Kuso yaro!"*

Hey, how'd he know my mom?

He kicked up, aimed at my groin. I shifted to the outside and punched down hard to the side of his thigh. He yelped and his leg went numb; it buckled underneath him as he tried to get his footing.

The couple woke up.

Perfect.

The guy scrambled away. The girl started screaming. Wonderful. Now I had a soundtrack while I worked.

Of all the train cars I could have picked, I had to choose this one. Awesome.

The killer swiped at me with the blade. It caught a piece of my jeans and sliced a slash open above the knee. He wasn't fooling around. He'd been aiming for the femoral artery. Slicing that— even on me—would cause me some serious problems.

Time to end this.

I stomped down at his arm and nailed him above the elbow. His hand jumped open and the blade skittered out, across the aisle.

The killer winced—I could tell he was close to passing out from the pain. He fought it back and got to his feet again, his right arm hanging limp and useless.

He'd earned my respect—the guy was a fighter.

He kicked, shooting his left leg out, and then tried to close with a left punch to my face. He caught a part of my chin and I saw stars. Damn, this guy could hit. There must have been a lot of banged up trees in his neighborhood because he punched like he spent hours working them over.

Lucky me.

I dropped and elbowed him in the stomach and heard his wind rush out of him. I shifted and got him between me and the couple he'd been after.

The killer's eyes widened. I could see the sweat along his hairline. I could smell what he'd had to eat. I knew he was close to losing consciousness, but he was trying to draw deep on his warrior spirit to come up with another attack.

It never happened.

Even as he started to shout and rush me, he stopped. Air flew out of his lungs, followed by a reddish pink trickle of foamy saliva from his mouth. I heard the raspy breath.

And knew even as he fell.

His own knife stuck out of his back. It had punctured his heart and right lung.

The young guy stood behind him.

Hands still shaking.

The train rolled into Jimbocho Station and the doors opened.

The young guy and his chick bolted.

Leaving yours truly and the dead killer on the train car as swarms of people started coming aboard.

Shit.

I took a last look at the killer. Something drew my eye to his wrist. It had been concealed during most of the fight but now I could see the faint black ink of a tattoo poking out from his cuff.

Oh, lovely.

The yakuza. Japanese mafia.

That was about the very last thing I needed.

Check that, the last thing I needed were a whole bunch of Japanese getting an eyeful of me standing over a corpse.

I grabbed my bag and hoofed it out of the train station, too.

The immigration official's voice echoed in my head. "Welcome to Japan, Mr. Lawson."

Yeah. No shit.

CHAPTER TWO

After nearly knocking myself unconscious due to the low overhang in the subway station not built to accommodate "giant" foreigners like me, I managed to get up to street level before the first police cars showed up. I wasn't worried about having my face captured on some type of video surveillance system because most of Japan's train stations don't have them. Something about violating a person's privacy that causes a loss of face maybe.

In this case, it sure helped me out.

I was in the middle of the Kanda district. It's known for its extensive assortment of bookstores that range from the multifloored superstore chains down to dusty old antique booksellers who stock some of the oldest books I've ever seen. I usually feed my need for old martial arts books in places like this. The last time I was here I bought two hundred bucks worth of glossy martial arts magazines, not realizing how much the things weighed in my backpack until it was too late.

Right now, I needed the bookstores to avoid the cops.

I ducked into the corner branch of the chain store and scooted up two flights to the windows overlooking the street, pretending to find fascination in the wrestling magazines stocked nearby.

The last time I'd feigned so much interest in a magazine was years ago, just before my centennial birthday. I was getting ready to meet with the members of the Council, the group of old vampires who govern my race, about the job I was going to perform for my people.

We've been around a long time.

Roughly ten thousand years ago, a branch of early humans broke away from the normal evolution track. Whereas normal early humans drank the blood of mighty animals they'd slain believing they would gain the dead creature's strength, early vampires drank the blood of other humans we'd slain thinking much the same.

The crazy thing? We were right.

I've never been a fan of what I need to drink to survive. It's just never settled with me and even calling it "drinking blood" freaks me out. I prefer to call it "juice." We get our supplies from a network of blood banks all over the world, carefully siphoned off to the community. Some of my race prefer to hunt in the vampire subculture where no one would even bother to ask questions if they got bled a little.

Over time, our bodies developed a means of distilling the life-force energy—what they call ki in Japanese, chi in Chinese, or even prana in the yogic traditions—from the blood we drank. The ingestion of this life-force energy meant we lived longer—hundreds of years—and had above-average instincts and reflexes. We can see extremely well at night. And we have incredible powers of regeneration.

Wood kills us, though. I don't quite understand how aside from the basics they taught us in school: according to a very ancient elemental theory, wood upsets the life-giving energy of earth. We're from the earth; wood therefore kills us. It's pretty tough being a kid and trying to avoid splinters.

Down on the street by the station, two city morgue employees in dark blue uniforms brought the sheet-covered body of the yakuza assassin out and loaded him into a special truck. I spotted what looked to be the homicide investigator, set off from his uniformed counterparts by the long trench coat he wore, the way he ordered the uniforms around, and the cigarette dangling out of his mouth. The antismoking campaigns hadn't reached most of Asia yet and Japan still had millions who sucked nicotine into their lungs on an hourly basis.

It didn't take them long to clear out, however. I could see the detective shaking his head as he walked back to his own car. I knew what he was thinking: no good witnesses. And Japan had enough tall foreigners running around that it would be tough to pick me out of any lineup in case anyone had eyeballed me.

The detective ran a hand over his buzz cut; he looked ex-military. The way he moved and the way the trench coat hung, he was solid muscle even though he couldn't have been much over five feet eight inches tall. With a final glance around, he ducked into his car and then drove off.

I was safe.

For right now.

The magazine felt heavy in my hands. I smirked. Same way it had felt back when I met with the Council that first time. None of us had any idea what to expect. To us, the Council was just a bunch of old fogies. But then the wait was over and I was led down a long carpeted hallway to their inner sanctum. They faced me, their faces impassive. Inscrutable.

They put me through a series of puzzles and problems that tested my reaction time to various stimuli. And after that, they sat me down at an oblong table. In front of me, there was a pile of old junk. I saw a dagger, some sort of goblet, a ceramic bull, and a bunch of other crap. They told me to root through it and see if anything appealed to me.

I found a small set of scales mixed in with the other junk. The tiny chains jingled as I picked it up. For some reason, I just liked them.

It brought a smile to their faces. It also garnered me my profession. The scales were the symbol of my new role.

We're called Fixers. Mainly because it's our job to make sure the Balance, the delicate, tenuous, and ultrasecret coexistence between the vampires and the humans, remains unbroken. Undetected. And if it gets thrown out of whack, we make it right.

Or we try to. Sometimes, trouble has a knack for not really caring about secrets or vacationing vampires looking to keep a low profile in a foreign country.

I slid the magazine back onto the rack. What the hell had I gotten myself mixed up in back there? Why would the yakuza want to murder a young couple like that? It didn't make sense.

Of course, I didn't need to keep myself involved in it any longer. I'd managed to cut the lines and damned if I wasn't going to make the most of it by getting myself to my hotel and then off for some martial arts training with the grandmaster of ninjutsu.

I hoofed it five blocks to the east to the next subway station farther up the line and hopped an express train to Kashiwa, which sat a few miles outside of the center of Tokyo.

On board the train, the schoolgirls were out in full force. They all looked like carbon copies of one another with the same reddish brown straight hair, ultra-hiked up plaid skirts and sweaters on, topped off by saddle shoes and tube socks. A lot of these girls spent their afternoons hawking their bodies to corporate lackeys who traded money for sexual favors. Dip into any phone booth in Japan and you'll find pictures and cell phone numbers for girls who'll turn a few tricks for a new Louis Vutton handbag or a couple of bucks.

Some years back, Japan lowered the age of consent to fourteen to dispel rumors that the country had a problem with pedophilia. Why bother trying to prosecute people for something they'd do anyway? It was easier and less embarrassing to simply lower the age of consent.

Unreal.

I've been around a long time and still Japan seems entirely freaky to me, especially when they pull shit like this. And don't ask about their standards for environmental pollution.

I settled into the corner of the train and tried to ignore the incessant giggling bubbling out of the gaggle of schoolgirls closest to me. They hear rumors. They see that foreigners are taller than Japanese men. That they're bigger than Japanese men. Naturally, they theorize that all parts are bigger. I don't know if they're right. I don't make a habit of checking out naked Japanese dudes.

The train rumbled down the tracks and while the schoolgirls tried to take my picture with their camera phones, I kept my eyes closed and head down. I didn't need a starring role on the gaijin Web site right now.

It didn't take long to reach Kashiwa and as soon as the doors opened, I was out of there. I took the stairs going up from the train platform. Being six feet tall in America isn't unique by any means. Plenty of men are taller than I am.

In Japan? I'm some kind of mutated giant. As I walked, a veritable sea of heads floated about six inches below my eye level. It's always weird walking through the crowds. You draw stares. Sometimes a lot of them.

Before I went to the hotel, I had to make sure I hadn't inadvertently picked up any surveillance. That meant a trip to the Starbucks coffee shop located right outside the train station.

The place was jammed with more teen schoolgirls.

And more giggling that started reminding me of fingernails being dragged down a chalkboard.

Since I don't drink coffee, I ordered a hot chocolate and a fresh-squeezed orange juice. The girl behind the counter didn't look like the rest of her counterparts. She actually looked Japanese.

And she was beautiful.

Usually, when I speak Japanese, I get a surprised look. When I thanked her, she just smiled at me.

"You're welcome." A pause and a smile graced her face. "Lawson."

My turn to be surprised. "Excuse me?"

She nodded at a small table toward the back of the shop that was mercifully unoccupied. "Sit there."

I took my hot chocolate and orange juice and sat there with my bag nestled close by. This day wasn't shaping up well at all. In country for less than three hours and already I'd been involved in a fight, a murder, and now I had unknown locals who knew my name. Not to mention the feeding frenzy of schoolgirl lust I seemed to be causing everywhere.

Not good at all.

She came over and sat down two minutes after I'd polished off my hot chocolate. She gestured to the empty cup. "You enjoyed it?"

Her English was perfect. There didn't seem much point in speaking Japanese. I nodded. "It was great."

She frowned. "And now . . . orange juice?"

"You've never had chocolate and orange together before?"

"I don't think so."

"You're missing out on a great treat. Dark chocolate orange creams are pretty much heaven on earth." I took a sip of the fresh-squeezed orange juice. Not bad. Judging by the tanginess, it had been squeezed about two hours previously.

The Japanese woman kept looking at me. Finally, I put the cup down and looked at her. "You know my name. How?"

She smiled. *"Fyar, Chuldoc, Erim."*

"Malang, dol Hachvem." The response jumped out of me instinctively. That recognition code used by Fixers is ingrained in us all. The woman said, "Duty, Loyalty, Honor," and my response was, "Before all, the Balance." I took another sip of my juice and set the

cup back down. "Now that that's settled. How'd you know the code?"

"My name is Yuki Matsuda."

"'Snow on pine trees'?"

She nodded. "Your Japanese is excellent."

"As is your English. How'd you know the code?"

She frowned. "You're surprised that I know it?"

"Yep. Considering it's not the kind of thing a Japanese woman working at a Starbucks in Kashiwa would have a need to know."

She smiled again. Something about her eyes crinkled when she did so. I tried to keep my mind focused on the conversation.

"If I were just a Japanese woman working at a Starbucks in Kashiwa, you're right. I would have no occasion to know it. But I'm not."

"Working at Starbucks?"

She laughed. "A Japanese woman."

I raised my eyebrows. "Sure look that way to me."

"Your reputation precedes you, Lawson."

I nodded at the schoolgirls. "Yeah. I seem to get that a lot."

"I'm not talking about your abilities as a Fixer."

"You're not?"

"I'm talking about your appreciation of women."

She made it sound like some type of college art course. "I don't know what you're talking about."

"Maybe this will help: I'm the Control for this sector."

I almost snorted my orange juice, which would have been painful and annoying. Not to mention my stock with the giggling schoolgirls would have taken a nose-dive.

"Excuse me?"

"You heard me. How else would I know the appropriate code words? How else would I know how to spot you?"

"Blind luck?"

She smirked. "You don't believe that."

"Forgive me, Matsuda-san, but—"

"I'm a woman."

"Yeah."

"And the service doesn't have women in it."

"Exactly."

"Not that you know of, at least."

I looked at her and smiled. "Well, you've got me there."

She leaned back. "You're handling it better than I expected. Most Fixers would be insulted to know a Control was a woman."

I took another drag on the orange juice. "I've had plenty of preconceptions turned on their heads lately. I'm trying to reform myself."

"A wise move."

"How long have you been here?"

"Since my shift started this morning."

"That's not what I meant."

"I took over the post a month ago. I worked in Brazil previously. It was easier for me to blend in there."

I knew what she meant. Brazil had a large Japanese population. "How long have you been in the service?"

"I worked operations for twenty years starting in 1980. In 2000 I was asked to move into the Control position in Brazil. I took it."

"But now you're back here."

"It's my home, after all. The previous Control retired to New Zealand and they needed someone back here. It's better cover than you could imagine. No one suspects a woman, after all. Especially here in Japan."

"And the Starbucks gig?"

"A little extra money never hurts."

I laughed. "That's bullshit. You make plenty being a Control."

She smiled and waved my comment off. "I've been waiting for you to arrive, actually. I own this franchise, so it makes a convenient cover for me to operate out of."

"You've got your office in back?"

She nodded. "You wouldn't believe how tough it is to find office space in this town. I'm not even located in Tokyo proper, for crying out loud. Rents are atrocious even with our budgets."

"How'd you know I was coming?"

Yuki glanced around the shop. "Niles is a friend of mine."

I sighed and took another sip of orange juice. "He told me I'd be clean. Off the books. No one was supposed to know I was coming over here. Especially after that favor I did for him down south."

"He told me about your side trip to the Philippines. A little unexpected, wasn't it?"

"Just a little."

"It sounds like you did us all a favor disposing of Miranda."

"I wasn't crazy about our entire operations network being shopped around on a keychain flash memory drive."

Yuki frowned, seeing the look on my face. "You must be upset with him."

Was I? Truth was, Niles was about as good a replacement Control as any I'd had. Not that I'd had a lot, but after my earlier Control, McKinley, had turned out to be a traitorous scumbag, I'd been wary of getting a new one. But Niles had proven himself. "He must have felt he had good reason for letting you know I'd be coming here."

She shrugged. "Concern for a friend?"

"Concern?"

"I think he's worried about you, Lawson."

"Yeah, well, the last few months have been a nonstop shredder. I guess I've been feeling a little burned-out." The amount of orange juice in my cup was rapidly dwindling. I tossed around the idea of getting some more.

"I think he also wanted someone to keep an eye on you while you were here."

"He doesn't think I can take care of myself?"

She laughed again. "Believe me, Lawson, he knows you can take care of yourself. And I've seen enough operational files on you to know the same. That's not the point. He wants someone on your shadow to make sure nothing bad happens to you over here."

"Like what?"

Yuki eyed me. "You tell me."

"What's that supposed to mean?"

"There's a news report about a murder near Kanda not two hours ago."

"You think it has something to do with this tired Fixer?"

"I think that would have been the train you'd be on if you came into the country on time."

I smiled. "I could have taken the express."

"No." Yuki shook her head. "You wouldn't have risked being locked onto a train with only two stops. You would have chosen the other option. And that stops right near the heart of Kanda."

"Maybe. Or maybe I was able to shirk my instincts today."

"Are you going to continuously beat around the bush with me?" Yuki looked around the Starbucks again without seeming to. She had the nonchalance of a seasoned professional and I liked that. "Because we can continue this some other time if that's the case."

"Sorry, I've been trying to adapt to the Japanese mind-set."

She frowned. "We're not dealing with that right now. We're in vampire mind-set, so don't forget it."

"All right then. I was on that train. A guy came on and I thought he was on to me. I intercepted him when he attacked a young couple. Couldn't have been more than twenty years old, either of them. I had the situation under control until the guy stabbed the assassin in the back. Punctured his lung by the sound of it. He was dead. The couple vanished. I ran for it."

"No sense sticking around for the police."

"Exactly."

Yuki leaned forward and I caught a whiff of a delicate jasmine scent coming from her. She smelled good. "Tell me about the assassin."

I took another sip of orange juice. "He was yakuza."

"You're sure?"

"Tattoo creeping out of his sleeve. Yeah, I'm pretty sure."

"That's unfortunate." Yuki leaned back and frowned.

I shrugged. "Not really. As far as they know, the couple foiled the attack. I don't have to worry about being involved in it. There was no surveillance in the station. Witnesses were haphazard."

She nodded. "Japanese aren't used to deaths on their subways."

"Yeah."

"You want me to look into it?"

I shook my head. "Up to you. I don't see much need for it, though. Personally, I just want to grab a quick nap and then head to some training."

She smiled. "You're going to Noda-shi?"

I looked at her. "You know everything about me?"

"Almost."

"What's missing?"

She smiled again. "A few things. But there will be time enough to fill in those blanks when I see you again."

"And when's that going to be?"

She smiled and gave a wave with one hand. "Go get your nap, Lawson. Then train with your sensei. I'll be here—if you're so inclined—when you get back."

I was being dismissed. I stood and hefted my bag. "Well, it's nice meeting you, anyway."

Yuki's eyes crinkled again. "Even if it was a surprise to you?"

I shrugged. "Sometimes I actually happen to like surprises."

CHAPTER THREE

The room at the Kashiwa Plaza Hotel was just as I remembered it.

Small.

Walk in, hang your coat, and take your shoes off. To the left, there was a step-up bathroom that consisted of a toilet and a deep bathtub—again not exactly made for anyone large. Beyond that, a small bureau that I never used—I just kept my stuff in my bag. And then the bed itself that was only slightly larger than a twin bed.

On top of the bureau/desk sat a television set with a receptacle for coins.

Slot machine porn.

Throw a hundred-yen piece—about a buck—into the slot and you got five minutes worth of porn. Presumably, it never took anyone longer than five minutes to masturbate and reach orgasm.

Presumably.

If it did, it was going to cost them extra. Inefficient slowpokes that they were.

I sat on the bed and thought about taking a nap. I was tired. The jet lag never really affected me much coming over from Boston. It was the return trip that nailed me for a good week sometimes.

Fourteen-hour time zone slips are rough on the old body. Especially one as old as mine was getting. But I wasn't coming over from Boston the way I thought, and the side step to the tropics had worn me out a lot.

A shower might have been good, too, but again, I didn't really have time. I broke down my luggage and took out the backpack I carry for short trips. Into that I stuffed my training uniform.

Time to go.

The walk back to Kashiwa Station only took three minutes. One of the signs for the Tobu-Noda subway line was flashing. The train was almost ready to pull out.

I needed to be on it.

I dropped down the stairs, passing slower moving travelers on the way. Japan's nice about stuff like that. If you don't want to hustle your ass around, stay to the right on the stairs and let everyone pass you on the left. The same idea used to hold true for U.S. highways, but apparently that was a relic now, too.

I slid into the local train just before the doors slapped shut. Even though it was going on seven o'clock, the train was still packed with commuters and schoolgirls. I'd be standing for the trip.

The Tobu-Noda line took us out of the metropolitan Tokyo outskirts pretty quick. We lurched through the countryside. It's always easy to tell when you're getting out of the city in Japan. Subway station signs are usually written in English letters and hiragana in the heart of Tokyo. But the farther out you get, the signs go back to the Japanese kanji characters they borrowed from the Chinese language over a thousand years ago.

The subway signs were getting old.

After three stops, the train began to clear out. I slid into a seat and glanced around the train. I didn't think anyone would be interested in me.

And then I spotted another foreigner sitting in the next car.

That didn't necessarily mean anything, either.

Especially considering where I was headed.

I've studied a lot of fighting systems in my years on this planet. When I went through my Fixer training, they'd supposedly distilled all the fighting systems down into a set of comprehensive yet simple moves that anyone could master.

I later found out that believing there was never anything else to learn about fighting set me up for a lot of disappointment when it came to surviving hostile situations. Sometimes, near-death experiences have a neat way of providing some new perspectives.

So I went back to studying various systems on my own time.

Most of them suck.

Some were conceived thousands of years ago but have lost their edge. Other styles were literally drafted on the back of a restaurant napkin.

And I'm supposed to trust my life to that?

After a lot of research, I decided to look into ninjutsu, but not that silly Hollywood movie crap. The real thing.

As a system of martial arts, ninjutsu incorporates every aspect of personal survival ranging from the kicking and punching to the joint locks, throws, grappling, and weapons work that other styles shy away from. Intermixed with that is an incredible system of strategy and personal awareness that is unrivaled.

Needless to say, I dig it.

During the 1980s, the world outside of Japan experienced what martial arts folks commonly refer to as the "ninja boom." The veil of secrecy that the traditions had been shrouded in for more than a millennium was lifted and the system gained international notoriety.

That wasn't necessarily a good thing in my book.

The art tends to attract two types of people: those who are sincere and train their butts off without ever thinking they are masters of anything.

Then there are those who study for a few months, go to Japan and get some ridiculous high rank, and think they are the next coming of the ninjutsu messiah.

The grandmaster, being the ninja that he is, cares little if people only want rank. He happily gives it to them. And these deluded fools go around thinking they are gifted. They're not. The grandmaster is simply giving them what they want. It's a funny thing. I don't always agree with it because of the incredible numbers of idiots who now purport to be high-ranked ninjutsu teachers without the depth of experience and know-how to back it up.

But that's the way it is.

When the secrecy vanished, foreigners came over to Japan by the literal planeload. Some of them were honest and trained hard. Others only wanted rank. And still others are such utter failures at living their lives in their home country, they end up staying in Japan and eking out some pitiful living while they attend classes at the main dojo.

I knew of one moron who made his living as a street clown over here, for crying out loud. He used to wear expensive suits and looked like an absolute idiot.

Good to see that he really embodied the principle of keeping a low profile.

So the other gaijin on the train with me was probably headed the same place as I was: Hombu dojo for Friday night training at eight o'clock.

The wisdom of training so soon after traveling all day, getting into a fight, witnessing a murder, and then meeting the first female Control in the Fixer service—as far as I knew of—was very much debatable.

Truth was, I was exhausted.

But I was also here to train and rejuvenate my spirit.

The hell with sleep. As one of my old instructors once said, I could sleep when I was dead.

The train shambled into Noda-shi Station and stopped. The

gaijin on the other car stood at the same time I did. He had a backpack, too.

The locals in Noda-shi get a kick out of all the foreigners that come to this sleepy little town. Before they found out the last true ninja was living a few doors down, the only source of excitement was the Kikkoman soy sauce company located nearby.

I couldn't recall the last time soy sauce got me excited.

I walked down the platform and crossed the tracks. Running alongside the tracks was a narrow parking lot full of bicycles and mopeds. It was a shortcut to the dojo and you had to thread your way through it or risk some massive dominolike catastrophe that would send the bikes spilling all over the place.

Farther on, you walked by the swampish fetid-smelling reedy grass, crossed another street, and then down at the end of a one-way street in a small one-level building, you came to the dojo.

The lights were already on, the soft glow pushing into the night outside. I walked up the steps and slid back the shoji door.

Jesus.

The place was packed.

The dojo itself is maybe forty feet by thirty feet. There were probably eighty people packed into the space. I caught a smattering of several languages but the one that overpowered the rest was Spanish.

I sighed. A lot of dojos around the world sponsor these megatrips where a bunch of students come over with their teacher and train for a week or more. I guessed the dojo from the Canary Islands had a junket over here this time.

I changed into my uniform in the anteroom, which meant my butt was hanging out by the door. Beggars can't be choosers. Amid the sea of shoes, I managed to climb into my uniform and wrap my black belt around my waist. I nudged through several other folks and squeezed into a small space halfway down the right side of the dojo to stretch out.

At precisely eight o'clock I looked up and noticed that the grand-master had already made his entrance. No one really noticed him doing so. He glanced around with the same wide smile he always wore. A quick wave here, a pointed finger there was really as far as he went to saying hello.

But having him recognize me wasn't what I was there for.

I just wanted to train.

"You American?"

I looked up. The foreigner from the train. He had sandy hair and a freckled face that reminded me of Howdy Doody. I nodded.

"Name's Lawson."

"Henry. You got a training partner for tonight?"

"Nope."

"Me neither. You mind?"

I scooted over and made some room for him. He squatted down and began rotating his ankles. I took a deep breath. It felt good to be back here again. The last time I'd been fortunate to train in Japan, this dojo hadn't even been built yet. The grandmaster used to teach at the dojo of his senior students or over at the Ayase Budokan. These days, he still held class at Ayase, but this Hombu dojo was where he taught most often.

The clock high up on the wall gonged and someone clapped their hands.

Line up.

Traditionally, you're supposed to line up behind the grandmaster with the seniormost person seated on his far right and ranks in descending order go from there back and down.

It never works that way. Especially with eighty people vying for their place in line. It always amused me to see idiots who'd been training for a few years nudge out senior Japanese teachers who'd been training for upwards of forty years.

Pathetic.

Still, the Japanese didn't let it bother them, at least outwardly. I resolved not to let it get to me, either.

The grandmaster entwined his fingers into some of the esoteric Buddhist mudra and recited a quiet mantra only he could hear. His deep voice suddenly rumbled out, *"Shikin haramitsu daikomyo!"* Roughly translated, it meant that in everything we go through there exists the possibility of finding the one thing that will lead to our enlightenment.

We all repeated it, clapped twice, bowed, clapped again, bowed again, and then waited for the grandmaster to turn around. When he did, we bowed and said, *"Onegai shimasu."* It was a simple phrase that asked him to give us his teaching.

Then it was on.

Henry and I moved back and to the right as the grandmaster demonstrated defenses against weapons using a small dull-edged tool known as a kunai. The overriding principle was an idea of *juppo sessho* or ten-directional awareness. As usual, there were too many levels to the lesson to count.

The physical wasn't as important as understanding the underlying principles behind the movement and the mental and spiritual side of fighting they encompassed.

Henry was a fairly decent practitioner. He was confident enough in his own ability, but not stupid enough to believe he knew everything. Instead of either of us correcting the other, we simply tried to absorb as much as we could and continue from there. I was glad that Henry could take a throw and give me a little of the energy I needed to get the most out of my training.

Throughout the next two hours, we bent, twisted, locked, and grappled in every conceivable position. I was enjoying myself immensely, but somehow I couldn't shake this feeling of some type of impending doom.

I looked up a few times and noticed the grandmaster looking in my direction.

I thought nothing of it. He'd seen me before. Probably he was just looking around at everyone.

The clock gonged again at ten o'clock and we all sat down. Class was over. I was spent. My chest rose and fell a bit faster than normal. My training gi was soaked with sweat and I felt the healthy glow of post-workout happiness descend.

But only a little bit.

The grandmaster smiled and retrieved a bamboo sword from along the weapons racks at the back of the dojo.

"Godan test."

Henry winked at me. "Wish me luck."

I grinned. "Good luck." I scurried back with the other students who had either already passed it or hadn't taken the test yet. I was officially ranked at sandan—my third degree black belt—and was looking at another couple of years until I got my fourth degree black belt. After that, I'd start worrying about the test Henry was about to go through.

Along with Henry, about thirty guys from Spain all lined up with him. The grandmaster's face dropped when he saw the number of people waiting. It would be a long night for him as well.

The godan test is one of those weird things that is really tough to explain.

The premise is simple. The student kneels in seiza—sitting on his heels with his legs tucked under him—with his back to the grandmaster. The student closes his eyes and waits. The grandmaster stands behind him with the bamboo sword raised overhead. The grandmaster then focuses his intention to the point that he unloads the sword directly at the back of the student's head. The student is supposed to be able to feel that deadly intention and roll out of the way before he gets hit in the head with the sword.

That's the test.

It's fast. Over in the blink of an eye. You either have it or you don't.

The first of the Spanish contingent went up. His body was all jumpy.

Whack!

"No."

He was dismissed. Good thing the grandmaster used a bamboo sword. In the old days, they used a live blade and if you failed the test, you were dead.

Literally.

One by one, the entire Spanish contingent went up and all of them failed. Then it was Henry's turn.

I could see how nervous he was. He seemed like a nice enough guy. I wished him well mentally.

He sat down and closed his eyes.

Whack!

"No."

Henry got himself out of there, a dejected look plastered across his face.

"Anyone else?"

The grandmaster looked around the room. I did, too.

"You."

I looked back. The grandmaster's eyes were focused on mine.

I could have shaken my head no. It wouldn't have mattered. When the thirty-fourth grandmaster of ninjutsu tells you that you are going to take a test, you don't argue with the man.

My stomach suddenly hurt a helluva lot.

He nodded and gestured for me to come up.

My knees felt like rubber as I walked to the center of the room. I knelt down and closed my eyes. A million images rushed at me. I couldn't calm down. After everything I'd been through that day, it all seemed to catch up with me just then. My body shifted and bounced around. I could feel all the smallest muscles vibrating like they'd been touched with a live electrical wire. I felt like a dead frog in some high school biology class having its limbs torched for fun.

I thought I felt something.

I rolled.

Came up and opened my eyes.

The grandmaster hadn't even swung the sword yet.

"Come back."

I went back to my position and sat there. I closed my eyes again.

The grandmaster spoke from behind me. Was he addressing the entire class or just me? "You must give up to succeed."

What did that mean? Was I supposed to sacrifice myself somehow? But how?

I could feel my heart thundering in my chest. My breathing was coming too fast. Even with all my training, I couldn't seem to calm myself down—

Whack!

Sound had vanished in that brief black hole vacuum. I heard the grandmaster's voice. "No."

And in that split second of time, my day went from bad to worse.

CHAPTER FOUR

I'd never felt so self-conscious in my whole life. Despite the fact that everyone had failed the test that night, it felt like everyone was looking at me while I scrambled to get dressed and get the hell out of there. I was the solo guy, after all. I hadn't come over with a big group of fellow practitioners. As an unknown variable, I probably attracted more attention. And the last thing I wanted was to talk to anyone about my failure.

Over the years that I'd been training in ninjutsu, I'd spoken to other people who had passed the godan test and asked them what they'd felt. How had they known it was time to move?

People who have seen the test done but not gone through it themselves, or even outsiders who don't understand the background of the test, have a tendency to write the entire thing off as just some big joke. That it's just a game of chance with little to offer the practitioner. Smoke and mirrors, some of them say.

Nothing could be further from the truth.

The test itself isn't about acquiring some mystical power. It's about reawakening an instinct we all already possess, but one that has lain dormant for years and years to the point where most of us don't even know it exists. I knew of times in my own life where something had made me stop a split second before I would have walked into an ambush. That was the instinct I was trying to re-awaken.

I slipped my shoes on and stepped outside. The air in Noda that night bit especially cold. A slight rain was falling.

Perfect.

In the dim glow of bar signs that bled neon into the misty night, I walked back past the fetid reeds, snaked my way down through the bicycle labyrinth, and then back to Noda-shi Station itself. All the while, I tried to keep my disappointment from bubbling out of me in a sob fest.

Training meant the world to me. This stuff had saved my life countless times and perfection of my technique through tests for the body, mind, and spirit were what I enjoyed.

What had happened back there that hadn't enabled me to pass the test?

I slid the hundred and sixty yen into the ticket vendor and grabbed the tiny slip before passing it into the ticket turnstile. The gates opened and I climbed the steps, walked over to the other side, and stopped by a vending machine to slip some coins into it.

I was damned thirsty. A tiny can of Pepsi jetted out into my hand and I cracked it and sucked it down.

But that didn't do a thing to slake my thirst.

I needed juice.

I sighed and slumped onto the bench.

"Well, that sucked wet farts out of dead pigeons."

I glanced up. Henry.

He stood there, eyes wet, but not from the rain. For a brief moment, I felt jealous that he could allow himself to cry over the matter. My own emotions were still battling it out.

He slumped down next to me and toasted me with a can of beer that he'd gotten from another vending machine.

"To us."

I nodded. "The failures."

Henry sighed and downed the remainder of his Asahi before belching. "That didn't go as I'd planned it."

"At least you knew you were taking it."

He belched around the corner of the beer can. "Aren't you supposed to be taking it anyway? You're a black belt."

"Sandan. Still got a ways to go," I said.

Henry shrugged. "I'm just a first degree myself."

I sighed. Ranking in ninjutsu was a mess. Years back, no one would have dreamed of trying for their fifth degree unless they were a fourth. Nowadays, people just didn't seem to care any longer. "How long have you been studying?"

"Ten years. You?"

I looked at him. Ten years was a decent amount of time. And I'd seen enough of his skill during class to know that Henry might have been a first degree black belt on paper, but in reality he was operating at a higher level. Maybe he'd been orphaned—his teacher had moved on and he was by himself now. That would explain a lot. "About twelve years."

"Shit!"

I sipped the Pepsi. "Yeah."

"He really seemed like he wanted you to take the test, too."

"I guess."

Henry tossed his can into the recycle bin. "You coming back on Sunday to take it again?"

"I don't know." And the truth was, I didn't. I hadn't come to Japan to take the test. I'd come here to rest. To get some time to myself. Maybe to rediscover who I was. God knew that last year or so had been one hell ride after another back home in Boston. I was spent. Used and abused.

And frankly, I was damned tired of it all.

"I'll be back on Sunday," said Henry. "One of these times, I've got to make it. Just a matter of chance I guess."

I looked at him. "You honestly believe that it's just chance that gets you through that?"

"Nah."

"Leave that thought to the losers. It's not chance at all and you and I both know it."

Henry didn't say anything for a moment. Then he belched again. "I tried hearing the sword come at me—"

"No way, it's moving too fast. By the time you think you hear it, you're already hit. There's no way you can try to listen for the right time to move."

Henry frowned. "Yeah. Dammit. You're right. So what does that leave us with?"

I tried to smile. "I don't know."

The train rolled in. We got on and sat down in the car. There were only a few other passengers riding back in to Tokyo. "How far are you going?"

"Ueno. My girlfriend lives around there. I'll crash at her place for tonight and head home tomorrow. What about you?"

"Kashiwa. I'm only here for ten days or so, I guess."

"Vacation, huh?"

"Supposed to be."

"Well, if you're here on Sunday, maybe we can work out again. I had a good time training with you. You aren't like some of the other jamooks that live here."

"I'd say the same about you."

We were silent the rest of the ride to Kashiwa. As we rolled into the bright station, I stood and shook hands with Henry. "See you when I see you."

"You bet."

The doors slid open and I stepped out on to the platform. Another cold breeze swept in and ruffled my coat. I shivered slightly and suddenly everything caught up with me—the long flight, the training, and the heavy burden of not passing my godan test. All of it seemed to drop onto my shoulders. I wanted to collapse to the ground and curl up into a ball like some frightened little kid.

Maybe I should have just stayed home.

I climbed the steps leading out of the station. At the top, I stepped outside and stood near the railing. The rain had stopped now. All around Kashiwa Station, the bright blue and red neon on the department store buildings and other high-rises blasted at you a million different pitches for a million different things. Japan at night. It could be beautiful or it could make you feel like more of an outsider than you'd ever felt before.

Across the plaza, the light for the Starbucks was still on. I wondered how late Yuki kept the place open. I wondered if a hot chocolate and a fresh-squeezed orange juice would make me feel better.

Probably not.

I wandered back to my hotel and slid the piece of paper with my room number written on it across the counter at the sleepy-eyed desk clerk. He gave me my key and took the elevator up to the third floor. Rumor has it that after the majority of foreign tourists kept losing their keys, the hotel took to this practice so they could save some coin. To me, it still felt like I was asking for permission to go out and do something when I was a teenager.

The elevator doors slid open. I banked a left and then another left down a carpeted corridor to my room.

I slid the key into the lock and turned it.

My door opened from inside.

"Hi, Lawson."

My jaw must have dropped, because she smiled. "Wow, the genuine look of surprise. I don't know if that makes you look attractive or not."

"Jesus Christ."

Talya.

She stepped back and let me into the tiny room. "Not exactly. I'm a bit better looking, if I do say so myself."

"How the hell did you get in here?"

She eyed me. "You think they make locks any better in Japan than they do anywhere else?"

"Apparently not."

She came to me then and kissed me. Long. Hard. Her lips felt great on mine. I pushed back into her. How long had it been since we'd been this way? The last time she came to town following my run-in with Shiva, she'd only been able to stay for a day before she had to jet off to Mexico on some executive protection assignment.

Before she'd gone freelance, Talya had worked for the KGB, handling their most covert assignments. Usually this entailed Talya going it alone in order to take down a target. She'd seen action everywhere, from the hellish mountains of Afghanistan to the jungles of Borneo. She was probably the best human operative I'd ever had the pleasure of working with. When we first met, I knew instinctively that I was going to fall in love with her. And that was strictly forbidden in vampire society. Sex, yes. Love, no way.

I didn't care. She didn't care. But the Council found out and told me if I didn't end it, I'd be on the receiving end of my very own sanction.

So I lied.

Ever since, we'd kept our rendezvous on the down low. A brief encounter here and there, when we could both manage one around our busy schedules. If Talya's skills had been in high demand prior to the fall of the Soviet Union, she was even more in demand now that that cold war was over.

She was always on the go. Not that I expected her to slow down for me. But in the last couple of years since we'd met, our get-togethers always seemed to be some happenstance thing that popped up when they popped up. I wished we could have had some predictability to our encounters.

She stepped away from me. "Glad to see me?"

"Absolutely. I was afraid you hadn't gotten my message."

"My answering service needs an upgrade. Besides, I was away on an errand."

"Who for?"

Her eyes narrowed. "We swapping trade secrets now?"

"Not unless you want to." I sat down on the edge of the bed and rummaged through my luggage.

"What are you looking for?"

I glanced up. "I'm hungry, sweetheart. I haven't had anything all day."

"Well, we can go out for dinner, Lawson. This is Japan, after all. And it's only going on eleven thirty. I know a place around the corner that serves chicken knuckles and beer until three in the morning."

"Sounds great, but I've got to have something a little more . . . specialized first."

"Specialized—?" She stopped and her eyes grew wider. "Oh. That."

I nodded. "Yeah."

She shook her head. "Sorry. It's just that sometimes I find myself thinking that you really are human."

"Well, I'm not."

She frowned. "I know that, Lawson."

I glanced at her, aware that had sounded a lot sharper than I'd meant it to. "Sorry. I'm tired is all. It's been one helluva bad day."

"Well, I'm here now. So you can forget all the rest of that shit and concentrate on me."

I dug the small vials of juice out of my bag. "I've got to drink this."

"Go ahead."

"You sure you want to watch?"

"Why wouldn't I?"

"Because I don't think it ranks as one of the most appealing spectacles you've probably seen before."

"Just get it done already and then we'll go out."

I downed the juice and felt it hit me a moment later, spreading warmth into my system as the life-force energy slid into my body. I sighed and lowered the vial from my lips.

Talya's eyes stayed on me and I could see the concern in them. "Are you all right?"

"Yeah. Just tired."

"Come on, get ready. Let's go out."

I looked up at her and tried to smile. "I'd actually rather stay in. I'm dead tired."

Talya frowned. "Lawson, I haven't eaten anything in some hours myself. And I really want to go out. Why are you so down all of a sudden?"

"Because I spent a long time getting here, then I got into a fight on the subway en route to my hotel, then I went and trained tonight and failed a very important test, and now I got the shock of my life by you showing up here and nearly scaring the shit out of me."

I took a breath. What the hell? Why had I just snapped like that?

Talya didn't looked pleased. "I see."

I stood up. "Forget it, listen, I'm sorry. It's just that—"

"I know. I know. You had a bad day." She brushed past me. "I guess I sort of expected a little different reception from you is all."

"What kind of reception?"

"Oh, I don't know. Maybe the overjoyed-as-all-hell. Maybe the I'll-do-anything-you-want-to-just-because-I-love-you-to-death-and-want-nothing-more-than-to-see-you-happy reception. That would have been nice, too."

"Talya, I am happy to see you."

She looked at me. "I'm sorry you had a bad day."

I shook my head. "Forget it. Seriously. It doesn't matter now."

"Apparently it does."

"Talya, you're overreacting."

"Am I?"

"Yes. You are."

She nodded. "And you're not."

"Maybe I am, too."

"Maybe?"

"All right, I am. Fine. Whatever. Can we just go out and have a good time tonight?"

Talya sighed and then started for the door. "I don't think so, Lawson. I suddenly lost my appetite. And somehow, I don't think it's going to come back any time soon with you around."

She slammed the door to my room, leaving me standing there with an empty vial in one hand and an empty heart in the other.

If there's one thing life has managed to teach me it's that things are never bad enough that they can't suddenly get a whole lot worse.

CHAPTER FIVE

I'd been in Japan less than twenty-four hours and managed to make my life back in Boston look like heaven served up with a side of fresh-squeezed orange juice next to the hell I'd cooked up for myself here.

It was past midnight when I threw the covers off and decided that sleep had turned its back on me as well. I shucked on some clothes and slid out of the hotel past the dozing desk clerk.

The cold night air hugged the steel skyscrapers and gray concrete buildings all around Kashiwa. Street sweepers siphoned the trash out of the gutter and left the asphalt slick in their wake. I passed an alley and saw a couple of foreigners puking into the sewer grates—probably drank too much at the sushi joints down the street.

Classy.

I'd gotten drunk in Japan once before. The fifteen-minute walk from the bar back to the hotel took about three hours and at one point, I sat in someone's flower bed for a rest. Real estate is treasured in Japan and I felt pretty bad the next day when I woke up. I'd ruined someone's obvious slice of heaven thanks to my over-indulging. I left an envelope full of money on the doorstep of the home and quietly made a resolution never to allow myself to get so blitzed ever again. Getting smashed is okay in the privacy of your own home, but in a foreign country, it's never recommended.

At least for me.

The escalators leading into Kashiwa Station still ran even this late at night. I didn't feel like taking the steps two at a time like I normally did. Truth was, I didn't feel much like doing anything.

At the top, I leaned over the railing and studied the muted cityscape for answers.

I wasn't sure what questions I was even asking.

I just wanted to feel like my life was right.

I walked slowly. Now that the trains had stopped running, there weren't any people in the station thoroughfare. Even the various oddballs I'd seen earlier—the break-dancers practicing their moves to Eric B. and Rakim, Tupac, and Public Enemy, and the Mohawk-wearing protesters screaming about the United States getting bogged down in Iraq—were long gone.

Only the dull hum of a bustling metropolis remained.

Across the plaza, Yuki's Starbucks sign had gone dull green as well. Closed.

Was she still there?

She mentioned earlier that she used it as her base of operations, so I guess it made good sense. But if she was asleep, I'd be disturbing her by knocking on the glass.

I sighed.

Talya.

She'd certainly surprised me by showing up unannounced. And like a perfect ass-clown, I'd driven her away because I was too concerned with my own failure to celebrate the simple fact that she was here.

Here.

It seemed odd to me that she'd even gotten my message. I tried for weeks to get in touch with her prior to leaving Boston. I hadn't heard a thing. But I guessed that was just the way she operated. Talya hadn't gotten to be the professional hitter that she was by leaving her calling card every place she went. Predictability meant death.

She was anything but predictable.

And I managed to screw that up.

I didn't even know where she was staying. How the hell was I going to get in touch with her now? I needed to apologize. I needed to make her understand that it was my fault I'd screwed everything up.

My reflection stared back at me from a grimy puddle of water and I tried to grin. *Lawson, you are one sad fool.*

Maybe it was time to retire.

I smirked. How often had I said that? Truth was, evil seemed to be everywhere. Vampires seemed to be getting tired of their secret existence and every month I had another nutjob with delusions of grandeur ready to announce our presence with billboards and TV commercials.

And then there was the unresolved business with the conspiracy that had brought me up close with the Syndicate, an organized crime family in New York intent on unleashing a new designer drug that I'd put a stop to. Then the humans at the airport—conspiracy freaks who somehow knew about my race. That was a loose thread I still had to run down.

Too many bad guys.

Not enough heroes.

Every time I closed my eyes, I was back in New York. Back dealing with the aftermath of putting down the Syndicate. There'd been collateral damage. Teresa, my cousin's roommate, got caught up in the mess and I couldn't save her in time. I could still feel her hand go cold in my own. I could still see the fear in her eyes as she succumbed to death. I'd put her in harm's way and she'd paid the ultimate price for my carelessness.

I owed it to her to at least see the bad guys pay for what they did.

"It's late, Lawson-san."

I turned.

Yuki.

I tried to smirk but the gesture felt as hollow as it must have looked. "Just taking a walk."

She smiled. "There's nothing 'just' about your walk. You've been ambling around the plaza here for the last thirty minutes."

"Couldn't sleep."

"That much is obvious."

I smiled. Yuki wouldn't come right out and say anything directly. Or would she? Most Japanese would go at their conversations obliquely. If I kept dancing around the issue, she'd either get frustrated or allow me to fester in my inner turmoil.

"How did the training go?"

I shrugged. "The training went well."

"But—"

I looked at her. "You won't stop until you find out, will you?"

"Niles-san asked me to keep an eye on you. I am concerned for your well-being. If that means I must ask difficult questions, then I must resign myself to that fate."

"I took a test after the class. I failed it."

Yuki's eyes grew wide. "A test of unarmed combat? I find that hard to believe for someone like you."

"It wasn't a test like that. I mean it was. But it wasn't. Related, yeah. But not mano a mano. You understand?"

"Not really." Her smile was patient. Like she knew that I'd spill my guts to her if she merely hung around long enough. Sometimes I find people like that rather insufferable. Tonight, I wasn't sure what I was feeling.

"It was an important test."

"I'm sure it was. All tests are."

"Yeah, but this was really important."

She cocked her head. "Is it possible you built up your own expectations as to what this test entailed? Only to find it did not meet those expectations?"

"What do you mean?"

"Sometimes we put our intention into things that should be allowed to remain as they are. A test is simply that: a test. It does not determine the outcome of the universe. The universe doesn't care. This test is simply that. But rather than see things for the simplicity of what they are, we sometimes turn them into that which they are not. We mutate them into the unconquerable burdens that then weigh us down. We falter. Our confidence suffers. We fail."

A breeze blew over us as we stood there. "You're saying I should have simply enjoyed the test for what it was rather than what I thought it would be?"

She smiled. "Maybe. I don't know what the test was. But if I was taking it, I would choose to view it as only that which it is rather than that which it is not."

"You're starting to sound like a fortune cookie."

Yuki smiled. "Even a fortune cookie can be right sometimes, Lawson-san."

"True enough."

"You want some coffee?"

I shook my head. "I don't want to trouble you."

"Forget for a moment that I am Japanese, will you? It's no bother. Besides, I usually have a cup this late myself. Especially if I've been up working."

I glanced around. "How'd you know I was out here anyway?"

Yuki grinned. "I have video surveillance of this area. It feeds into my office. Very useful for keeping an eye on things."

"And you saw me out here walking around." I looked around for the video cameras, but knew I wouldn't be able to see them. They'd be too well-hidden.

"Looking like a puppy who'd lost his way, yes."

I glanced back at Yuki. "I look like a puppy?"

"Well, you did." She winked. "Now I am not so sure."

I smiled. "Thanks for the advice."

"It's only advice if you choose to use it. Right now, they are only words floating around in the night air."

"You're something of a poet, aren't you?"

"I'm something of everything." She nodded toward the Starbucks. "Come on. It's growing cold out here."

"I don't drink coffee, though."

"I know that. It was a colloquialism only."

Inside the Starbucks, I pulled a tall stool up to the counter while Yuki got me a hot chocolate. I waited until she'd made herself a latte and then joined me at the counter before taking a sip.

She held up her cup. *"Kampai."*

"Gassho."

We drank and I sighed. The heat of the hot chocolate spread throughout my body, followed by a snap of sudden adrenaline. I leaned back and exhaled. I felt great. It reminded me of another time when I'd been far from home and how energized I'd suddenly felt after eating a slice of specially made bread. I smiled at her.

"Special ingredient?"

She blushed. "My version of a hot toddy, I suppose. Yes, there's blood in it. I keep a private stock for myself. I've found it mixes well with the coffee."

"You can add hot chocolate to the list as well. It's fantastic."

"Now don't you come in here and order that every day, freaking out my poor girls. They'd be beside themselves having to deal with such an attractive man who drinks blood."

"I thought I looked like a puppy."

Yuki smiled and ignored me while she drank her coffee.

"Not to worry." I took another drag on the hot chocolate.

Yuki put her cup down. I could read concern etched into her face.

"Something wrong?"

She sighed. "I'd hoped to keep this strictly friendly tonight, Lawson. After all, you do look deeply troubled over this test of yours."

"But?"

She winced. "But I'm afraid we have some business to discuss."

I shook my head, the frown already creasing my face. "Forgive me, Yuki-san, but I'm not here for business. I'm here to recoup my strength."

She nodded. "The man on the train. The one you saw killed today."

"What about him?"

"You said he was yakuza."

"Had the tattoo, yes." What was she getting at?

"You don't recall the design of the tattoo, do you?"

"No. What difference does that make?"

She shrugged. "Sometimes no difference at all. But some of the *gumi*—the gangs—make a point to use tattoos to differentiate themselves. It's their calling card, so to speak."

"Okay."

"I pulled some strings in the police department. I got a look at the tattoo." She reached over the counter, pulled a photograph back and slid it over to me. In the black-and-white picture, I could see the hand outstretched. An intricate design featuring a tidal wave eclipsing a samurai warrior spun its way down the length of the arm.

"Nice work." I handed it back to her and took another sip of my drink. "I don't go in much for body art, though."

"I didn't show you that for an art appraisal. That design means nothing to the police. It doesn't show up on their yakuza database. None of the *gumi* use that design."

"But you know something about it."

"*So desu.* It is the calling card of a man the Council once believed was dead."

I put my hot chocolate down. "One of us?"

"Yes."

"But I saw this guy die like nothing. He wasn't one of our kind."

"The man behind this design employs humans. His version of Loyalists, I suppose. The *teppo*—the bullet—you attacked on the train—"

I held up my hand. "Hey, he was coming for me first."

She smiled but it looked pained. "Regardless, he was acting on the orders of the vampire who employed him."

"But why the young couple? What had they done to warrant a sanction?"

"I don't know."

I sipped some more hot chocolate. "Tell me about the man behind this."

"I don't know his name. No one does. He goes by one title only. That is the only way we've known of him since he first appeared on the scene almost twenty years ago."

"He's been around that long?"

"We believed—that is, the Council believed—that he died about ten years back. That was the official story, anyway."

I'd seen enough of the Council's assessments to know that they could be trusted about as much as some of the political machinations coming out of Washington, D.C., these days. That is to say, they couldn't be. I thought back to Cosgrove and Shiva.

Cosgrove had been my oldest enemy and I'd warned the Council about him numerous times. They'd dismissed my concerns until he came back to Boston and started leaving a trail of bodies around town.

And Shiva had been dismissed as a low-level threat as well when she'd been anything but low level. If I hadn't stopped her, things would have gone from bad to worse, real quick.

"All right. So this guy is still around then. And he's involved in what happened on the subway earlier." I still couldn't see why this had anything to do with me.

"Yes."

"And you're concerned."

"I am concerned because he is liable to be mightily pissed off, as you might say, when he finds out one of his men has been killed."

"But he won't know there's any other vampire involvement in it, would he?"

"This isn't the type of vampire to write things off to coincidence."

She was scared. I could see it now. And somehow, I'd caused her this source of fear because of my involvement.

I bowed my head. "I'm sorry to have caused you this inconvenience."

"Forget the manners, Lawson. I just want to make sure you're up to speed on what he can do. And who he is."

"What does he call himself?"

"We know him only as the Kensei."

I processed the word. "Sword saint?"

"Literally. Yes. He is said to be incredibly adept at *kenjutsu*—sword fighting."

"What ryuha does he study?" If I knew what family tradition he studied, it might give me some idea of how he would handle himself in combat.

Yuki shook her head. "Again, no one knows. But one thing is certain: if the Kensei is still alive—and it appears he is—then I am very concerned that your vacation will suffer as a result."

I looked at her as she said the next words.

"He will come to kill you, Lawson."

CHAPTER SIX

I finally managed to eke out some semblance of sleep a few hours later back at the hotel. The realization that my vacation was about to be disrupted didn't sit all that well with me. I'd been craving rest for the longest time.

And as usual, it seemed like my life wasn't my own to control.

At six the next morning, right after I'd showered, there was a knock at my door. I slid out of bed and peered through the peephole.

Oh, man.

I opened the door, praying this exchange went better than the one I'd had last night.

"Hi."

I smiled. "Hi, yourself. Come on in."

Talya slid past me and sat on the edge of the little bed. "I shouldn't be here."

"I've been thinking the same thing about myself these past few hours."

She looked at me, her eyes narrowing only slightly this time. "And I'm still pissed at you."

"Okay."

A big sigh worked its way out of her. "But I need your help."

I sat next to her. "You're in trouble?" She raised her eyebrows. I shrugged. "Hey, happens to the best of us sometimes."

Talya shook her head. "Not to me it doesn't."

I wasn't going to argue the point. "What do you need help with?"

"Finding someone."

"And you think I can help with that?" I frowned. "Talya, I'm not exactly the best choice for scouring Japan. I don't blend in very well here. I'd think you'd have a better shot at that since you've got some Asian blood in your veins."

She sighed. "To the Japanese, I'm as much an outsider as you are. Worse, I'm a woman."

"Come on, you don't still think Japan's a backward society, do you?"

Talya laughed. "Oh no, of course not." But the sarcasm was evident in her voice. She knew that women were still regarded as lesser beings here.

I ran a hand through my hair. "Where'd you stay last night?"

She smiled a little bit more. "Upstairs."

"Upstairs?"

"I got a room."

"You could have come back."

"Would you have wanted me to?"

I thought for a second. "Yes. I was going nuts wondering where you'd gone off to."

"That didn't stop you from taking a walk last night over to the plaza. A late-night rendezvous?"

"What? No." She must have followed me without me picking it up. "Wait—you mean Yuki?"

Talya's eyebrows shot up. "Oh, is that her name?"

I held up my hands. "Talya, relax. She's one of my kind. She's the local Control."

Talya's eyebrows jumped again. "I thought you told me there weren't any women in your service."

"Yeah, well, as far as I knew, there weren't. Turns out I was wrong. I stand corrected. She's one of the few."

"Tough spot to operate in, too."

"I'm guessing the Starbucks helps establish her front a little bit more."

Talya's piercing look stabbed at me. "You're sure she's not your type?"

I smiled. Sure, Yuki was a good-looking woman. But she was a vampire. And for some reason, with one notable and painful exception, I've never been able to get close to a female vampire since. It was probably just my own emotional baggage cluttering my preference, but nobody's perfect.

I cleared my throat. "You're my type, Talya."

"You mean that?"

"Absolutely." I took a deep breath and bridged the gap between us. I pressed my lips into hers and felt her press back. My heart jumped inside my chest. I felt Talya's arms around me, pulling me back down into the bed.

I don't know where her clothes disappeared to, but in no time they were off and we were rolling around like two animals desperate to rut. Our moans seemed suspended in the air.

And then we found each other. Locked together, we twisted in the sheets, grinding our skin together, fusing our bodies into one.

All that time we'd been apart, all the longing and desire that had built up, it rolled over us like a tidal surge, pulling us back down into each other's lust. We crashed time and time again until we lay there nestled together. Totally spent.

"And here I was thinking that I'd gotten just enough sleep," I said.

Talya laughed. "I was thinking the same."

I stretched my arms overhead. "Now I need another nap."

She rolled off of me and sat on the edge of the bed again. "I meant what I said earlier."

"About my help?"

"Yeah."

I rolled on to my side and propped myself up on one hand. "You want to tell me about it?"

Her eyes seemed sad. "It feels like it's been years since we saw each other last, Lawson. Years. You know?"

"It's been a while."

"Since that crummy one-day visit back in Boston."

I tried to lighten the mood. "Beggars can't be choosers."

She frowned. "It ought to be easier than this. It ought to be, but I know it can't be. You'd think loyalty and honor would count for something in this world. Do your service and at least get some reward for it."

"Loyalty and honor aren't necessarily the best choices of description for the Council. In their eyes, we're breaking a mighty big law."

Talya's face darkened as she stood. "I know the arrangement." She pulled on her panties and bra. Both of them were white lace and satin. I ran my fingers over the fabric on her backside, enjoying how smooth it felt to my touch. How her skin glistened under the satin material.

"I see you remembered."

She smiled. "Not that you noticed when we were busy getting naked."

"I was a little busy fighting off your attempted tonsillectomy."

She stood there clad in her underwear looking down at me. "Always the funny guy, aren't you?"

"Best way I know how to combat all the stress in my life."

"I used to wonder if I had any joy left in my own life." She leaned into me and kissed me again. "I figured out that you are the only source of happiness for me, Lawson. I don't like being away from you."

"I don't like it, either."

Her eyes were inches from mine. "Let's kill the Council and re-write the laws."

"Okay."

"I'm being serious."

I pulled back and away. "I'm not sure I'm being entirely face-tious myself."

She looked at me and then sighed. "Let's get breakfast."

I got dressed. "The restaurant downstairs is a smoking café. If it's all the same with you I'd rather not have to inhale a chimney full of smoke with my eggs."

"McDonald's?"

There were two in Kashiwa. Both of them had nonsmoking sec-tions. "Yeah. May as well. I can get orange juice there, too."

She pulled on her pants. "You and your orange juice."

"Well, it keeps me healthy."

Talya laughed again. "You don't get sick, silly."

"Well, not physically. But I feel like hell whenever you're not around." I wrapped my arms around her waist. "God I missed you."

She turned and looked up into my eyes. "I missed you, too. But we need to eat. And talk."

Kashiwa Station was alive with early morning commuters rush-ing to squeeze their way into the trains and ride into Tokyo central. Talya and I bypassed them and the gaggles of giggling schoolgirls as we rode the escalator back down to the street level. We walked across the street and past the enclosed marketplace where the Inter-net café sat halfway down.

We both chose the second McDonald's automatically. You or-dered outside on the street and then climbed to the second floor to find seating in the nonsmoking section. The benefit was that you could observe most of the main street from any seat on that floor.

Old habits die hard.

Talya started into a hash brown and said nothing for a moment while I sipped my orange juice.

Finally, she looked at me. "I came here to see you."

"I know. And it's wonderful."

She shook her head. "But I'm not being totally honest with you. I came here for another reason, too."

"For help. It's okay." I bit into the Egg McMuffin. They tasted the same anywhere in the world.

She looked at me. "Have you heard of organ trafficking?"

"Vaguely. A couple of urban legends about people passing out at parties and waking up in bathtubs full of ice cubes missing a kidney or something like that."

Talya shook her head. "Those are just simple tales. I'm talking about serious human organ harvesting here. Not just piecemeal shit."

This didn't sound like the kind of action Talya normally got herself mixed up with. "How did you get involved in this?"

She smiled. "It's not professional, if that's what you're asking."

"I guess I am."

"Would you believe I've got a soft spot for kids?"

I kept working on my sandwich. "Sure. Why not?"

"It sort of goes against the whole tough-girl killer image I've been trying to cultivate over the years."

I smirked. "Your secret's safe with me."

Talya paused. "I sponsor kids, Lawson."

"Sponsor?"

"You know those commercials on TV? The ones that hit you up for money by showing these awful films of children living in squalor?"

"Yeah, they usually come on when I'm eating."

"Exactly."

"You're doing that?"

She smiled. "I was taking care of some business in Detroit. I was eating in my hotel room and saw the commercials. But rather than get involved through the mail, I actually went to Africa and found myself a village. Lots of the most beautiful kids in the world. All of them full of life and vibrancy. I donated gobs of money to help get the village up to a good standard of living. It's where I've been spending a lot of my free time these past few years."

"I wondered about that tan of yours. You didn't seem to be the sun-worshipping type."

She smiled. "I don't know, maybe it's my biological clock telling me it's time to have children of my own. I don't know. I haven't thought it all the way through yet. But something really made me want to get involved with those kids."

"I think that's wonderful."

"So did I."

"Something happened to change your mind?"

She took out a picture and slid it across the table to me. I nearly choked on my juice. "Jesus Christ."

The grainy photo showed what I guessed was once the body of a child. But only the skin and bones remained. In fact, it looked almost like it had been completely gutted. All of the organs were gone. Like someone had just torn them out and left the husk behind for dead.

When I looked up again, Talya had tears rolling down her face. She dabbed her cheeks with a napkin. "Look at me, crying like some little girl. I'm sorry. It's just that I knew that boy."

"Don't apologize for feeling some emotion, Talya." I glanced at the picture again and felt the anger welling up in me as well. "Who did this? And why would they do it?"

Talya sniffed and sipped her coffee. "I haven't exactly figured out everything just yet."

"But you've got something? Some type of lead?"

"There's a market for human organs in Asia and Russia. I ran down all the major buyers in my old homeland and came up with a trail that brought me here. Don't mistake me, when you contacted me and suggested we meet up, I was all for it. But I also knew I'd be coming here anyway. I've been to all the other hot spots for organ trafficking: Hong Kong, Shanghai, and Kuala Lumpur. None of those places led me where I needed to go."

"The trail leads here."

"Yes. And as much as I hate to involve you in my work, I feel like I won't have any chance of finding a way to stop this horror unless you help me."

I took her hand. "You know I'll help you. No question about it."

She smiled. "Thank you."

"No thanks necessary. I'm glad to help if I can. But I think I should tell you that we aren't liable to get very far unless we get some help from a local."

Talya's eyes narrowed. Like many other covert operative professionals, she equated getting more people involved with operational security risks. I couldn't blame her.

But I also knew my own limitations. And while I could shake all the trees I wanted to back home, this was a foreign country and my luck would run out pretty fast. Despite speaking fluent Japanese, I was under no false illusions about my own chances of finding clues here.

No. We'd need help.

"You have someone in mind?"

I finished my juice. "Yeah, I think you'll like her."

And I was sure she would. All I had to do was make sure Yuki didn't freak out when I brought a human around to her store. Otherwise, I'd have a Council sanction slapped down on me faster than I could blink.

And that wouldn't be any fun at all.

CHAPTER SEVEN

After we finished eating at the McDonald's, we hoofed it back up the escalator to the raised plaza. When we reached the top, Talya glanced around and saw where we were headed and raised an eyebrow.

"Starbucks? This is your big and mighty ally that will help us out?"

"What? You got a better idea?"

"Not yet." She smirked. "I must admit I hadn't considered a corporate sponsorship as a means of stopping child organ theft."

"Funny." I nudged her in the ribs. "I've gotten help from a lot less likely places than this in my time," I said. "And besides, they know what I like here."

"I'll bet."

I grinned. "What's that supposed to mean?"

Talya stopped me. "Lawson, I'm part Asian, remember? I know you've got some sort of thing for Asian women."

I shook my head. "Not really. I happen to think of myself as a fine purveyor of women no matter what their skin color. Provided they happen to be beautiful, I could care less where they're from." I spread my arms. "They all find a home within my libido."

Talya's eyebrows jumped. "Really."

"Sure."

"A three-armed Venusian with five breasts?"

"Bring it on."

Talya smiled. "You would, too. Wouldn't you?"

"Well, someone has to have the experience. You know, for posterity and all that."

She smirked. "You're a slut."

I grabbed my chest. "I prefer the term 'manho.'"

Talya punched my arm. "Let's get some coffee or whatever it is you like to drink here."

It was my turn to stop her. "We get in there, you think I'm human, got it? No vampire stuff."

Talya frowned. "I'm a little beyond Tradecraft 101, sweetheart."

"Just checking."

Inside, there weren't as many schoolgirls as there were in the afternoon and evening. Thank God. There's really only so much giggling and inane commentary I can stand before I flip out.

But what the place lacked in schoolgirls, it made up for in busy commuters stopping by on their way to work for a quick jolt of caffeine.

I went to the counter and ordered for Talya and me. I also asked if Yuki was around. The counter girl bowed once and vanished into the back office.

Yuki emerged a moment later and smiled when she saw me. "*Ohayo gozaimasu.*"

I bowed once. "*Ohayo.*"

Yuki came around the counter quickly, but stopped short upon seeing Talya sitting near the window, looking out on the plaza. She stuck with Japanese. "Who is she?"

"A friend."

Yuki's eyes narrowed. "What sort of friend?"

"Someone I owe my life to. And no, she doesn't know what I am. As far as she's concerned, we're all humans, okay?"

"Is that so?" Yuki busied herself with wiping down a nearby counter. "Why is she here?"

"She needs some help."

Yuki looked at me. "She calling in a marker?"

"Yeah. You could say that."

"And you brought her here?"

"Yuki-san, she asked for my help, but this isn't my playing field. There's not much help I could give her, you understand? I'm out of my operational depth here."

Yuki paused and then sighed. "So, you're asking for a favor, too."

I gave a very slight bow to show how serious I was. "I would owe you, yes."

She shook her head. "Lawson, enough with the *giri* bullshit, okay? I don't really go in for that all that much if I can possibly avoid it. I'll do you a solid; it's no sweat. But only if I can do it without compromising our security."

"I wouldn't ask for anything else."

Talya stood as we approached and bowed lower than Yuki, showing an extended amount of respect. When Talya came back up, she smiled and said, *"Namae wa Talya de gozaimasu. Dozo yoroshiku."*

I could see Yuki was mildly impressed. She bowed in return. *"Hajememashite."* She smiled at Talya. "But since I'm quite at ease using English, we can dispense with Japanese. Especially if we're discussing things best not overheard by too many people." She winked. "I do appreciate your consideration in using my native tongue, however. Thank you."

Talya smiled at her and it was warm enough. "If what Lawson says is true—and I have every reason to believe it is—I shall be the one thanking you before too long."

"We'll see," said Yuki. "What can I do for you?"

I listened without really listening as Talya outlined the reason she was in Japan. Truth was, my mind was wandering. I was thinking about the godan test. A lot. Tomorrow was Sunday and there was early morning training. That would mean another opportunity to take the test over again if I wanted to.

To be honest, I wasn't so sure what I wanted.

It was tough trying to explain it even to myself. I hadn't much thought about the test prior to coming here. I'd come here because it felt like the right thing to do at the time. I was spent and burned-out and in the past, Japan has been a place where I can recover my soul and feel better about stuff. I can return home with a fresh mind and a clean heart. Plus, there's nothing like being away to make you appreciate what you left behind—even if it's a city filled with rogues and scumbags.

But now that I'd actually sat down and tested, part of me felt like it was some sort of challenge that I had to meet again and overcome. If overcoming was the proper way to even look at it.

I didn't know.

What I did know was that I still felt like shit for not passing it on the first try last night.

I'd heard other people talk about it in the past. Some of them had failed it numerous times. They'd consoled themselves by barking about how it must have been some sort of guessing game and that sooner or later they'd get it right and guess correctly.

I didn't buy it.

The godan test had been used for more than a thousand years to determine if a student was ready for advanced training in the art. It wasn't something to be taken lightly. And as far as I was concerned, only a damned fool would ever think it was a guessing game.

"How does that sound, Lawson?"

I snapped back to reality. "Sorry?"

Talya sighed. "You see? Just like him to fall asleep when we're talking about important matters here."

Yuki eyed me. "You're still thinking about your test, Lawson-san."

"Yeah."

Yuki looked at me like I was a small child who had misbehaved. "The more you think about it, the more it will become that which it is not. You will know when the time is right to take it again. Don't force the issue."

"I'm trying not to." It would be a losing battle trying to explain what I was feeling to anyone who hadn't taken the test.

Yuki nodded at Talya. "From what she tells me, there is only one man who can be responsible for the organ trafficking that has apparently grown to epidemic proportions."

At least we'd have a lead to go on. "And that would be?"

Yuki smiled but there was no joy in it. "The same man I have warned you about. The Kensei."

Oh.

Nifty.

I sighed. "So it seems we have a common enemy."

"Apparently." Yuki sipped some coffee that the counter girl had brought over. "I am not yet through running down possible leads for you, Lawson. But I expect I will be by this evening. Would you both like to stop by then?"

I glanced at Talya who shrugged. I nodded at Yuki. "That would be great. Are you sure that's enough time?"

Yuki frowned. "Lawson, I run a pretty tight ship around these parts. I'm expecting information from a good source of mine. I have used him for years and he's never failed me. Some young DJ who spins hip-hop and rap down in Rappongi at a place called Tony Tony's."

"Catchy."

Yuki shrugged. "Makes no difference to me as long as his information is good."

"And it is?" I glanced around Yuki's shop. I wondered what people would think if they knew what we were discussing.

"Grade A. Top-level intel. He's cheap, too, which is always nice. Means I can keep my expense reports down." She smiled at Talya and me.

"Always a good thing."

Yuki smiled. "Well, our bosses seem to think so."

Talya seemed to be happy about the possible lead. "How does this man get in touch with you?"

"Mao?" Yuki shrugged. "He swings by on his way to downtown."

I smiled. "His name's Mao?"

"Sure. What the hell. Gives him a street cred I guess. You know Japanese kids; they all have to have some crazy hook to their name. Helps differentiate them from the rest of this homogenized cesspool."

I cocked an eyebrow. "Are you waxing philosophical on me, Yuki?"

"Who, me? Nah." She sipped her coffee. "I'm happy toeing the company line, you know that."

I grinned. "Well, we'll check back later then."

Talya and I stood up. Yuki watched us. "You going anywhere special?"

"Maybe down to Ueno," I said. "I haven't seen the Meiji Shrine in a while. Be a nice way to spend the day. Just relaxing."

Yuki nodded. "You do that. And try not think about what you'll be thinking about all day long."

"Thanks." But I think we both knew that wasn't going to be easy.

Talya nudged me and we left the Starbucks. As we walked, I could feel Yuki's eyes on us the entire time. I hoped we'd passed the masquerade off well.

"You think she bought it?" Talya's voice wasn't that loud. She might have suspected that Yuki would have the entire area wired for video and possibly even sound.

I kept us walking back toward the train station. "We did the best we could, right?"

"Yes."

"Well, then I hope she did. Otherwise there'll be one helluva bad surprise waiting for us when we come back here tonight." I sighed. Hiding the fact that Talya and I were together was becoming irksome to me. I wasn't all that certain how much longer I felt like putting up with it.

"She seems nice, though."

"Yeah, she is." I shrugged. "I haven't seen her in an operational capacity yet, so I can't comment on how cool she is under pressure."

"You told her about your test, though?"

"Yep. She saw me out walking last night. She's got this whole area wired for video surveillance. She sees everything."

"You sure she hasn't got audio, though?"

"I doubt that very much. Look." I pointed and on cue the giant video billboard came to life with thundering music and an obnoxious speaker hawking all sorts of electronic junk and sports tickets.

I glanced at Talya. "You listened to that all day and it'd drive you nuts."

"She could filter it out. They got this new device on the market that can separate audio signals into various different channels so—"

"I'm not concerned, Talya."

"Okay."

Inside the station, we bought our tickets at the vending machines. The annoying thing about Japan was that you could leave your hotel with a bankroll of paper money and after a day of riding all over town on a gazillion trains, you'd come home with pockets filled with twenty pounds of metal coins from all the ticket machines.

It really sucked.

I checked the schedule and saw we had about one minute before an express train left the station. We hustled down the stairs and jumped onto the green JR train moments before the doors slid shut and the train shot out of the station, accelerating as it raced down the track.

The seats were warm. Talya was warm, too, as she leaned against me. I pressed back into her. It felt good being over here with the woman I loved riding next to me.

Weird how things work out sometimes.

I just hoped Yuki didn't suspect anything.

As the homes raced by the window, I thought about what she'd said.

The Kensei.

Who was this guy? And what was he doing trafficking organs on one hand and looking to kill a young couple on the train on the other? And why did he use human assassins to do his dirty work for him?

It didn't make sense.

In fact, it made about as much sense as the godan test had made last night.

That fact didn't leave me feeling very cheery.

I wasn't even all that happy when Talya looked up from my shoulder, kissed me lightly on the cheek, and whispered, "I love you."

Well, that cheered me up a little.

CHAPTER EIGHT

Just outside of Harajuku Station on the Yamanote Line, the Meiji Shrine sits as testament to the great achievements of the Emperor Meiji. One of the tallest *torii*—gates—in Japan stands near the entrance. It's made of *hinoki* cypress wood that is more than 1,700 years old. That was almost as old as my good friend Wirek back home, even though I felt sure he'd debate that with me. Being an Elder, Wirek's life span was a good deal longer than mine due to the ancient rituals they go through. I've never understood it, but then again, I've never really asked about it, either.

We passed under the gate that stood almost forty feet high and kept walking along the gravel pathway. All around us, thick stands of tall bamboo and pines leaned in, lending their shade. Our feet crunched the gravel as we walked. Early tomorrow morning, the monks who manned the shrine would be out to rake it carefully again.

I was a little surprised there weren't many tourists here today.

The sun shone overhead, casting warm beams down on our skin and I almost forgot about everything else as I walked along the path with Talya on my arm.

How would it be to live a life like this all the time? To never have to worry about righting the wrongs? To not have to be one of the few who stood up to the onslaught of evil—to have to shoulder all the burden?

Could I get used to it?

And what about Talya? She looked serene and lovely. Her hair framed her eyes just right and I thought myself the luckiest guy around.

We drew close to the cluster of temples. To the right, I could see a traditional wedding party getting ready to have their ceremony performed by a Shinto priest. The bride was dressed in an elegant white bridal kimono, called a *shiro-maku,* offset by bright red borders.

The Shinto priest moved them all over and began to recite his prayers. I tugged Talya along. It would have been rude to stay and watch something that was of no concern to us.

Talya pointed at a board by the big temple. "Why are all of those wooden plackets hanging from there?"

"They're called 'ema.' You write a prayer on them and hang them from the board. The priests collect them and then burn them. Supposedly, your wish will come true."

Talya had a mischievous look in her eye. "I think I might try that."

I smiled. "You're kidding."

She looked at me. "I'm not silly enough to think I can do it all by myself." Her eyes narrowed. "What about you, Superman?"

She had a fair point. We bought the blank wooden plackets. Talya produced a thick black marker from her purse and proceeded to write her wish down on the board. She handed me the marker and then went to hang it on the board.

I stared at the blank wood for a moment. What was it that I wanted? What did I need to pray for? I'd always been one of those guys who didn't think I deserved it if I couldn't get it based on my own hard work.

But lately . . .

I took the marker and wrote my wish down on it. I felt a bit odd as the words seemed to jump out of me and onto the small piece of wood. I looked at what I'd written when I finished and exhaled.

"You done?"

I held the wood out to her. "A good friend of mine used to have a cool philosophy."

"What's that?"

"In the spirit of full disclosure."

Talya's eyes never left mine. "No secrets."

"Yeah."

She glanced down at the placket but didn't take it. "You need to hang that on the board now. Otherwise, it won't come true."

"I suppose it wouldn't." Still, it felt unreasonably heavy in my hand. Almost as if I didn't want to hang it there. Or it didn't want to be hung.

She pointed. "You really want it to come true?"

"I think maybe I do. I wasn't sure when I started. But then it just sort of came out of me."

"I guess that's a good thing."

I watched her for a second. "You didn't read it."

She smiled. "No."

"You don't want to?"

Talya turned back and studied the Shinto wedding party. "I don't need to, Lawson."

I walked to the board, moved a few of the other plackets aside and placed mine behind them. For some reason, while I hadn't minded Talya seeing it, I didn't want it being seen by anyone else.

Talya moved off to the left side of the temples, exploring the side buildings devoted to lesser gods and goddesses. Japan's religions have always been an interesting mix. At their core, Shinto is a nature-based religion focusing on gods and goddesses connected with nature and the environment. Then there are Buddhist influences as well. Zen mixes into it. Esoteric mind sciences also have their place in the pantheon of belief systems.

Talya took a long breath. "The air's so incredible here. It's tough to believe we're actually in the middle of one of the most heavily polluted cities in the world."

A fresh breeze blew over us. I almost shivered. "All the trees. They clean the air."

Talya sighed. "I wish they could clean my soul."

I looked at her. "You've had a rough spell of late, haven't you?"

"Rougher than I ever dreamed it would get."

"Sounds like we're two of a kind, sweetheart."

She looked at me and smiled again. I could never get tired of that. "Why else do you think I'm with you?"

I shrugged. "I thought my magnificent butt might have had something to do with it."

"It might have . . . last night."

I put a hand to my chest. "You're making me feel so . . . cheap."

Her smile dipped at the edges. "I came here to track down this man who traffics in organs. I came here to see you. But I think I'm here to recharge my batteries. Sounds weird, doesn't it? I've been here before and never felt like this. What's different this time that I should feel so at ease and at peace here?"

I shrugged and slid a grin across my face. "Could be the company you keep."

"Maybe." She leaned in and kissed me. "You saw that couple getting married back there?"

"I saw it."

"She looked beautiful." Talya sighed. "You ever think about that?"

"About brides? Sure, I got a thing for chicks in wedding dresses."

She smacked my arm. "About getting married, silly."

I looked at her. "You know, when I met you three years ago,

I never ever would have figured that I'd someday be standing in Tokyo surrounded by holy temples and discussing marriage with a former Soviet assassin."

"Well, I never thought I'd ever fall in love with a vampire."

"Touché."

"You didn't answer the question, Lawson."

I could hear the crows in the trees now. We must have been disturbing them. Their raucous caterwauls lit up the afternoon air and shattered the relative peace and quiet.

I took another breath and sighed. "It's a weird concept for me, I guess. I mean, marriage? I'm a Fixer."

"Well, maybe you won't be a Fixer forever."

"Yeah, someone'll probably shoot me dead first."

Talya sighed. "You've got a real talent for spoiling the mood, pal. I don't like thinking about you dying."

"If it makes you feel any better, neither do I."

She leaned against the wooden walls and crossed her arms. "I mean, I know what we are. What we both get ourselves into. This trip is a perfect example of that."

"How do you mean?"

"You ever notice how things just seem to happen to us? You came here to escape work for a while and then I show up and dump a heap of shit in your lap."

"Well, I sort of stepped into some five minutes out of the airport. So, you didn't ruin anything for me. Hell, you made it worthwhile."

"Yeah, but—" She stopped. "You don't get it?"

"I'm trying."

"What we do, what we are, it just seems like bad stuff follows us. You ever think that standing up for what's right—that being soldiers of good—makes us a magnet for the bad and evil forces at work in our world?"

"'Soldiers of good.' I like that."

"Lawson . . ."

"Sorry." I looked around. I could barely hear myself over the cawing crows. "I guess so. The problem with things these days is that being good is too difficult. People want to take the easy way out. They avoid conflict because society's programmed them to ignore it, to turn the other cheek. But then there's that saying, you know?"

"What saying?"

"All it takes for evil to triumph is for good men to do nothing."

Talya nodded. "But the burden."

"I know. You stand up to someone and you become a target. Other people think less of you for fighting for what's right. For calling people on their bullshit. For stopping the tide of evil. It's not an easy job. But someone's got to do it."

Talya frowned. "Yeah, well, I'm not so sure I want to do it anymore."

"You serious?"

"Look at me. I'm getting older. I'm tired. I just found out the children I've been working hard to save have been mutilated for someone else's agenda. My spirit's worn through, Lawson. Part of me thinks retiring now might just be the wise thing to do."

I looked up at the sky. "I wish I had it that easy."

"Why don't you?"

"Not the way our society works. I left a lot of loose ends after my last mission anyway. And a lot of people lost their lives. Some of them didn't deserve that."

"Collateral damage is way of life for us." She shrugged. "Just one of those things."

I shook my head. "No, it's a way of life for bombs that go rogue. It's a way of life for cowardly terrorists who don't give a rat's ass about killing innocents. But for surgical professionals like us, it's unacceptable."

Talya came close to me. "You've been hurting, too."

"Probably more than I'd care to admit."

"I think you just did."

"Yeah."

She kissed me again. And as her lips touched mine, I felt the warmth of her breath touch me, the fullness of her lips.

Everything stopped.

Even the crows.

Which is why in the next second I shoved us both to the floor even as the first bullets splintered the walls where our heads had been a moment before.

CHAPTER NINE

One of the worst things I can imagine is being in the middle of a shoot-out without a gun. Fortunately for me, because I was so stupid and hadn't asked Yuki for a firearm loaner, I didn't have to imagine it any longer.

I wasn't armed.

We rolled right, toward the doorway. Talya grimaced as some shards of splintered wood rained down on us as more gunshots exploded nearby.

She looked at me. "I'm not packing!"

That was the big problem with Japan: guns were about as illegal as they come. Getting ahold of them in the country was tough. And I hadn't even thought about acquiring any just yet. Neither, apparently, had Talya.

Could I blame it on the fact we hadn't been here long enough to think about firepower? Sure. I could.

But I didn't.

Truth was, the responsibility lay with each of us for not thinking far ahead enough. Even after I'd been warned about the Kensei, I still hadn't considered a gun. Maybe I was so used to having one on me, I simply didn't even know I was without it. That was the danger of becoming too reliant on a weapon.

For right now, the trick was to get out of this mess without getting plugged full of holes. Then we'd head back to Yuki's and see what sort of weapons she could score for us.

All the more since someone had apparently just declared open season on me.

Or Talya.

Or both of us.

"Gotta move." I tugged on her arm. "Let's go."

I could see the shooters advancing now. Three of them. Sunglasses helped to hide their faces, but they were Japanese. And they didn't look like they wanted to give us a hug.

Empty shell casings glinted in the sunlight and littered the ground as they kept up a steady rain of lead.

They were still almost a hundred feet away, coming at us across the courtyard.

Something didn't seem right.

Why had they opened fire so early? I would have waited to get closer before I let loose.

Talya ducked through the doorway. "Lawson! Come on!"

I ducked through also. More bullets slammed into the wall behind us. I could hear people screaming now. Gunfire in Japan, especially at a crowded tourist attraction like Meiji Shrine, was unheard of.

Until now.

The police would get here fast. Real fast. But I didn't particularly want to stay around. Being questioned by the cops is one of those things you just don't want to ever have to endure in a foreign country if you can possibly manage to avoid it.

And I wanted to avoid it.

We scrambled down the side path. Talya led the way. A few yards farther on, the path was deserted. People had managed to vanish in

the short space of time since the start of the unannounced fire-
works display.

Talya veered left into a thick stand of bamboo trees. "This
way."

I followed, concerned that at any moment our gun-toting posse
would come barreling around the path and make sure their bullets
found us for good. I had no way of knowing if the bullets had
wooden tips that could kill me. I had to assume they did.

Talya snaked her way through the undergrowth, and then led
us around to the right. I could hear more commotion now from
somewhere in front of us. Talya crouched down, lying in the dirt,
and put a finger to her lips. I got down next to her and tried to
quiet down the hammering heart in my chest.

Just a little bit farther, the main path must have been there. I
could hear voices now. But unlike the other voices that were loaded
with fright and concern, these voices didn't sound worried at all.

They sounded angry. As they rattled off the machine-gun Japanese, my mind translated it automatically.

"Where did they go?"

"We don't know, sir."

"They were here and then they vanished? That's impossible. I
want them found. Both of them."

"Yes, sir."

I heard the crunching away of feet on the gravel. It sounded like
they were heading back to the temples to search again. But just as
I was about to shift and relieve some of the pressure on my arms,
Talya held me down. She pointed slowly out ahead of us again and
made a single gesture.

I understood.

Someone was still out there on the path.

I made a gesture I felt sure she'd know. Should we take him out?

Talya frowned. And shook her head no.

The fact that whoever this guy was didn't seem the least bit fazed by the approaching storm of police sirens left me feeling unsettled. Anyone else would have been in a hurry to hightail it out of there.

Not this guy.

Who was he?

And why didn't he have to worry about the cops?

The gravel crunched close by again. "They have vanished, sir. We couldn't find any trace of them."

"Fools! You think this was easy to set up? You think something like this can be arranged on a whim? Are you aware of how much work went into finding them in the first place?"

"Sir—"

"Shut up. When I want you to talk, I'll order you to."

Another voice. "The police are coming, sir. We should leave now."

A long pause. And then, "Very well."

Now the gravel path erupted in noise as three sets of feet walked away. Beside me, Talya let out a long breath. I did the same. After a moment, I shifted and finally sat up, wiping bits of dirt and branches off of me.

Talya looked at me. "Who the hell was that?"

"Would it be too presumptuous to say it was most likely the Kensei we've been hearing so much about?"

"Maybe not. But somehow I didn't think he'd be the type to launch a shoot-out at a temple."

"What I don't get," I said, "is why they opened fire from such a long ways away. It was foolish on their part. Unless they were expert marksmen, there's no way they'd have hit us with pistols."

"They should have waited," said Talya with a frown.

"Exactly. Why risk alerting us like that when they could have virtually guaranteed the kill if they'd held back and gotten closer?"

"Orders?"

I frowned. "What—they were told to not kill us?"

"Only to make it look like it was a hit." Talya got into a crouch. "Wouldn't be the first time I've heard of something like that."

"But why?"

Talya shook her head. "I don't know."

I sighed. "We can't stay here."

"What do you suggest?"

I smirked. "First things first, we need some weapons. I don't want to find ourselves in a situation like that ever again without any guns to shoot back with."

"I feel like a damned amateur," said Talya. "How could I forget to get a gun, for crying out loud?"

"Maybe you were just so happy and excited about seeing me that you forgot." I smiled at her.

"You wish." She stood and brushed off the front of her jacket. "We'll have to be careful finding a way out. The cops are liable to have the entire area cordoned off."

"You know this place better than I do apparently."

She looked at me. "What do you mean?"

"How'd you know about the path in here?"

She smiled. "It's not much of a path now, is it? I just thought it made better sense to get our tails into the brush rather than stay out on the gravel path where we could be picked off."

"Good thing you did, too."

I could hear running feet now. The police had arrived.

Talya held a finger to her lips and gestured for me to follow her. We threaded our way back out onto the gravel path and then cut across the park and finally found ourselves on the outer perimeter.

Talya pointed at a police checkpoint to our right. "But farther on there's nothing. We can get out that way and make our way back to Ueno Station."

"Sounds good."

We eased ourselves over the metal barriers and then melted into the ground. We waited until the light changed and then let ourselves be carried along by the crowd crossing the street. Despite the commotion of the firefight, the rest of the populace seemed relatively oblivious and swarms of people carried us along in the tidal swells.

At Ueno we bought new tickets and then caught the train.

Once aboard, we both slumped into the seats and took a moment to catch our breath. No matter how many times I've been in combat, the adrenaline never leaves you. And the dump afterwards is always a tough thing to reconcile. It leaves you tired and worn down. There's not much you can do about it except to just let your body get it out of its system and then carry on. Looking at Talya I could tell she was going through the same thing. It doesn't necessarily take long, depending on how often it happens to you, but it can be exhausting.

The train rattled on back to Kashiwa. I didn't want to even think about spending another day in Japan without a gun.

No way.

In Kashiwa, we exited the platform and caught the escalator back up to the top of the platform. The schoolgirls were back all around us. They kept flashing Talya evil looks as if she had singlehandedly ruined their chances of bedding me. She grinned.

"You know, I don't think they like me."

"Well, you throw off the whole curve. They know they've got no shot with me when you're around."

She laughed. "Still got that silver tongue."

"I thought it was gold."

"Not always."

We stepped out into the bright sunlight of the afternoon and were immediately set upon by a megaphone-wielding woman who was loudly demonstrating the continued U.S. presence in Iraq. A few other protesters stood nearby handing out flyers. The majority of Japanese simply ignored them. Across the way, the break-dancers were spinning on their heads to something that sounded like Public Enemy. On the giant jumbotron video screen, a huge dinosaur lumbered across. A young girl hawking a new sports drink followed that image.

I took a breath. Only in Japan.

"Lawson."

"Yeah?"

Talya pointed. "Look."

She was pointing across the plaza.

At the Starbucks.

"Cops."

Lots of them, too. And they had yellow crime scene tape all over the place. I had to push through another gaggle of schoolgirls to see the twenty or so officers loitering around nearby.

"What the hell?"

And then I spotted someone I'd seen before.

Back in Kanda.

Yesterday.

The same detective type still wearing his long overcoat and smoking another cigarette. He surveyed the scene and kept glancing around as if he were waiting for something.

Or someone.

"I saw that guy yesterday."

"Which one?"

"Trench coat. He was outside the train station where I ran into that assassin. But that was Kanda. This is Kashiwa."

"You think this is outside his jurisdiction?"

I shrugged. "I don't know a damned thing about the operational areas of Tokyo's finest. He might belong here. I just think it's odd he shows up at two crime scenes within twenty-four hours of each other."

"Perhaps we should get closer. Maybe find out a little something about our unnamed police inspector."

I looked at her. "I'll do it. You watch my back. No sense both of us getting tagged if that guy gets suspicious."

Talya frowned but nodded. "All right. Watch yourself."

"You, too."

I pressed my way forward through the crowd. At the yellow tape I attempted to slide underneath. A uniformed cop held up his hand and barked at me in Japanese. I smiled and answered in Japanese as well, albeit a bit rustier than the normal fluency I have.

"Sorry. I just wanted coffee."

"No coffee. This place is closed."

The detective turned then and eyed me. He took a drag on his cigarette and then wandered over. Something about his eyes . . .

"Something we can do for you, sir?"

I pointed. "I just wanted to get some coffee. They make a good cup of it here."

He exhaled a thin stream of smoke. "You didn't see the tape?"

"I don't read Japanese."

"But you speak it."

I shrugged. "Audiotapes. They're all the rage now for learning foreign languages."

He smiled but it was forced. "Well, there's been an unfortunate incident here. I'm afraid you'll have to find someplace else to have your prized coffee." He turned and started to walk away.

"What happened inside?"

He stopped and turned back to face me. "Why?"

"Just a curious gaijin."

He smirked. "Yet another one. And I wonder why the gods see fit to keep sending me more of them to deal with."

I said nothing but waited. He kept staring at me. Finally, he took the cigarette out of his mouth and crushed it underfoot.

"There's been a shooting here. A woman's dead. The owner of this place."

I rocked back.

Yuki.

CHAPTER TEN

As much as I try to never let my emotions show themselves on my face, sometimes something hits me hard enough to rattle my cage. Hearing that Yuki was dead was one of them.

Usually, no one notices my momentary slips.

Today was a different matter.

Mr. Homicide Detective noticed.

His mouth twisted a bit as he regarded me. "Are you all right, sir?"

I recovered fast. "Huh? Oh, yeah, sure. Just odd to see a shooting over here. Japan's usually safe, you know? I'm more used to hearing about this stuff in America. You know, crime capital of the world and all."

"Indeed." He lit up another cigarette. "And where are you from exactly?"

"Boston."

He nodded. "A lovely city. I visited once when I was younger. Back before I had a job with responsibilities."

I grinned. "Those were the times."

"Indeed. And what is it you do for work, Mr. . . . ?"

"Lawson. You want to see my passport, too?"

He inhaled and smiled. "Do you have it on you?"

"Of course."

He exhaled a long thin stream of smoke into the crisp air. "In that case, no."

He seemed a bit odd. Part of me wondered why he hadn't wanted to see it. There was no mistaking the not-so-subtle interrogation he was conducting. I wondered if Talya was seeing all of this. I corrected myself. Of course she was.

"You know my name. It seems I should know yours as well."

He nodded and his hand flashed into his coat faster than I would have thought possible. When it reemerged, it held his card. He presented it with a vague bow.

"Tetsuo Nakahashi. At your service."

"Nakahashi-san—"

He held up his hand. "Please. Call me Moko. It's a helluva lot easier."

"Nice to meet you, Moko."

"And I'll call you Lawson, okay? That makes everything easier for all involved."

I nodded. "Fine with me."

"So you knew Ms. Matsuda well?" He dropped the question with as much grace as I would have expected from an obviously seasoned member of the police force.

I let the question hang there for a second. "Not well at all."

His eyes swept over mine. "You're sure about that?"

I sighed. "All right. Fine. You got me. Truth is, I've been coming here quite a bit."

"Why so?"

"For her."

"Ms. Matsuda?"

I nodded. "Yuki. Yeah. Look, I know it sounds strange. But I'm staying at a hotel close by and when I discovered there was a Starbucks here, I had to come in for a taste of home. And then I saw her."

Moko's eyes lit up. "Ah. And let me guess it was love at first sight for the adventurer from a faraway land."

"I wouldn't call it love."

Moko grinned. "Did she know?"

I laughed. "God, no. I don't think she was interested. I wasn't even sure on how to approach the situation. I'm not real good with the women."

Moko's eyes narrowed so much I thought he might have closed them. "That seems unlikely. You're a handsome enough man, Lawson."

I bowed. "Thanks, but even if that were true, it's only part of the battle. You still have to know how to talk to them."

"Well, language doesn't seem to be a problem."

"Nerves, mostly." I shrugged. "It's always been a problem for me."

He stomped the new cigarette and lifted the yellow tape. "You want to take a look?"

I frowned. "What?"

"One last time? As a courtesy to you, I could let you through."

"Are you sure?" This was weird. Why was Moko granting me access to a crime scene? Did he have suspicions about me? I made a mental note to stay alert to any signs he might be getting too close.

He seemed completely unfazed by my question. "I'm heading the investigation. I call the shots here."

I shrugged. "All right then."

I ducked under the yellow tape and Moko led me past the cordon of uniforms wearing amazed looks that a gaijin was trespassing on their crime scene. Moko barked a few commands to redirect their attention and then we were inside.

Shards of glass littered the floor. I couldn't tell if stray bullets had broken the glass or if they'd deliberately trashed the place. Moko led the way to the rear of the counter where I saw the sheet.

Yuki.

I exhaled. Moko's face wore a grim expression. "This should not have happened here."

I didn't know what to make of his comment so I said nothing. I knelt down next to the sheet and stared at it. Moko placed a hand on my shoulder.

"I'll give you a moment."

I looked up. "Why?"

"Maybe it's easier to say the things you wanted to tell her now that she's dead." He walked away before I could protest.

And in fact there was something I wanted to say to Yuki. Or, more accurately, give her.

I eased the sheet back and her face came into view. Her expression seemed serene. I eased the sheet lower. I could see the entry wound right above her heart. Whoever had shot her, they knew where to plug her. Judging by the powder burn residue on her clothes, they'd gotten fairly close before doing the deed.

Bastards.

I checked the time on the cheap watch I wore and as I did so, I pressed the side button twice. A tiny compartment sprung open and a small tablet popped into my right hand. I nudged Yuki's mouth open. Her incisors were extended, the way they do when a vampire dies. The tablet would cause them to retract and Yuki's body would resemble a normal human being.

No traces.

I pushed the tablet in under her tongue. Yuki was still fresh enough that the saliva in her mouth would break the tablet down and cause the necessary reaction.

I drew the sheet back up.

The tablet was a recent invention that we'd been issued. We were supposed to use it on ourselves if we found ourselves about to die or seconds away from death. I didn't think they'd mind me using it on Yuki.

Moko came back just then. "All finished, Lawson?"

"Yeah." I stood. "Thank you."

His eyes never left mine. "I'm glad I could help ease your pain."

"I just wish I could repay the favor for Yuki."

Moko took a breath. "Indeed."

"No leads, I assume."

Moko laughed. "I've only just arrived here. Even I take a few hours to work my miracles."

"I'm sorry."

He held up his hand again. "Forget it. I understand your anxiousness. If someone had done this to a woman I admired, I would feel the same way."

"Thank you."

"Would you like me to let you know how the investigation progresses?" His eyes betrayed no hint of whatever his intentions might have been.

"That would be wonderful."

"Where can I reach you?"

I nodded back outside. "I'm staying at the Kashiwa Plaza Hotel."

"All right. I'll leave you a message there if anything comes up. I should warn you, though, these things sometimes have no rhyme or reason." Moko frowned. "I could bore you to tears with the number of cold cases I have in my files."

I nodded. "It happens in America that way, too."

"Forgive me for saying so." Moko fixed me with another stare. "But you seem to be the type of man who has seen a lot of this before."

"A lot of what?"

"Death."

"My parents died when I was young. A break-in that went pretty horribly awry. I was sleeping over a friend's house when it happened and the next day I walked in on their bodies. Something like that, it doesn't leave you. Ever. And as much I hope to never see things like this again, it seems to find me."

"Well, here's hoping it doesn't find you that much more on your vacation in my beautiful country." He grinned. "That would not do at all."

"I agree."

"Otherwise"—Moko winked—"I'm going to be a very busy man. Good day, Lawson."

I bowed again and stepped back outside. The air bit into me again. I could see Talya hovering in the midst of a crowd several hundred meters away. I began walking back to my hotel. Talya was enough of a pro to know that she shouldn't make immediate contact with me once I'd been inside the crime scene.

And what I was hoping she'd do was hold back and see if I picked up any surveillance on the way back to the hotel. Something about Moko rubbed me as slightly suspicious. Like he might just know more than he was letting on. Or that he was just a bit too interested in me.

And things like that have a tendency to make me nervous.

I moved through the station past the ticket machines and kept walking through the concourse. Outside, instead of taking the stairs, I rode the escalator down. Might as well make it easy for them.

At the bottom, I crossed the street and stopped in the convenience store where I picked up some mango chewing gum. While I paid for it, I spotted Talya walking past the doorway, headed for the hotel.

I walked back down toward the hotel, stepped inside the main lobby, and immediately got nailed by the heavy curtain of smoke that hovered by the restaurant. I moved fast and got my key before catching the elevator.

As the doors closed, Talya stepped inside.

"Where'd you come from?"

She smiled. "Trade secret. I could tell you but then I'd have to kill you."

"Someone took out Yuki."

Talya frowned. "One of yours?"

"Near as I can tell. They knew to shoot her in the heart. Powder residue was from close up." I leaned against the back wall of the elevator. "What are we mixed up in here, Talya?"

"I don't know yet. But we'll find out. We owe Yuki that much." She pressed the third floor. "Who's your new friend?"

"Name's Moko. I'm guessing he's the homicide inspector for this neck of the woods."

She nodded. "Seemed very interested in you."

"Did I have any hangers-on when I left?"

She shook her head. "Nope. Moko came outside and watched you walk away. I can't tell whether he thinks you're holding back on him or if he's just after your ass."

"Gee, what a conundrum."

"Well, he had himself a cigarette and then went back inside. And none of his uniformed goons followed you, so I figured we were all set. You get your chewing gum?"

I grinned. "Yeah."

"You going to offer me a piece?"

"I've got one in my mouth. I'll tongue wrestle you for it when we get back to my room."

Talya shook her head. "We've been in your room all the time. You come up to my place now."

We stepped off the escalator and she led the way down the carpeted hallway. Then she opened the door to her room and we walked inside.

I took a breath. "I love what you've done with the place." It was a carbon copy of my room. Talya slid her shoes off and lay down on the bed.

"Did Yuki have any family?"

"I don't know. I'll find out. Make sure they know what a good operative she was."

Talya sighed. "I'm tired, Lawson."

"Well, these shoot-outs have a way of wearing you out."

"Not just the goons we ran into. Everything." She stretched her arms out. "Who would have thought Japan could be so dangerous?"

"Danger's everywhere. You know that."

She propped herself up on a pillow. "We could find an island somewhere in the South Pacific. We could live there and never give a damn about any of this shit ever again."

"Tempting." I lay next to her and stretched. Yuki shouldn't have been a target. But she'd been shot because of Talya. Or me. Or both. "I've got to go back there later."

"Why?"

"I've got to sanitize the place."

"There's stuff there?"

"Yeah. Video surveillance, reports, and Yuki will have some weapons there as well. I can't let Moko find that stuff. He does, and things will go south for us real fast."

She eyed me. "That's later, though, right?"

"Yeah."

She kissed me lightly. "Then we'll talk about it later."

"Okay."

Talya moved closer. "Right now . . . just hold me."

CHAPTER ELEVEN

It was midnight when I slipped out of bed and got dressed in the darkness of the room. Talya slept soundly as I finished dressing. I looked down at her and smiled. It felt damned good to have her back in my life. Where she belonged, as far as I was concerned. The hell with what the Council might think or deem appropriate.

I made the decision not to wake her. I had to go sanitize Yuki's office and make sure there was nothing left behind that could tip off any inquisitive souls about the existence of the vampire world.

I was especially concerned about Moko. Something about him today hadn't settled well with me. I felt like there was a whole other side to him that I wasn't seeing. He might have been a homicide detective, but he wasn't like any that I'd ever met before. And I knew a lot of cops.

Some folks happen to hate them. Personally, I know plenty of good ones and I've certainly met my share of bad ones. At the end of the day, they've got a job to do like anyone else. I try to keep that in mind.

Maybe I was making too much out of Moko's apparent interest. Maybe.

I went to my room and got ready. After changing clothes, I slid out of my door and took the elevator down to the first floor. The counter attendant snapped awake as I approached and I handed him my key. He scrawled the room number down on a piece of paper and handed it back to me. I pocketed the slip and walked out into the cold night air.

This time of year in Japan is normally pleasant. But the nights can still get cold. I'd dressed light for this evening's jaunt. Bulky coats can get cumbersome when you're trying to break into some place. I'd chosen black slacks, a black turtleneck, and a navy poplin jacket. I wore black sneakers on my feet. I had a balaclava in my pocket that I could slip over my face if I needed to.

I took the steps two at a time getting back up to the top of the concourse. I glanced around just to make sure Moko or anyone else hadn't set up a surveillance screen on me while I'd been asleep. I wasn't in the mood for any unexpected surprises. But after fifteen minutes of doubling and tripling back on myself, I didn't see anything that set off alarm bells.

Nothing.

That was a bit of good news.

The yellow crime scene tape still stood out like a giant wart on the concourse. Fortunately, the train station was almost deserted. The trains had just stopped running. This time of night, the only people still out were drinking at the local restaurants that stayed open later than the others.

That lessened witness reliability if anyone saw me.

I doubted they would.

I took my time maneuvering closer to the entrance to the Starbucks. I was trying to figure out how exactly I was going to get in there. The doors were motorized and slid back like you were entering the bridge of the *Starship Enterprise*.

The cops would have turned off the power hours ago.

But there had to be another way inside.

It took me another fifteen minutes of scrunching myself along a thin lip of concrete to get to the back of the building and locate the small door that read SUPPLY ENTRANCE in Japanese.

I slid my lockpicks out and was inside in another minute.

I eased the door shut behind me and took a deep breath.

Exhaled it slow.

Listening.

Waiting.

Anytime you enter a new territory, you don't just barge inside. You wait.

You see how the environment reacts to you. Once you acclimate yourself to your surroundings—cataloging the various ambient noises and smells and other inherent properties—you move. Slowly at first. Always slow and controlled. Moving fast is for when you're being chased.

My eyes adjusted quickly. Vampire eyesight is much better than a human's. Darkness doesn't pose much of a problem for us.

Boxes lined the back of the store. I eased my back along them. I used a sidestepping motion gleaned from my years of ninjutsu training to continue working my way toward the front of the store. I'd have to be careful out there. The giant glass windows would let anyone walking by see me.

I didn't want to be seen.

I could see the doors now.

I crouched by the counter and moved behind it. On the floor, there was a vague chalk outline of where Yuki's body had lain when I'd seen her earlier. I bowed my head for a moment and paid her the respect she deserved. Dying for the cause is an honorable way to go.

But she shouldn't have died like this.

I made a solemn vow to find whoever did this and bring them to justice.

My kind of justice.

Off to the left of the counter, I saw another door. There were two locks on this one. It took me twice as long to pick my way through them and finally enter Yuki's office.

A bank of small television screens stood along one wall. They were all dead. When the cops had shut off the power earlier, they'd killed the cameras as well. I started looking for the videotape storage facility but all I came up with were rows of CDs.

Then it hit me.

I was in the land of electronic marvels. Videotapes? Not a chance. They were passé. Yuki was recording things on CD. It made sense because it saved room and space was at a premium in Japan.

There were ten CDs in total.

Under the desk was a safe. It had a cipher code lock that only accepted alphabetical keys. I looked the safe over and decided there was no way I was going to be able to pick it.

That meant guessing at the combination.

I don't like guessing.

Ever.

But sometimes I have to do it.

I tried all the usual ones: Yuki, Matsuda, you name it, I tried it.

What finally opened it was the same Fixer greeting we all used: *Fyar, Chuldoc, Erim*. I had to input it in our language of Taluk, but the door finally opened.

Twenty minutes after I started. I had an accumulation of sweat building up along my hairline, but I wiped it off and stared into the safe.

I saw the two handguns. SIG Sauers. 9mm. I took them out in their holsters. They were in perfect condition. Judging by the smell of oil on them, Yuki kept them in meticulous shape. Was she expecting to have to use them sometime soon?

Or had she used them lately?

Didn't matter.

What mattered was that I was finally armed.

I grabbed the three boxes of ammunition, too. I slid the magazine out of one of the SIGs and loaded it, slid it home, racked the slide to chamber a round, dropped the magazine, and topped it off with another round again. Finally, I slid the holster on behind my right hip where I liked to wear it. I put the other gun in my pocket along with the ammunition.

I eased the door to the safe shut and locked it again. No sense making it easy for anyone else who might come along. I looked around the room.

Yuki's computer sat dead on the desk in front of me.

Inside it, there was probably a lot of information I could use to try to figure out who the hell the Kensei was and what he was up to, aside from trafficking human organs.

But the power was off.

Even if I found the power switch, turning it on would have been suicide. The bright green neon sign would come on and all the lights and every drunk stumbling fool outside would know someone was inside the Starbucks when no one should have been.

Uh-uh.

It just wasn't an option.

Could I take the computer with me? It wasn't a huge desktop machine but a laptop Apple computer.

I was going to need a bag for all my groceries if this kept up. Maybe I should have brought Talya after all.

But the computer was bolted to the desktop. It wasn't going anywhere.

I got down on my hands and knees and tried to see if I could pry it off the desk.

But then I froze.

My ears had picked up a noise that didn't belong.

Someone was inside with me.

They were moving very stealthily.

I eased myself out from under the desk and crouched low.

Talya?

Had she woken up and found me gone and decided to come over herself to help?

I doubted it. She couldn't know if I'd mistake her for an opponent and put her down without finding out. It was too risky even if she had woken up. Even if she'd wanted to come over here, she wouldn't have.

No.

It was someone else.

I heard a dull scrape now. The sound of a shoe on the floor.

Rubber by the sound of it.

They were closer.

I had the SIG and could use it, but I didn't have a suppressor on it. And the gun going off would be just as bad as me lighting the place up.

I'd have to do this by hand.

Great.

Another scrape came even closer. Where the hell was he?

Then I saw the shoes.

Thin-soled rubber. Black.

The way they moved, I could tell I was going to have my hands full. Sometimes you can just tell by the way people move that they know how to handle themselves. They're always balanced.

Tough.

Ready for action.

I waited until the shoes had gone past me before I came up behind the guy.

Slowly.

I kept my head lower than his, trying to stay in his blind spot.

I could just make out the silenced pistol he carried in his left hand.

That ruled out any friendlies.

Even Moko wouldn't have cause to carry a silenced pistol.

No, this was a bad guy.

I clamped my left hand around his left wrist while I snaked my right arm under his neck and jerked back. Trying to disarm a gun-wielding attacker is always a monster. But you don't go after the gun. You go after the limb that controls the gun. By locking his left wrist I could effectively keep the gun from pointing at me.

My goal was to choke him out and then ask him some questions later on.

It didn't work.

As I jerked up under his chin, he immediately put his chin down, blocking my attempt to cut off his airflow. He'd been trained.

I immediately went for the nerve point under his left ear by using the knuckle of my right thumb to drill it in there.

He dropped his weight, going with the force of the thumb and started to turn back into me.

Mistake.

By doing so, he extended his left arm and gave me the opening I was looking for. I abandoned the thumb strike, got my right arm out of there and slid to my left, getting an armbar on his left arm.

He grunted and tried to roll out of the lock.

His face slammed into a counter.

I could hear his breath now.

Or was it mine?

I dropped my right knee on his left elbow and then dropped all my body weight on it as well. The gun skittered away.

I heard the crack a second later.

But he didn't scream out in pain as his elbow shattered.

He just grunted.

Whoever'd trained this guy had done a damned fine job.

With his left arm useless now, the attacker tore himself free and knocked me back at the same time. He came up about eight feet from me and planted a kick right into my sternum.

I sucked fire. My diaphragm spasmed and I couldn't get any

oxygen into my lungs. He came at me hard now, his right hand chopping down toward my exposed neck.

I brought my hands up in an X and deflected the strike.

As I came up, trying to slide inside of his arms to elbow him in the chest, he kicked me again.

I dropped.

The floor felt cold.

Sweat soaked my back.

I still couldn't breathe.

Another kick thundered into my lower back. It sent me sprawling forward.

My hands pawed at the floor.

And closed around his gun.

My reaction was automatic.

I spun, thumbed the safety off, and fired three times center mass.

In the quiet of the night, I heard the gun spit thrice and the sick wet splat of the rounds striking home. The guy moaned and dropped like he'd taken a cinder block to his head.

My lungs finally started working again and I flushed myself with oxygen.

I crawled over and looked at the guy.

Dead.

So much for questioning him.

Funny how having your life on the line suddenly makes you choose different options in the name of survival.

I went over him with both hands. No papers. No identification of any kind.

What he did have, however, were two grenades.

Grenades?

What the hell?

Still, it solved a problem for me.

Ten minutes later, I'd placed the CDs on top of the computer and then taped the grenades on top of them followed by the body of my recently deceased attacker. With a string around both the pins and spoons, I wound my way back to the rear door of the Starbucks. When I'd gone as far as the string would allow, I braced myself and yanked the string.

Far off, I heard the sound of the pins and spoons hitting the floor.

I hauled ass.

Three seconds later, two explosions rocked the Starbucks. I knew that the attacker's body would act like a tamping agent and send most of the blast through the CDs and the computer, effectively ruining any evidence that might have compromised the vampire nation.

I walked back to the hotel.

Behind me, flames were already starting to devour the remains of the Starbucks.

And Yuki's respectable legacy.

CHAPTER TWELVE

I walked back to my hotel as the high-pitched whines of sirens filled the night. I didn't glance back, I just kept walking. I'd make sure Yuki got some sort of special commendation when I got back to Boston. It was the least I could do for her and the work she'd done.

Still, not being able to access her computer left me dry in terms of having a lead to follow. Somehow I had to find out who this Kensei was and try to find him. Without Yuki, Talya and I were going to have a really difficult time tracking him down.

I stopped at the convenience store and bought some orange juice. I stepped back out into the night air and drank it down nice and fast, the way I do sometimes when I'm pissed off. The cold headache came over me and I winced but shrugged it off. Pain after all, is a physical thing.

It can be controlled.

Well, physical pain anyway.

There were some things that hurt more that couldn't be so easily erased or minimized.

I stood there for about twenty minutes, letting my system come down from the adrenaline of combat. The stars overhead seemed to wink at me. I took another sip of juice and then headed for the hotel.

The hydraulic doors at the hotel entrance swished open as I broke the motion sensor. The curtain of smoke still hung heavy in the lobby. I could see someone sitting in the fake leather chairs puffing away like there was an emergency need for added pollutants in the air and he was the only one who could supply them.

I walked to the counter and slid the piece of paper across to the desk clerk. His eyes hadn't grown any more alert since I'd left. He slid my key across to me and I turned for the elevator.

"*Komban wa.*"

Uh-oh.

I knew that voice.

I turned.

Moko, the ever-vigilant albeit soon-to-be-riding-the-cancer-pony homicide detective stood in front of me, hands thrust deep into his overcoat pockets with a cigarette dangling out of his mouth.

I gave a quick bow. "*Komban wa.*"

He grinned. "Almost too late to be saying 'good evening.'"

"Almost."

"This time of night"—he shrugged—"most people in Tokyo are long since dead asleep."

"Most are. Not me."

"Apparently."

"I don't sleep well. I'm restless. I suffer from tremendous insomnia. It's almost debilitating sometimes."

The corners of his mouth turned up. "I was not asking, Lawson-san."

"Consider it a polite admission then, on my behalf." I glanced around. There didn't seem to be anyone else with Moko.

He tipped some ash off the end of his cigarette. "You're wondering why I'm here."

"Sure. You said yourself it was late."

Moko smiled. "I've been drinking."

"A lot of people drink. Nothing wrong with imbibing a little."

"May we sit down? I'm afraid the sake has weakened the state of my legs to the point that standing for a long time makes me fall over rather unexpectedly." He winced. "It is my shame to bear alone."

I sat with my back to the counter, watching the front door. I wanted to be able to see if any reinforcements came through. I hadn't smelled anything heavy on Moko's breath. Certainly nothing that would have indicated he'd been drinking the rice wine sake.

I took another sip of my almost empty orange juice. I wondered how long I could nurse the carton and make it look convincing. I'm much more of a get-to-the-point kind of operative, but I was dealing with Moko and the Japanese are never direct about anything. I had to give him time to get comfortable before he opened up.

Moko sighed. "I am still troubled about the tragedy that befell your friend this afternoon."

"Yuki."

"*Hai.* Miss Matsuda. Your . . . affliction, as it were." His eyes twinkled slightly.

"My fantasy more likely." I shrugged. "At least at this point it seems that's all she will ever be."

"Why would anyone want to kill her, Lawson-san? I mean, tonight I have been asking myself this question over and over again. I was even unable to enjoy the company of several rather attractive barmaids who would like nothing better than to entertain the chief of homicide for the Tokyo Metropolitan Police."

I smiled. "Now that is definitely a tragedy."

He eyed me. "You have not seen these women. You would certainly agree with me if you did."

I smiled. "I think it's a tragedy anytime anyone is unable to enjoy the benefits of a woman's company."

He laughed. "So true."

I took a final sip from the carton.

Moko glanced around and then he shrugged. "The only thing I have been able to come up with is that perhaps there is something I have overlooked."

"Overlooked?"

"Yes. So I say to myself, 'Moko, you old tiger, what is it that eludes you here? What is the lone clue that might reveal more about this truly sad and bizarre circumstance?'"

"What did you come up with?"

He smiled again, but it seemed less than happy. "I came up with you, Lawson-san."

"Me?"

He nodded. "Yes. You knew her. Apparently."

"So did a lot of people." I frowned. "She did serve coffee for a living after all. Probably to thousands of people."

"Perhaps. But you are . . . forgive me . . . a gaijin. Naturally, you stand out in my mind more."

"You're not doing much to bolster my confidence in the notion that Japan has abandoned its distrust of foreigners, Moko-san."

"As I'm sure you are aware, Japan has two distinct sides. The *omote*—outside—and the *ura*—inside. What we say on the outside is very often not how we truly feel. Japan may say she treats everyone with the same attitude, but we do not. And unfortunately, in my quest to rid my city of crime, I must sometimes indulge the age-old attitudes that others find distasteful."

"Even if you find them distasteful yourself."

He nodded. "Particularly if I do."

"I see."

Moko leaned forward and lit a fresh cigarette. "Is there something you wish to tell me?"

"Do I need a lawyer, Moko-san?"

"Not unless you have something to hide."

"I confessed everything this afternoon. That I only knew and admired Miss Matsuda—Yuki—from afar."

"Were you aware she had video surveillance cameras of the entire area set up inside her back office?"

How in the hell had he known that? The doors had been locked. I could feel Moko's eyes watching me like a hawk. If I hadn't been wearing a black turtleneck, he might have even been checking to see if the pulse in my neck jumped.

"I was not aware of that. Is that something that people do over here now? Some sort of voyeuristic fetish thing?"

"Not that I know of, but then again, I don't necessarily find the time to explore all the new fetishes the younger kids find fascinating." He toyed with his cigarette. "She kept the video records burned onto computer CDs. Sort of interesting, don't you think?"

"Not really."

He leaned forward again. "What I think is this: most women who own a Starbucks coffee shop do not employ an elaborate security system that scans the outside area of their store."

"You see? That's where we differ. In America, we're a bit more security-conscious ever since the tragic events of 9/11. We've got cameras everywhere now. That's why I wasn't too surprised when you mentioned them."

"We have security cameras, too. However, most of ours cover the inside of our stores in order to catch perpetrators who might wish to steal something."

"But these were not."

"No. They watched the approaches to the store only."

"Well, that is a bit odd." I hefted my empty container. "So, you've seen the CDs?"

"I have only seen one of them. The one that was from earlier today."

"Anything interesting on it?"

"You."

"Sure, I stopped there earlier. Had a hot chocolate and a large fresh-squeezed orange juice." I held up my container. "In case you hadn't noticed, I'm a real fan of orange juice."

"There was a woman with you."

"Was there?"

"A gaijin, like you."

He got that right in more ways than one. Still, this was rapidly disintegrating. Moko was starting to become a bit of an annoyance. Trouble was, I liked the salty bastard. And he was doing the job he'd been paid to do. I got the impression that he was a lot like me.

It was unfortunate he was becoming a bit of a thorn in my side. I didn't want to have to take him out.

I smiled at him. "Would you believe she's my girlfriend?"

"I might believe anything," said Moko. "Provided I have a good reason."

"She is."

"And yet . . ." Moko's voice trailed off.

I nodded. "I know. I have all these unresolved feelings for Miss Matsuda. I'm with one woman and yet felt like I might have loved another." I leaned forward now. "It pains my heart to not be able to resolve it."

"It would seem that the universe has resolved it for you." Moko frowned.

"Seemingly."

"Some might even hazard to wonder if you yourself took care of that problem on your own."

I shook my head. "They'd be wrong to think that."

"So why did you go for a walk tonight?"

"I couldn't sleep."

"You said that already, Lawson-san."

"I think the stress of not knowing how to resolve my feelings is still with me. Yes, Yuki is gone, but I am still in a quandary about how to tell my girlfriend that I may not be in love with her after all."

Moko smirked. "And I thought I had trouble with empty-headed barmaids."

"We all have our own troubles. Who is to say which are more heavy to bear?"

Moko glanced at his dwindling tobacco and sucked on the filter. The cinder glowed red and I tried not to breathe when he exhaled. "You have found yourself in an extraordinary situation, Lawson-san."

No shit. But before I could say anything, Moko's pocket buzzed. He reached into it and extracted a cell phone.

"Excuse me."

He listened and I leaned back into the chair, waiting. Moko's face darkened. He spoke some words quietly and then hung up. He looked at me for a long minute and then stood.

"I have to go."

"Trouble?"

His eyes bored into mine. "Curiously, there's been a fire at the Starbucks."

I stood. "What?"

"A body has been found. Unfortunately, it's mostly blown apart. Miss Matsuda's office was also destroyed, along with all the other CD surveillance disks."

"Good heavens."

He nodded. "It's interesting to me that you always seem to be close by when tragedy strikes, Lawson-san. Forgive me for saying so, but you are either an extremely unlucky man, or else you are more mixed up in this than you are letting on."

I shook my head. "Unlucky. That's it."

He sucked on the cigarette and then flicked it into an ashtray. "I'll be in touch."

Moko turned and in a flash, he'd exited the hotel lobby. I exhaled and stood there watching the doors for a long time.

Close.

Too close.

And the revelation about Yuki's CD was not a good one. If Moko had one of them in his possession, I needed it back. It would have a picture of the Kensei entering her shop. Or at the very least the thugs who had killed her.

I owed it to her to get it back and hunt them down.

It was the least I could do.

I stepped on to the elevator and leaned against the wall, still trying to steady my heartbeat. Moko was a bloodhound. I knew he smelled something amiss. He'd keep on tugging at the thread until it all came unraveled. Not that I'd done anything to give him cause to be suspicious, but he had good instincts. And he'd been a cop long enough to know when he was sniffing in the right direction.

Not good.

I sighed and stepped off the elevator. Suddenly, I wanted to sleep a long time and never wake up. At my door, I slid the key into the lock and opened the door.

Inside my hotel room, it was dark.

I flipped on the light switch.

"Hiya, Lawson."

A whole other party was waiting for me.

CHAPTER THIRTEEN

Things did not look good.

There were two pistols aimed right at my chest. The two goons holding them didn't look like they'd lose sleep if they had to pull the trigger. Combined with the fact that my hotel room was about the same size as a shoe box, fighting didn't seem to be the most prudent move.

At least not yet.

"Where ya been?"

The goon looked as Japanese as they come but his speech led me to believe he'd been raised in the States. Or else they had *Hooked on Slang* in Japan.

I eyed him. "I was out . . . probably killing one of your friends."

He glanced at the other guy. Neither of them said anything. But the lead goon gestured with the gun. "I think we'll be going on a little trip now, if you don't mind."

"Sure. I was just going to catch some sleep, but this sounds like more fun anyway."

"Before we leave, it will be necessary for you to leave the weapons you took from the coffee shop here."

I smiled. "You know about those?"

"I can see them under your jacket." He pointed with the gun but kept it far enough away from me that trying to take it out of his hand would have been foolish.

I nodded. I withdrew the two pistols and the extra magazines and ammunition and put them on the bed. The lead goon glanced at them and then back at me.

"Don't try anything or we'll have to kill you."

I nodded. "And I'm assuming someone wants to meet me before you do that."

"You catch on fast, gaijin."

"Lucky me."

"Lucky us if we get to kill you and your girlfriend."

"Where's Talya?"

He just laughed. "Don't worry about her. She's not in any position to help you. I'm not sure anyone is."

Shit.

"We're going to walk outside now. And then we'll get in the elevator."

I opened the door and stepped back into the corridor. What were the chances that some dazed drunk traveler would stumble upon us and give me a chance to take these guys down?

Not good.

We reached the elevator bank and I pressed the call button. A moment later the doors slid back.

I stepped inside and glanced at them in the mirror. Technically, I had a better chance now than I'd had in my room. If I disarmed them and was able to interrogate them, I could get some information.

Unless they lied.

That's the problem with questioning someone without the use of drugs. You just can't be sure if they're telling the truth. And if the rumors about this guy, the Kensei, were to be believed, these guys would rather die first than cough up any good intelligence.

Better to settle back for the ride and let them take me where I needed to go anyway.

In the lobby, we passed the counter clerk who had given up on trying to stay awake and was passed out behind the counter. Of all the times for the Japanese service industry to fail, it had to be now.

I was glad to see my luck was improving so steadily.

Outside the hotel, a black Buick sat idling by the curb. It hadn't been there when I'd come in earlier. I must have missed one of the goons giving it the signal to roll around.

Point of fact, most American cars in Japan belong to the yakuza, who import them for their size and prestige. Must be a penis thing. The driver stepped out and opened the back door. I felt the gun in my ribs and climbed on in. The two goons joined me a second later.

The driver got back in behind the wheel and I heard the locks engage.

I looked at the lead goon. "You got a name, Sparky?"

"Does it matter?"

I shrugged. "I always like knowing who I'm going to kill in the future."

He laughed. "You're a funny guy, gaijin. You can call me Kozo." He nudged the other goon with his elbow and the two of them had a good laugh over it.

"So, where are we going?"

Kozo leaned forward. "You said it yourself, gaijin. Someone wants to meet you. Real bad."

"Real bad?"

"Yeah."

I glanced out of the window as the streets zipped past. "So, Kozo . . . where'd you learn your English, anyway?"

"Brooklyn."

I glanced back at him. "And you came back here?"

"It's the homeland, man." He looked proud of himself.

"Dig it." I looked out of the windows again. We'd passed

through most of Kashiwa already. Traffic was nonexistent. The night seemed darker looking out until I realized they'd tinted the windows.

Kozo piped up again. He seemed to like the sound of his own voice. "Don't bother trying to figure out where we're going."

I looked back at him. "Why not?"

" 'Cause you got a one-way ticket, brother-man. You ain't coming back here, if you catch my drift."

I smiled. "You shouldn't have told me that."

"Why not?"

"Ruins the suspense. There's no shock or surprise now when we get there. You'll muscle me in to meet whoever it is that wants to meet me. We'll have some playful banter. I'll pretend I'm impressed and then you guys will empty a couple of magazines worth of bullets into me. That'll be it."

Kozo frowned. "Yeah?"

"Kind of boring," I said.

Kozo seemed to be trying to process this and I smiled at the other goon. *"Namae?"*

He glanced at Kozo, who just nodded. The second goon looked back at me and frowned. "Tetsuo."

I inclined my head. He started to return it and then stopped and frowned at me some more. I smiled.

We traveled for about twenty more minutes before I caught a whiff of fish. I'm not a huge seafood eater. I've been working on expanding my culinary palate, but the smell of raw fish really nauseates me. Back when I was chasing the Syndicate in New York, they had their headquarters near the Fulton Fish Market and I nearly lost it every time I had to be there.

I wondered if we were near the Tokyo Fish Market.

I could see vague neon through the windows, but nothing that stood out as a landmark. But judging from the way the Buick was slowing down, we must have been getting close to our destination.

"Almost there, gaijin."

I looked at Kozo. "I have a name, you know."

He shrugged and switched the pistol to his other hand. "Dead men don't need names."

I sniffed. "You get that from an old spaghetti Western or what?"

"Sure, hombre. Whatever."

I heard a heavy garage door opening. The Buick rolled inside what appeared to be a huge warehouse. The garage door came down behind us, squeaking and protesting the entire way.

"Little WD-40 would take care of that," I said. "Maybe give the impression you guys care about your business image and all."

"Shut up," said Kozo.

My household tips never seem to go over well.

The Buick's engine shut off. I felt the familiar twinge of butter-flies fluttering around in my stomach. That's combat for you. The driver's door opened.

The right door opened.

The smell of the fish market rushed inside and I wrinkled my nose in disgust. "Maybe a couple thousand pine tree air fresheners would be good for this joint."

Kozo gestured with his gun. "Get out, funny man."

I stepped out. The warehouse was stacked high with all sorts of crates and boxes. I could read some of the kanji markings on them. Most seemed bound for Russia or Europe. Some of them were des-tined for the States.

Kozo stepped out behind me. He nudged me with the gun again. I was getting tired of having my ribs poked. I moved toward steps leading up to a catwalk.

"Your friend is waiting for you up there."

I looked at Kozo. "My friend?" Did he mean Talya? Had they already brought her here?

"Just keep walking."

Tetsuo brought up the rear. The driver stayed positioned next to the Buick. Good thing. He was built like an Abrams tank and the thought of having to deal with him didn't make my day look any brighter.

I crested the steps and followed the catwalk down for about forty feet before it ended at a door. I glanced back at Kozo. "Should I wait for you to make the proper introductions or just barge on in?"

Kozo frowned. "Now that wouldn't be very polite."

"My point."

Kozo brushed past me. I looked back and smiled at Tetsuo. He frowned and kept the gun trained on me.

Kozo knocked on the door.

From inside, a bark rang out. Kozo turned the knob and the door swung in.

It was dark inside.

Totally.

I walked in and glanced around, looking for vents or anything that would introduce ambient light into the room. I saw a desk and then the room went dark as Kozo closed the door behind me.

Nothing.

It was almost as if we were standing in some sort of sensory deprivation tank.

But somewhere ahead of me, I could hear breathing.

"Leave us."

Cultured. He spoke English with a vague British accent. It sliced through the air and behind me I could hear Kozo and Tetsuo fade back out of the room.

When the door shut, the voice spoke again. "I trust you had a satisfactory trip on your way here?"

"Well, the guys didn't serve an in-flight snack, but otherwise I have no complaints."

There was the briefest of pauses. "I was told you fancied yourself as some type of comedian."

"Who? Me? Nah. I'm just a sarcastic, cynical prick. If that's your idea of comedy, well, then I'm your man."

"I don't find such an attitude amusing."

"Too bad. I don't do imitations."

"You realize you are about thirty seconds away from dying?"

I smirked. "Welcome to my world."

He laughed now. "Yes, I thought you might say something like that."

I kept glancing around, hoping to see some sign that Talya had been here. But I couldn't make a damned thing out in the darkness, even with my eyes. "What have you done with Talya?"

"Talya? Ah, yes, the woman. Your . . . girfriend."

"Whatever."

"You know it's illegal for you to be in love with a human?"

I sighed. "Listen, I've heard all that bullshit before. I don't expect you're going to shed any new light on the subject so let's just move on past it, okay? Why don't you tell me why I'm here?"

"You are here because you are becoming a thorn in my side."

"Really." I didn't think I'd been in Japan long enough to be a thorn in anyone's side. At least not yet. Unless this guy knew about my run-in on the train.

"Yes."

"You mind clueing me on what I did to piss you off?"

"You've been investigating my business."

That got my attention. "You the guy who traffics in human organs?"

"Somewhat."

I shrugged. "Okay, you got me there. Although, honestly, I haven't been able to find out all that much. And I don't even think I've been poking into your business at all. In fact, this might be really sort of jumping the gun on your part. You could have at least waited until I'd made a real nuisance of myself."

"I decided it would be better to be proactive. Rather than wait for you to bumble upon my affairs, I decided to move first."

"'Bumble'?"

"Call your unusual method of doing your job by whatever label you wish. It strikes me as rather bumbling, however."

I frowned. "Yeah, well, I try to impress. Especially idiots like you who hide in darkened rooms afraid to even face the guy they claim they're going to kill."

I heard a sharp intake of breath. Guess that pushed some buttons.

"I am not afraid of someone like . . . you."

"Yeah, well, how about some lights in this place?" If I could just get him to switch on some lights, I'd have a much easier time of things.

"We don't need lights to see."

"Yeah, but we need some ambient light for crying out loud."

"Is that what you really want?"

I sighed. "Wouldn't have said it otherwise."

"Very well, Lawson. You will have your wish. Although it may well be your last."

"Hang on then, I wanna change it to a ménage à trois. No sense wasting a final wish on lights, after all."

He sighed. "Honestly."

"Sorry."

A tiny bit of light crept into the room. Vague shadows revealed tiny details at first. As my eyes adjusted, I could see more. And more.

I saw a body in front of me.

Tall.

Lean.

White?

More light came into the room.

I saw more white now.

And then the full force of the pale translucent skin struck home.

At about the same time as the voice spoke again.

"I am the Kensei."

CHAPTER
FOURTEEN

He was tall. Sickly thin almost. And his pale skin reminded me of another albino I'd killed recently—Cho, who ran the Syndicate in New York City.

The Kensei eyed me up and down. "So, you are the infamous one. The Fixer they all speak of in hushed whispers. The one they fear above all others."

Hushed whispers? "I usually go by Lawson."

"And now that you've seen me?"

"I liked you better with the lights off."

He smiled. "Honest even though it might well pain you. I suppose I can respect that."

"Great. Now I can die happy."

"Oh, you will die, Lawson. Have no worries about that."

"I'm not worried."

He regarded me with cold, unblinking eyes. "You know, I must admit I was exceptionally pleased to learn that you would be coming to Japan."

He knew? How was that possible? The only person I'd told back in the States was Niles. And in turn, he'd alerted Yuki. But apart from them, no one else was supposed to know. Yuki was dead. As far as I knew, Niles was still alive.

But it didn't make any sense. If Niles was dirty, he could have had me killed a million times before now. It must not have come from him, either, then.

But who did that leave? I'd been in the Philippines directly before this, but I'd plugged all those holes before I left. Miranda wouldn't have been able to tell this guy anything.

The Kensei smiled. "I find it amusing watching the inner turmoil you're working through right now. You're trying to figure out how it is that I knew you would be coming here. You're wondering if perhaps someone isn't as good as they made themselves out to be. Maybe you're thinking it was Miss Matsuda?"

"She's dead. Not much good being a traitor if you're dead."

He nodded. "True. And she wasn't. She was one of those annoying individuals who cling to a sense of honor as if it's their sole lifeline or purpose in life. Pathetic."

"Nice to know there are still some people who cherish that."

"It led to her death." He spat. "She was a fool."

"There's nothing pathetic about dying with honor."

He waved me off. "Bah, you're nothing but a gaijin. You can't presume to speak to me about honor or some samurai Bushido code as if you know it better than I."

"I think I do, though. Because there's nothing honorable about trafficking human organs."

"We'll get to that in time."

I was still trying to work out who might have tipped this guy off that I was coming. "Is Niles dirty?"

His eyes narrowed and then widened. "Your Control."

"Yeah."

"You think he is?"

"I think the number of people I told about my trip here are few and far between. I'm going down the list of candidates."

"You can cross him off your list."

"Yeah?"

"He's not dirty, either."

"Well, thanks for being candid with me."

He shrugged. "Doesn't matter much. You'll be dead soon."

"So, how'd you know?"

"Would you believe me if I told you I have excellent surveillance abilities? That I can tap the phones of anyone I choose to, no matter where they are in the world?"

"Probably not."

He shrugged. "Well, you're right. I don't. But I do know some people placed higher up than you or I. And they are most forthright with useful information."

"And these people . . . they told you."

"Niles, as far as I've been able to figure out, was able to keep your trip here 'off the books.' But the people I work for had his phones tapped. And when he placed a call to Yuki, the pieces fell into place."

I frowned. This was becoming a bad case of déjà vu. When I'd taken down Cho and his bunch of Syndicate goons, he'd alluded to someone dirty within the vampire governing body who was calling the shots, steering things into certain areas that weren't good for the vampire race and would risk exposing us all. I hadn't had time to run it down before I came over here. Now it seemed that I was hearing about it again. And I didn't like it any better than I had when Cho had bragged about it.

"That's convenient for you."

"We visited Yuki to see if she might be convinced to discontinue her investigation into my activities. She stubbornly refused to do so. We had no choice, therefore, but to kill her."

"You know she had that entire area under video surveillance?"

The Kensei's eyes registered a tiny fragment of shock. "I was not aware of that. No matter, I'm told the bomb blast you helped manufacture destroyed any of the evidence which would point to our existence."

"Yeah, I thought so, too. I was wrong."

"What's that supposed to mean?"

"One of the CDs with the video surveillance footage escaped. It's in the possession of a certain somebody."

"That's unfortunate."

I nodded. "Yeah. And guess what?"

"Yes?"

"It's got the footage from the time of day you and your boys paid Yuki a visit. Right now, there are probably a dozen police computer experts extracting facial data from that CD. Pretty soon they'll be showing your ugly mug all over the television. You won't be able to go anywhere or do anything."

He waved this off with vague amusement. "I'm not too concerned."

"No?"

"You can see my skin condition?"

"Yeah."

He spread his arms. "I cannot go out in public like this."

"But you just said—"

"I go out in public, but when I do, it's with the help of a latex mask specially fabricated for my use. The police will pull images from the CD, certainly, but it will not be my image they extract, but the image of my mask."

"Lemme guess: you've got plenty more where that one came from."

"Exactly."

I thumbed over my shoulder. "What about Kozo and Tetsuo?"

"Easily replaced."

"Nice to see loyalty pays such crappy dividends in your organization." I pointed a finger at him. "Your theories on employee retention and motivation need a lot of work."

"They knew the risks when they got involved with me."

I ran a hand through my hair. Had it gotten warmer in there? "Is everyone here a vampire?"

"Do they need to be?"

"I'm just curious."

"Why?"

"Because when I get out of here, I need to know who to kill for breaking the law. My jurisdiction doesn't usually apply to humans."

"You've made exceptions in the past."

I shrugged. "Sure. But it's not a habit or anything."

He smiled at me. "And you think you'll be getting out of here?"

"Yeah."

"Indeed. What gives you such confidence?"

I smiled. "Now, that would be telling."

He frowned. "You're a fool. And I don't like fools."

I smirked. "Well, I don't like you much, either. I mean, what's to like? You're a monstrosity. A freak."

The color of his skin changed. His eyes narrowed to mere slits and his voice drew low to a whisper. "You will die here."

I held up my hand. "Listen, would you mind turning around so I don't have to look at you?"

He ignored me. "You recently were in New York City."

"That's right. I killed a bunch of traitors."

"You must be proud."

"I'm never proud of having to kill those who would threaten our existence. But it's my job. And better them than the harm they would cause us and the innocent lives that would be lost."

"Such complete and utter sanctimonious bullshit." The Kensei looked like he was going to throw up.

"Call it what you want, I don't really care." I looked around. "You never answered my question: where's Talya?"

"How many died in New York?"

"Bad guys?" I sighed. There'd been plenty of them. "A lot."

"How many?"

"Well, there was Raoul, Kohl, Boxcar, D'Angelo—although he wasn't in New York. And some half-pint scrubby mutant named Cho."

The Kensei's eyes flared. "Do you see any similarity between Cho and myself?"

"Aside from the fact that you're both scum? Just the albino thing."

"Yes. That's the unfortunate side effect of our condition."

"You both have the same condition? Weird. What was it—a chemical explosion that caught you both?"

"It was the drug-induced pregnancy our mother was forced to endure at the hands of a deranged scientist intent on altering her physiological makeup."

I didn't like the sudden realization that was sweeping over me. I didn't like it at all.

The Kensei nodded. "That's right, Lawson. Think it over. Let it come to you. I can see it trying to penetrate that thick skull of yours."

I sighed. "Brothers."

"Yes."

"Great."

The Kensei walked behind his desk and removed a long black sheath from the underside of it. "Do you know anything about the circle of honor? Are you familiar with it?"

"Somewhat."

"You know how in ancient times, the samurai would avenge the death of a fallen friend or family member in order to close the circle that had been opened by the wrongful death?"

"It's only wrong from your twisted perspective."

The Kensei smiled some more. "Yes, you could argue that point, I'm sure. I, however, choose to view it only from my perspective. And looking at things from here, you are the guilty one."

Naturally. "I've been getting bum raps all my life."

"And now it's my turn to close the circle."

"Now?"

He unsheathed the sword from the sheath and nodded. "Yes. I think now is the best time."

"You won't be able to swing that much in here. It's too close."

The Kensei pointed the sword at me. It gleamed in the dim light. How he was going to kill me with that was beyond me.

His eyes ran from the blade up to mine. "You've no doubt noticed this is a traditional katana."

"Yeah."

"Not like your famed wooden bokken."

He knew about that? God, this guy was piped in. "Nope."

"And you're wondering how this piece of metal would kill you, being what we are and all."

"Maybe."

"Look at the edge, Lawson."

I leaned in just a bit. I could see an oily residue clinging to the cutting edge now. Almost like a thick syrup.

"What is it?"

"You know what it is."

I sniffed the air and I could smell it now.

Turpentine.

"Distilled from pine trees, it will kill you as easily as having wood introduced into your body." The Kensei laughed. "Isn't technology wonderful?"

"You aren't the pioneer you think you are. I know someone who used turpentine on the shuriken she used to carry."

"Is that so?"

"Yeah. But I killed her."

"Too bad."

"And I'll kill you, too."

"I don't think so, Lawson. It's time for you to die right now."

He swiped through the air then so fast I barely had a chance to lean back just out of the cutting arc. The tip of the sword sliced a few threads of my turtleneck open. I stumbled back over the chair and fell back on my ass.

Which is when the door to the Kensei's office exploded in.

Light poured in.

The Kensei shrieked.

A concussion blast went off.

And I passed out.

CHAPTER FIFTEEN

"You okay?"

"I feel like shit."

I heard her laugh and knew everything was okay. Despite the undulating throb in my head and the high-pitched whine in my ears that threatened to drown out anything else, I felt safe.

For the moment.

"Where is he? Where'd he go?"

"Gone."

I sat up and tasted the acrid smoke still lingering in the office. "What the hell did you use to blow the door in?"

"Well, since you decided to go off on your own and cut me out of the loop, I had to improvise."

"Literally."

"You bet. It's an old shirtsleeve formula I learned when I was going to school in the Urals."

I smiled. Talya didn't ever like referring to her time with the KGB. To her, that was another time and place. Another era entirely. I was cool with that. God knew there were plenty of things in my own past I had no desire to ever speak about again.

"Judging by the smell, it must contain some wonderful ingredients."

Talya nudged me. "You know where we are? It's not exactly the States where I can get my hands on anything I need at the local convenience store."

"If we were in the States, you could have bought a flash-bang off a kid on the corner."

"Good point." She got her arm around my back and stood me up. "I'm guessing your friend isn't a huge fan of bright light, huh?"

"Albino, I think. He looked like an extra from *The Omega Man*. This is the second one I've run into in the last few months. I'm getting tired of it."

Talya looked at me. "An albino vampire?"

"Yeah, I know."

"Kind of odd, isn't it?"

I smiled at her. She looked great. "Since when has my life ever been anything but?"

"Another good point."

"Besides, they have albino alligators, don't they?"

"I thought that was an urban legend."

"Really? You sure?"

"No."

"We'll leave it alone then." I checked the Kensei's desk. There was nothing inside that would give us any information about where he might have gone.

"So much for that."

"You mad I came in when I did?"

I smiled. "You kidding? Any longer and I would have bought it. He was getting ready to make sushi out of me."

She glanced around the office. "Nice to know my timing's still as good as it ever was."

"You bet." I looked out the doorway. "Say, how'd you get in here past all the guards anyway?"

"Weren't many to speak of. I took out one guy down by the entry area. That was about it."

"Oh."

"Why 'oh'?"

I pointed outside. "Looks like we're going to get our chance to deal with the rest of the happy campers now, then."

Talya turned. "Oh, shit."

There were about six of them in total. Not a ton by any means, but I wasn't all that anxious to take them on. My head was still spinning. And these guys were probably highly trained vampires. The Kensei didn't seem the type to employ human thugs. But I could have been wrong. Only one way to find out.

I glanced at Talya. "You didn't bring any weapons, did you?"

She smiled. "I stopped by the hotel room before I headed out."

I frowned. "Yeah?"

She handed me one of the SIGs I'd liberated from Yuki's office. I checked the slide and saw a round in the chamber. Yuki, like Controls everywhere, had had plenty of the modified ammunition that we used to kill bad guys. I looked back at Talya. "Have I told you how much I love you lately?"

She hefted her pistol. "Not nearly enough."

I yanked the gun and fired. The bullet tore into the chest of one of the goons who'd crested the steps while we were talking. Talya jumped and spun. The goon spilled back down the steps and crashed into his brethren.

"Remind me later to rectify that situation, will you?"

Talya smiled. "You bet."

I braced on one side of the doorjamb. Talya took the other. I glanced at her. "How do you want to play it?"

"Would it be foolish to think one of them might have a rocket launcher or a grenade somewhere out there that they could conceivably lob in here to fry us with?"

I held up a finger. "Now, now, we must never assume."

"My point. I'm not exactly thrilled about staying here."

"You want point or you want me to take it?"

She frowned. "What is with you guys always having to lead when we dance?" She ducked out of the doorway and fired a single shot. It nailed the next guy on the stairs right between his eyes. Talya had opened his third eye for him and done it on the run.

Talya grabbed cover by a crate. "Go!"

I ducked and fired on the run. I made the crate and scrunched next to her. "I ever tell you how much effortless lethality turns me on?"

"I'm getting the idea that pretty much everything turns you on, Lawson."

"You say that like it's a bad thing, my dear." I shot another goon trying to climb up and flank us on the left side of the walkway. He screeched and spun down to the ground, crashing onto a stack of more crates that splintered as his body hit them.

Talya pointed. "We need to get down there. Lots more cover."

It was a twenty-foot drop. "Can you make it?"

"I was the best in my parachute class." She grabbed the railing, shot, and then dropped. I watched as she hit the floor of the warehouse, tucked, and rolled perfectly behind a larger stack of crates.

What a woman.

She stuck her head out and fired off two more shots. The rest of the goons were keeping their heads down. Talya glanced up at me and nodded.

I grabbed the rail.

A shot rang out.

Splanged off the railing near my hand.

I lost my hold.

Fell.

The ground came up fast. I turned in midair, let my feet come down first, and then immediately went with the momentum, rolling to where Talya was still squeezing off single shots.

"Nice recovery."

I came up in a crouch, pissed off. "You tag the bastard that shot at me?"

"Yep."

"Damn. I wanted him."

But then the firing stopped. Talya looked at me. "They run out of bullets?"

"Maybe."

I got my face down next to the ground and snuck a peek. Two of the goons were standing there.

Out in the open.

Maybe fifteen yards away from us.

One of them had ripped off his shirt. I could see an elaborate tattoo slithering across the muscles of his chest and abdomen. A sheen of sweat basted his already unkempt appearance.

"Gaijin!"

I looked at Talya. "You think they're calling me?"

"Could be me, too."

"True."

She smirked. "But I'm more like a half gaijin. Must be you."

The voice rang out again. "Gaijin!"

I looked at Talya. "You think we tagged all the others except these two?"

"Yeah."

"Okay." I stood up, but kept my profile low. I glanced around the crates. The other goon had stripped off his shirt, too. A dragon flew across his shoulders and neck.

I stepped out. "What?"

"Put your gun down, Lawson. We'll fight the way this ought to be done."

"And what way is that?"

"Your skills against ours."

I frowned. "Two against one? That hardly seems fair."

"One-on-one," said the lead goon. "You and your bitch there."

I glanced at Talya. "You know, I don't think he likes you very much."

"Probably never seen a woman kick ass in this backwards country."

"I think you might have something there." I looked back at the two goons. Both of them were now engaged in working themselves up with elaborate martial arts moves in the air. Sweat cascaded off their bodies. I could hear their breathing.

I glanced back at Talya. "These guys are pretty serious-looking."

Talya stuck her head out. "Is that supposed to impress us?"

"Probably just you. I don't think they care about me, aside from possibly spilling my blood."

"Well, now I'm turned on."

"Better than Viagra, huh?"

She laughed. "You know what you're going to do?"

I nodded. "Oh, sure."

Talya stayed close behind me.

I walked out from behind the crates. The lead goon smiled at the other goon and they started walking toward me. I could already smell their perspiration.

"You guys might want to look into some deodorant. You stink."

"That won't matter much when we get through killing you both," said the lead goon.

I stopped.

Talya stopped.

The goons stopped.

We were about fifteen feet away now.

I smiled. "You guys ever watch movies?"

"Sure."

"You like *Raiders of the Lost Ark*?"

"Indiana Jones. Very good film."

I nodded. "I think so, too." I smiled some more. "You want to know what my favorite scene is?"

"What is that, gaijin?"

"When Indiana's in the square and that huge Arab comes out with the sword and he does all those crazy swings and cuts in the air trying to make Indiana feel like a big ol' chump. You know that scene?"

They laughed. "Yeah. It's a good one."

"Glad you agree." I jerked my SIG up and pasted them both in rapid succession. Two shots to the lead goon and two more to his cohort. Blood tore itself out of their bodies and splattered the walls around them as they spun to the ground already dead.

I shook my head. "Good intelligent help is so hard to find these days."

Talya nodded. "It would certainly seem so."

I glanced at her. "This was a first for you, huh?"

"What's that?"

"Losing your cherry like this."

"Excuse me?"

"Killing vampires." I gestured around us at the bodies. "These cats are all bloodsuckers. And today you took some of them down."

Talya's eyebrows waggled a bit. "Well, this is certainly one for the books. Now I can add another race to my kill ledger."

"You have a kill ledger?"

"Don't you?"

I grinned. "Oh, well, sure, you know, I would and all, but I keep running out of room in the damned thing."

"Now that's a shame. Mine's this cute little Hello Kitty number I picked up in Hong Kong. Lots of flowers and stuff. Girly-girl, y'know?"

"I'm almost scared to ask you if you're joking around."

"Then don't, silly."

We stepped over the bodies of our attackers. Talya glanced down. "The teeth thing, is that normal?"

"Yeah. When we're dead, they come out."

"How are you going to cover this up?"

I smiled. "I was hoping you might have some more of those shirt-sleeve formulas handy. Maybe a little something along the incendiary firestorm lines? Like I want to burn this place to the ground in no time flat. With nothing left behind but charred remains that no one will be able to identify."

Talya glanced around. "Hmm, I think maybe I can whip a little something up."

"Get to work, Chef Talya. I'd like to get the hell out of here before the cops show up."

CHAPTER SIXTEEN

True to her word, Talya managed to whip up a little something that turned the warehouse into a blazing inferno in a short time. We hightailed it out of there and got a good distance away from the scene.

Watching the warehouse blaze across the predawn sky was somehow beautiful. The flames illuminated the dock area and yet the fire itself seemed quite contained. I mentioned this to Talya, who sniffed as if I'd insulted her.

"I wasn't going to burn down the entire waterfront, Lawson."

We hung out for a few more minutes, watching the fire trucks douse the flames. There was little left behind of the Kensei's building. A few blackened timbers jutted out of the concrete and that was it.

"Time to head back to our hotel?" Talya eyed me.

I smiled but then stopped. I saw blue lights flashing across the way. Cops. "Hang on a second."

Talya tugged at my sleeve. "Lawson, I don't want to hang around here and watch my wizardry being subdued by firemen. Besides, they might see us."

"We can't be seen here. Just keep your head down for a second, okay?"

She grumbled but did as I asked. I kept my eyes on the growing crowd of police and fire crews.

And then he showed up.

Moko.

He slid out of the black car like smooth honey pouring itself out of a jar. The ubiquitous cigarette dangled from his lip and judging from the expression on his face, he was none too pleased with having to investigate yet another potential crime scene. And he didn't even know about the bodies Talya and I had left behind for him.

I'd hate to be his therapist.

I watched him stalk around the scene for a while but something seemed a bit unusual. I kept turning it over in my mind.

"He's not surprised."

"What?"

I glanced down at where Talya was resting with her back against a steel container. "Moko, the homicide investigator that was at Yuki's."

"What about him?"

"He's not surprised."

"By what?"

"This. The fire."

Talya sighed. "Lawson, you ever think that maybe the guy's just a hardened cop who's seen so much crap in his career that this kind of thing doesn't affect him anymore?"

"You think I'm reading too much into this?"

"Maybe. I just can't see why him not looking surprised would get you all riled up."

There was more to it than that. "He's been on everything I've been involved in since I got here. The incident on the train, Yuki's, the hotel lobby last night, and now this."

"So? It's his jurisdiction, isn't it?"

"Yeah."

"Can we go now? Your suspicions of conspiracy are starting to wear me out."

She was grinning but I could tell she meant it. "All right. But something still strikes me as odd."

Talya leaned against a metal container. "You know what strikes me as odd? That I haven't had much to eat all day and my stomach is ready to kill me if I don't feed it."

"You got a preference for food?"

"Sure. Whatever I can digest."

"How about raw blowfish?"

"Funny." She glanced around. "Can we leave now?"

"We've got another problem?"

"Now what?"

"Our hotel."

"What about it?"

I sighed. "It's compromised. They know where we're living. They tagged us there. We can't risk the Kensei coming back for us now that you've managed to piss him off." I came down from the vantage point and stood near her.

"Me?" Talya punched my arm. "This was a team effort, pal. You'd better not forget that."

I smiled. "I won't."

"Let's get some grub first and we can worry about the lodging problem later. I'm not all that concerned though. Worse comes to worst, we can bunk in one of the slumber coffins near a train station."

"What about our stuff?"

"You think we can't get in and get out fast enough to grab our clothes? How long's it take you to pack, anyway?"

"No time at all," I said. "Come on." As we left the area, I cast another look over my shoulder between the crates. I could still see the tendrils of smoke rising slowly into the morning sky. But Moko and his black car had vanished.

Already?

I frowned. That didn't make sense, either.

Fortified with a hearty breakfast, Talya and I grabbed a train back to Kashiwa. We bounced around a few times to shake off anyone who might be tailing us. Japan's a tough place to lose surveillance, though, because the rest of the population looks fairly homogenous. Talya and I stood out. Me more than Talya.

But we played it as best we could and I think we were clean by the time we got back to the hotel. Talya went in first. I followed two minutes later.

Moko was sitting in the lobby again.

I caught a glimpse of Talya in the nearby restaurant. She must have spotted Moko and known something was up.

I felt damned lucky to have her along with me on this trip.

I walked over to Moko. "This is getting to be a habit."

He stood and shook my hand. His cigarette smoke swirled around us. "You have a minute?"

I sat. "Sure."

"How'd you sleep last night?"

I gestured to my clothes. "Does it look like I slept last night?"

"No."

"Because I didn't."

Moko's eyes seemed to radiate sympathy but I knew it wasn't sincere. "That dreadful insomnia keeping you awake, huh?"

I nodded. "Yeah."

"Another night spent wandering the streets of this lonely town?"

I grinned. "Just obeying the whims of my soul I guess."

"Listen to the two of us, huh?" He tipped some ash into the nearby ashtray. "Poets at heart."

"Well, reality has a way of fashioning even the strangest into an odder sort."

"Ain't that the truth." Moko stabbed out his cigarette and started another.

I pointed at the pack of cancer sticks. "Your doctor know you're doing those like a machine gun?"

"Nope." He inhaled hard and then let a thin stream of smoke issue forth from his mouth. "I haven't seen a doctor in about fifteen years."

"Really."

"Really."

"You got a reason for that?"

Moko shrugged. "Deniability. If I don't know about it, it can't kill me." He smiled.

"Interesting philosophy."

"I used to think so."

"Used to?"

"Well, lately, the way things have been happening around this town, I'm starting to wonder if maybe I shouldn't poke my head up from my ostrich hole and see exactly what the hell is going on."

"You think something's going on?"

"I know there is. Just a matter of finding the right nut to crack is all."

I smiled at him. "Some nuts are tougher to crack than others."

"Yes. That is a problem. What I've found over the years is you have to study the nut and somewhere along its natural fault line, you'll find just the right position to focus your attack."

"I didn't think all nuts had natural fault lines."

Moko laughed at that. "It's rare you find one that doesn't."

"But they do exist."

"I have yet to find one."

"Maybe some day."

"Maybe."

He sat there puffing away on his cigarette.

I sat there looking at him.

He smiled at me.

I smiled at him.

"You that nut, Lawson?"

"Which nut is that?"

"The one without a fault line."

"Oh, I've got plenty of faults. But I'm not sure I'm the type that can be cracked. I keep my faults pretty well hidden, I think. Something to do with my natural state of arrogance."

"You think so."

"Yeah."

"Maybe you do keep them hidden." He shrugged. "Or maybe you just think you do."

"Meaning what?"

"Meaning that you think you're being covert and all, but I'm not buying it for one second. And I haven't been buying it ever since you stuck your nose across the crime scene tape at Miss Matsuda's."

"Really."

"Yeah."

"Well, suppose you go ahead and tell me what you think is going on here and if I can help you out, I'll be glad to."

"All right." Moko inhaled and the tip of his cigarette burned bright. He unleashed a mouthful of smoke. "I think you know exactly who killed Yuki."

"What happened to Miss Matsuda?"

"Oh, we're beyond polite now. Now, we're getting into the serious shit."

"Okay."

"I think you know who killed her. What's more, I think you're out to even the score."

"Maybe I hate seeing a good woman gunned down like she was an animal."

Moko kept going with his theory. "Maybe you've run afoul of whoever plugged her, too. Maybe they want you now just as bad as they did Yuki. Maybe they waited in your room last night and grabbed you when you came in. Maybe they brought you to a crummy warehouse down near the fish market and intended to kill you there. But maybe somehow you managed to get away and leave behind a trail of bodies and a burning husk of a building that somehow managed to burn itself to the ground without turning the rest of the waterfront into an inferno. Rather unnatural, that last bit."

Nice to know Talya's incendiary device did the trick. I grinned at Moko. "That's one helluva lot of maybes."

"Sure is."

"Maybe not the best way to build a court case, either."

"Only if you plan on going to court." There was no mirth in his smile this time. Moko probably settled things out of court a lot.

"Yeah?"

"Yeah."

"You going to be judge, jury, and executioner on this?"

"If I have to."

"It's an interesting theory, Moko-san, but I'm afraid you're wrong."

"Am I?"

"Yes."

He nodded. "That why your real girlfriend is sitting in the restaurant trying to pretend she's actually enjoying drinking the awful crap they pass off as coffee around here?"

I almost laughed. Moko was pretty sharp. "You don't like the coffee?"

"It was better at Yuki's."

"Really."

He took his cigarette out of his mouth and regarded it as if it were some nectar of the gods. "I'd been watching her for a while. I used to go in there quite a bit as well. Not when you did. I was there before you arrived."

"And?"

"And I knew she was into something."

"Into something?"

"Something . . . different."

I frowned. "That's an interesting choice of words."

"The something or the different?"

"Yes."

"It's the truth, isn't it? She was into something."

I looked at Moko. He stared back. I took a breath. "Yuki was just doing her job. And she paid the ultimate price for it."

"And now what?"

"Now?" I shrugged. "It's my job to make sure the people who did her get done themselves. By my hand."

It was Moko's turn to sit there and not say anything. I wondered if he'd start espousing police protocol and how civilized societies don't do this kind of thing. After a moment, he put his dead cigarette butt in the ashtray. "Would it be silly to suggest we team up?"

I thumbed in Talya's direction. "I've already got a team."

Without looking, Moko asked, "She any good?"

"One of the best."

"And you?"

"Fixing problems is what I do for a living."

"Some living."

"It has its moments."

"This one of them?"

I smirked. "I'm not here to kill you, Moko. I want the person responsible for Yuki's death, though. And I mean to see it gets done."

Moko sighed. "You're asking me not to interfere."

"I'm asking you to look someplace else for a while."

He stood and shoved both hands into the pockets of his overcoat. "I don't know if I can do that, Lawson."

"You don't want me as an enemy, Moko-san."

He looked down at me. "I'm not your enemy. You just don't know what I am . . . yet." He turned and walked out of the lobby.

And I just sat there.

CHAPTER SEVENTEEN

With the Kensei apparently back in hiding and Moko out there looking to do his best to impede my progress, I wasn't feeling particularly good about my situation. On one hand, I didn't want to have to take Moko out. He struck me as having some deeply ingrained sense of samurai honor and I respected that.

At the same time, I had a score to settle with the Kensei. And for Yuki's sake, I was going to get him. Talya had her own agenda as well. The Kensei just happened to be at the top of her list.

"We're not doing well."

I looked at her as she sipped the cup of coffee from a small stand near the train station at Kita-Narashino, a part of Tokyo that looked like a cornfield of ferroconcrete apartment buildings. We'd spent much of the morning hopping trains to take other trains to take still more trains. As far as we could tell, we didn't have any surveillance on us.

Then again, it's always tough spotting the professionals.

I sipped the bitter green tea and watched the flocks of salarymen weave their way through other crowds bound for the office buildings down near Ginza and Shinjuku.

"We're doing something, though."

Talya shook her head. "I'm not used to operating like this. I want to find this fucker and hit him dead-on. Enough of this try-to-find-me stuff. I've got kids who need avenging."

"And I've got a friend who needs avenging as well." I glanced around the stand and saw no one of interest. "But the Kensei hasn't gotten where he is by being stupid. It takes guts and know-how to stay alive in the underbelly of Japanese society. The yakuza control everything over here and if he's managed to stay around, he's got to be damned good at what he does."

Talya sighed. "We don't even know enough about him to make hunting him a worthwhile venture."

I finished the cup of tea and set it back down on the small plank of wood that served as the counter and eating area. The man running the stand swiped it away before I could even thank him. I slipped some yen across to him and he bowed again. I glanced at Talya. "Let's walk."

Outside the stand, Tokyo was looking to bring down another overcast day on us. Dark gray clouds bloated with rain and smog hugged the tops of the buildings closest to us, obscuring the topmost parts. I felt a spit of drizzle starting up.

"Better get back to the subway."

Talya frowned. "We going somewhere?"

"We need an umbrella."

Talya looked up. "Shit. More rain."

I pointed. "The train stations have scores of umbrella orphans sitting in bins. We can borrow one or two for now."

"And where are we going?"

"Something I just remembered that we haven't had a chance to check out just yet."

"And what's that?"

I led the way into the train station and sure enough, we found a couple of expandable umbrellas in the stand by the cashier. I mumbled a quick *"Domo"* and we found our way down to the platform. I directed Talya toward the very end where no one else stood.

"Remember Yuki mentioned someone she got her information from? Some sort of DJ whiz kid named Mao?"

Talya's eyebrows shot up. "Oh, yeah. All this saving your ass has kept me so busy, I almost forgot about him."

I nudged her with my elbow this time. "I think it's about time we had a talk with him, don't you?"

"Sure as hell beats doing what we're doing right now." Talya sighed. "So much for your vacation, huh?"

"What's that supposed to mean?"

She smiled but it looked like a life's worth of pain was concealed within. "You came here to recuperate. You came here to get away from all the bullshit that plagued you back in the States. I meet up with you and I've got my own agenda. And suddenly you get dragged into it? Hardly seems fair to me."

"Well . . ."

She tugged on my arm. "And if I were you, I'd be really upset at whoever disrupted my plans. In this case, that'd be me."

I grinned. "You want me to be mad at you?"

"Aren't you?"

"Yeah, I'm really pissed that you saved my life yesterday when the Kensei was intent on killing me."

Talya turned away. "Lawson, you wouldn't have been in that situation if it wasn't for me begging you to help."

"You didn't beg. And I knew the risks. I accepted them freely. My choice, my destiny."

She looked back at me. "You say that too easily."

"What, like it's practiced? Maybe it is. Maybe it's just a fact for both of us. Look at what we do. Look at the lives we've chosen for ourselves."

Talya frowned. "Please don't talk to me about choice. And for that matter, I never thought I'd hear you say your life was filled with choice."

She was right, of course. Since when did the illusion of choice enter into my life? My role in vampire society had been predestined before my birth. I'd sat before the Council on my centennial birthday and they'd laid out the various items in front of me. For some reason I'd been drawn to the small sets of scales.

Scales of justice.

The symbol of the Fixer service.

With just that small action, I'd been drawn into a secret society within an already secret society. Our numbers weren't great, but what we did could profoundly affect the entire race of vampires. I was a protector, a judge, a jury, and an executioner, an intelligence-gatherer, a commando, a cop, and now an ally to a human I happened to love.

And I was talking about choice?

I tried to grin and failed, so I sighed instead. "Well, you had a choice when the Soviet Union collapsed. You could have gone and done something else entirely."

"After twenty years of service to the motherland? What was I supposed to do—open a coffee shop?"

I aimed a finger at her. "Hey, don't knock Seattle. It's filled with ex-Communist spooks, I hear."

Talya half smiled. "How you're always able to find something to make light of never ceases to amaze me."

"That's good, because I suck at card tricks."

She shook her head. "This your way of telling me not to worry about it?"

"Does it work?"

"Maybe."

"Fair enough." I could hear the rumble of the train coming toward us. Japanese passengers all stood dutifully in the neat yellow lines marking exactly where the doors of the train would pop open. Talya and I waited until the train had stopped there and all the rest of the passengers had filed on before hopping aboard ourselves.

As usual, I got plenty of looks being a shade over six feet tall. Some of the people moved out of the way as if standing too close to me would be bad for their health. Come to think of it, my recent past had certainly proven that theory in spades.

Talya's voice was close to my ear. "Where are we headed?"

I glanced up at the train map above the door and saw we'd have to make a connection. "Shinjuku."

"To find Mao."

"Right now, that guy's the only lead we've got. May as well track him down and find out how he's able to come by such grade A intelligence. If we can find the Kensei that way instead of waiting for him to try to kill us again, I think that would be a good step in the right direction."

"Agreed."

The cityscape shot past us as we screamed along the track. We'd grabbed an express train that would deposit us in the heart of Tokyo. We'd transfer to a local line for the short hop to Shinjuku.

Outside, the rain fell heavier, sending streams of water down the train at forty-five degree angles as the velocity and wind speed combined to influence the rain. I could just barely hear the steady patter of water atop the train car. Talya leaned into me and she felt nice and warm. I would have much preferred spending a day like this wrapped up in the blankets of our bed back at the hotel.

But the Kensei had ruined that for us as well. Earlier this morning we'd both checked out of the Kashiwa Plaza Hotel and stowed our gear at a storage facility close by Ueno Station. For rest we had two choices: one was the coffin hotels that were basically sleeping tubes tucked into honeycombs of space by train stations. The advantage was absolute privacy. The incredible disadvantage was the fact that it was impossible to fight your way out of a bad situation from a cylinder six feet long.

The second choice made better sense: love hotels.

They were also situated near train stations, but had the advantage of larger rooms. Basically, they were flophouses for getting it on in good style. A lot of schoolgirls and older businessmen hooked up and made arrangements to meet for a little mutual gratification.

Love hotels had the added advantage of anonymity. When you entered, you simply slipped your money through a slot. The proprietors couldn't see you and you couldn't see them. Japan's obsession with saving face enabled folks to screw without having to be shamed by it.

In this case, we'd use that to our advantage.

If Talya felt like a little mutual gratification at the same time, who was I to argue?

She pulled my head toward her, keeping her voice low. "What was the name of that bar again—Tony Tony's?"

I nodded. "Named after a band in the States I think, if my memory serves."

The train rolled into the station and we hopped out. After switching lines, we wandered through the neck-high crowds and found our way down to a darker station, deeper underground. The local train puttered into the station and we found two seats on board. I felt the heat instantly creep up my backside and spine.

"Lawson?"

"Yeah?"

"I think my kundalini just woke up."

She was smiling. That was a good sign. I nudged her and we sat there watching the bricked walls of the subway tunnels pass by the windows. The train seemed almost deserted.

The lights flickered and went on and off again. In a second they came back on, but I found myself surprised that a train on the Tokyo subway system would be in this bad a state of disrepair.

"Lawson."

"Yeah?"

"I've only been to Japan a few times, but I don't recall ever seeing the lights go out on a train."

"I was thinking the same thing."

Talya eased away from me. I went the other way. I could hear the wheels of the train jumping over the tracks. My vision started to tunnel and I fought to keep myself fully aware. I took some deep breaths, fully oxygenating my blood. I could have used a sip of juice to really keep my wires primed, but that would have to wait.

Talya made it to the end of the car and stayed in a sort of semi-crouch by the doorway. I could see the dim outline of one of the SIG Sauers in her hands. She seemed relaxed.

Lithe.

Lethal.

Her eyes swept all sides of the train.

Waiting.

I made it to the other end and mirrored her position. This way, we could cover the entire car without compromise. I drew my own gun and thumbed the safety off. If things went down, I wasn't going to buy it trapped on some dingy piece of shit train in a foreign land.

The train shook some more. The lights flickered again and went off. Talya didn't say a thing and neither did I. My vision showed nothing moving in the darkness. I didn't think anything was in the train car with us.

I wanted to bring the gun up and start firing but that wouldn't have been professional. Nor would it accomplish much. What it would do was waste bullets and tell any potential attackers exactly where I was. That would also compromise Talya.

Were we even under attack? Was I jumping to conclusions? Was this my body's way of trying to convince me I was ready for my godan test? That I could actually sense the premonition of danger somehow?

But if it was just me being irrational, then why was Talya so concerned?

No.

Something wasn't right.

I wasn't guessing or being paranoid.

I needed to *listen* to my gut—to my instinct.

And when I heard the sudden implosion of glass somewhere on the car, I knew things were about to get a whole lot worse.

CHAPTER
EIGHTEEN

I heard Talya fire first, the muzzle flash bright in the dim light of the train. The Soviets must have instilled the whole "spray and ask later" philosophy in her.

I couldn't blame her. In the fringes of my vision, I could make out some forms slithering in through the busted window glass. What—had they somehow jumped on a moving train?

I aimed at the window and fired twice. I heard a squeal or a screech and saw something fly back out of the train. I hoped to hell it landed on the tracks and got promptly serrated into a million gushy pieces.

Talya's gun spat twice more. She was picking her targets now. Aside from the explosion of the gunshots, there were only two sounds: the rushing air from the tunnel outside the busted window and a low hissing breath that reminded me of snakes.

I pivoted without thinking and shot once. Too close to me, I saw someone dressed in black screech and fall away. Whoever it was had gotten much too close to me for comfort.

Talya's gun erupted twice more and I was about to call down for an update on her status when my own pistol was stripped away by something that felt like five scalpels. The blades bit into my skin and drew flaps of skin away. The entire car filled with a heavy copper tinge of blood.

Not good.

A kick landed in my stomach and I rolled left to compensate for the force. I came up with my hands shielding me. Again, my vision caught a glimpse of something slinking around. And again without thinking I fired off a volley of kicks and punches.

I made contact but the new guy knew how to take hits. He shifted and went with the pressure rather than resisting. With my vision now narrowed, I was bleeding badly and had to feel my way in.

Pain was an issue but my surging adrenaline seemed to be keeping that at bay for the moment. God knew what kind of shape I was going to be in later.

If I survived.

I went low and slammed the top of my head into his abdomen. I heard a rush of breath and kept my hands down to ward off the knee strikes I knew would be coming. Instead, I dropped my weight and brought the assailant down to the ground with me.

A barrage of elbows landed on my upper back. It hurt like hell and I saw stars for a moment until I was able to use my shoulder to pump his diaphragm. I felt tension and kept the momentum going forward.

I rolled and let my right foot come down smack onto his head. There was a dull crack and then he lay still.

My breathing was coming in spurts and I had to consciously stop to flush my system with a few good deep inhalations. Losing oxygen and blood together would spell bad news for me.

I heard a final gunshot and got to my feet. I was shaky as hell. Somehow I knew when this was over, my hands were going to be a mess.

"Lawson?"

I stumbled and grabbed a pole. My bloody hands slipped right down to the floor and I fell, knocking my chin on the seat rest. So much for my fashion model career.

"Here."

In the darkness I could see Talya threading her way through the bodies. The wind rushed over me and I found it tough to breathe. I was fighting to stay conscious. Then I sensed Talya close by. Her warmth seemed like a blanket and I wanted nothing more than to draw her up to my chin and fall asleep.

"You're hurt."

"Feels fine." But I knew it wouldn't much longer.

"There's blood everywhere."

I tried to grin. "I believe some of it is theirs."

The train rushed out of the tunnel, blinding us with brilliant daylight. The gray clouds had apparently retreated in favor of rendering Talya and me blind again. I blinked a few times and then looked around the car.

There was blood everywhere. And a lot of it seemed to be jetting out of my hands. My right hand had a long jagged laceration running from the wrist to the tips of my fingers. My left was slightly better.

"A knife?"

"Worse, I think." I pointed to the guy closest to me. "Look at his hands."

Talya bent and examined the guy. "What are these—claws?"

"Maybe the Kensei is a big fan of the X-Men. Got his boys outfitted with Wolverine's claws."

Talya didn't laugh. I didn't mind. Sometimes my jokes suck. But the expression on her face worried me.

"Problem?"

She looked up. "This guy's actually got claws."

"What?"

"It's not some glove. These things are organic claws. Not metal.

Fingernails, but incredibly strong and long and sharp. No wonder he was able to slice you open like that."

I glanced around the train. There were four other bodies in here with us. Talya came over and set about examining my hand.

"You need a bandage or you're going to lose a lot more blood. I don't think that would be a very good idea."

"What—you wouldn't give me a little hit if I needed it?"

She nudged me. "We went through that once. No offense, but I don't really want to do it again."

Back when we'd first met, Cosgrove had bled Talya of nearly all her blood. I'd given her an infusion of mine. Talya had been shaken to the core by it. "I'll try not to be offended."

She knelt next to one of the goons and stripped off his T-shirt. Brilliant dragon tattoos rippled across his muscled body. The calling card of the yakuza gangs. Talya looked at me.

"We're really batting a hundred here if we draw down this much heat from the man." She came back and started to wrap both of my hands in the fabric. My blood seeped through the thin material, but it would eventually clot enough and stop. The plus side of being a vampire is the accelerated coagulating properties of our blood.

But I was in rough shape and we both knew it. "I'm going to need medical attention."

Talya nodded. "You know anyone in the underground here?"

"I think so."

"All right then." Talya helped me to my feet. As she did so, I got another look at the bodies of the men we'd killed. Something didn't seem right.

"Let me down for a second."

She resisted. "You need to rest."

I pulled away from her and walked to the closest corpse. I bent down on shaky knees and looked into the mouth of the goon.

One single canine extended from the gum line like a lone stalactite jutting down from the top of a cave.

One.

I let his lips slip back and stood. "What the hell is going on here?"

Talya checked the other bodies. "They've all got one tooth, Lawson. Just one."

One canine didn't make sense at all. I looked at the base of the collarbones of each man.

No birthmark that identified my race.

"They're not vampires."

Talya frowned. "But the tooth . . . ?"

I shook my head. "There's no birthmark on them."

"Maybe they got it removed when they did the tattoo."

I looked at her. "You don't understand. The birthmark that marks us all is something we can't ever erase. It's on us no matter what we do to our skin. It's not something topical. It comes from within and it's watermarked on every layer of skin we have. You could use acid to wipe it out and a day later it would be back."

"But if they're not vampires, what the hell are they?"

"With one tooth?" I shook my head. "I don't know."

The roar of the wind lessening brought me back to reality. And our reality was that we were going to be entering a train station very shortly. And with four bodies, a busted window, and much blood splattered about, things were going to get crazy unless we managed to vanish before then.

Luckily, I was working with Talya who understood the situation and didn't need explaining to.

"The window's our best bet."

The landscape rushed by us outside. "You ever jumped from a train before?"

She smiled. "Lots of times. Just not by using a jagged glass-busted window as support."

I ducked my head out. We were about a mile away from the station. I could see crowds milling around the platform.

"Got to be now."

Talya kicked out the bottom rim of the glass and then hoisted herself up on the frame. She looked at me. "Remember to run in the same direction as the train is moving."

"Thanks."

She kissed me on the cheek. "Just a friendly reminder, oh, wounded one."

I watched her leap from the train and land on deeply bent knees. She ran for a few steps and then rolled off to the side of the tracks on the gravel.

Road rash was going to be a bitch today.

I got up on the edge and felt the wind rush through my short hair. The platform was coming up even closer now. I took a breath, felt myself go woozy and then just leapt into the air.

I came down hard and tried to stay upright to run with the train. My legs buckled and I went down. Luckily, my rolling saved me and took me down a steep embankment. I rolled and opened my body up to stop the forward momentum. Bits of gravel and rocks bit into my back.

I came to rest in a puddle of grimy water. It soaked my backside and I smelled something awful. A dead rat lay nearby, bloated in death.

Great.

"You okay?"

I looked up in time to see Talya getting closer.

"Lawson, you all right?"

She didn't wait for me to answer but moved over and got a hand under my right arm, trying to hoist me up. My legs felt really shaky.

"You don't look so good, lover boy."

My stomach rolled. "I don't feel particularly nifty, either."

Talya felt my neck. "Your pulse isn't exactly thrilling me. You've lost a lot of blood."

I glanced back at the station as I heard the first police wailing sirens cut through the air. "No time to think about it. We've got to get out of here."

Talya's face showed deep concern. "You need a doctor. What's the name of the guy you know?"

"We're actually close. His name is Kennichi. Lives maybe a block from the station, if I've guessed right."

The daylight had once again yielded to the gray oppressive clouds again and rain was now pissing down on us. The water merged with my blood and turned it into a river of pink dripping off of my arms.

Talya peered back at the station. "Cops'll start down the track soon."

"If they haven't spotted us already."

Talya nodded. "Can you walk?"

"I think so."

I took a step and felt my legs trying hard to stay locked in position. My stomach lurched and I felt my gorge rising in the back of my throat. It didn't seem to make sense that a wound was having this much effect on me.

The look on Talya's face as she helped me stumble along didn't help, either.

"Sweetheart . . . I feel like shit."

"You're pale. Something's wrong with you, Lawson."

I grinned. "That's some bedside manner you've got there. I suppose you don't dress up like a nurse?"

Talya frowned. Another sign she was concerned. "You think you're going to be able to make it to your friend's place?"

I nodded but my muscles were feeling really slack. "It's just over there."

Somehow we managed to make it to the road and I took a deep breath. "I need to rest."

Talya helped me sit down. "I'm getting a taxi. Don't go away."

I watched her move off in a sprint. I don't know where she was getting the energy to run after having leapt from a speeding train. Quite a woman she was. I felt like three tons of shit had just been dumped on top of me.

I thought about Japan. I thought about the fight we'd just had and how surreal it always was being in combat.

A breeze blew over me and I shivered.

Shit, I was going into shock.

Where was Talya?

I slumped back without realizing it. The ground felt strangely warm. Inviting. My eyes felt heavy.

I gave in and blackness embraced me.

CHAPTER NINETEEN

"Byoki ni naru, dayo."

"I know he's sick, idiot. Do something to make him better."

From behind the veil of darkness, I could hear the voices. I picked out Talya's as the pissed-off woman speaking English. The other one I hadn't heard in a very long time. I tried to open my eyes.

"Kennichi-san."

The room swam into view as a molten mass of bright light and pale green walls. Two forms stood over me. Kennichi's face bounced into view. He was still wearing those ridiculous large black-framed glasses with the thick lenses.

"Ah, Lawson-san. This is good you are able to open your eyes."

"Probably about the only thing that feels decent right now."

Kennichi nodded. "I was able to staunch your wounds. The cuts were fairly deep. You lost much blood, but I think you should be able to recover . . . given your genetic makeup."

Talya tried to smile. "Just don't think you're getting any from me."

"Always so reassuring to hear from my true friends." I took a breath and listened to the rattle in my lungs. Kennichi heard it, too, and his face betrayed him again. "What's going on with me?"

"I don't know, Lawson-san. The wounds seem to have been taken care of. They are already starting to heal, but this . . . your lungs . . . I don't know what causes it."

I looked at Talya. "A toxin?"

She shrugged. "Plenty of them around that could do this to someone. I wouldn't have thought your kind would be susceptible to them, however."

"Learn something new every day, I guess." I closed my eyes and tried to picture the fight again as it had unfolded. On cue, my hand started to throb. I opened my eyes and looked down. Kennichi had wrapped the entire limb in gauze. I looked like I had a puffy white glove on.

"There must have been something on those blades they cut me with."

Talya leaned back. "Something our friends have been working on?"

"Maybe."

Kennichi pulled out his stethoscope and placed it on my chest. I could see the lines in his forehead deepen. "There is much buildup of fluid in your lungs. You need to expel it."

"Sure. I'd love to oblige. Any idea how to do it?"

Kennichi nodded. "I'll return shortly. Do not attempt to go anywhere."

I grinned. "Are you kidding? How the hell would I walk out of here now?"

Kennichi sighed. "I do not know. In fact, I still do not know how you managed to leave my care the last time you were badly wounded and I told you to stay still. And yet, you somehow did it."

I grunted. "I had places to be."

Kennichi nodded. "Such a stubborn fool. But listen, my friend, if you leave now, there is every chance you will die very soon." He vanished out of the office, leaving me alone with Talya.

She thumbed over her shoulder. "He really going to get something for you or is he just giving us a private moment to strategize?"

Kennichi was a good man. "Maybe both."

She leaned closer and I stared into her eyes. "What do you need me to do?"

"Just keep looking as beautiful as you are right now."

She laughed and kissed my forehead. "You won't say it."

"Say what?"

"What you know I need to do."

"I don't want your blood, Talya. I've got some juice back at the lockers in—"

"Lawson, Kennichi is right, you know that? You are one stubborn son of a bitch."

I started to protest, but my lungs seized and I started coughing hard. A wad of sputum flew from my mouth and stained the opposite wall. Even from where I was lying down, I could see it was bright red.

"Damn."

"I'm leaving." Talya started to pull away, but I grabbed her hand.

"Wait."

She turned back. "We need to know what was on those blades. That means I have to go back and find the bodies."

"Place'll be swarming with cops."

"Probably."

I sighed. "Moko might be there."

"The guy you've been running into all the time?"

"Yeah."

Talya shrugged. "That's assuming he can even see me."

I took another breath and heard my lung rattle like worn shutters again. "This isn't like other countries, Talya. The folks guarding the scene won't be lazy security guards you can easily bypass. They'll be professionals who will not take any chances if they think you're an imposter."

Talya sighed. "I've operated all over the world and you know what? The experiences have taught me a lot of things. But of all of them, one thing remains consistent no matter what: sentry duty is a bitch and a half to pull. Eventually, everyone—and I mean everyone—gets bored. All I have to do is wait until that happens."

I was too tired to argue. I just nodded. "Be careful."

Kennichi's head reappeared followed by the rest of his body through the curtained door. "And hurry. We must know soon what it is that infects Lawson. Or he will die."

Talya nodded, blew me a kiss, and vanished. Kennichi watched her go and then looked back at me. "She is a lovely woman."

"Yeah."

"And you are a tired old man."

My eyes widened. Kennichi was laughing now. "I thought that might get your attention."

"So much for Japanese customs."

"Lawson, we are old friends, you and I. And it's good to see you again. After the last time, I had no idea if you had lived or died once you left my care."

"I would have sent word . . ."

Kennichi nodded. "*So desu.* But it was not the right time. I understand."

I'd screwed up. Writing Kennichi to thank him for patching me up had been on my mind, but as usual, the job and life had intervened. And now, here I was again, back on his slab expecting him to help me, the ungrateful prick that I was.

"I should have written. I'm sorry."

He nodded, brushing it off even though that was the last thing he was doing. "I see the years have impressed on you the need for companionship."

"Talya?"

"Yes."

"Well, she's not really . . . I mean, she's not exactly—"

"Sure seems to be." He smiled at me some more and then held a small cup up to my lips. "Drink this."

"What—" But Kennichi pushed the cup at me and I felt the hot liquid wash into my mouth, sliding down the back of my throat. I sputtered and coughed and swallowed some more.

I started to protest, but felt a jolt of energy hit me like a brick. "What the hell is that stuff?"

"Old family recipe."

"Tasted a little like sake."

"It is part sake."

"And part . . . blood?"

Kennichi smiled. "You think you are the first vampire I've treated here? My family's service to your kind goes back many hundreds of years. What is the term you use for humans who know of your kind?"

"Loyalists."

"My family was among the first."

I could feel the juice coursing through my system. I felt marginally better. "I never knew that."

Kennichi smiled. "Well, you left so fast the last time you were here we never had a chance to discuss it."

I coughed some more, but it wasn't as severe. "Any more of that stuff in the back room?"

"Yes. Plenty. But for now, you must only ingest a little bit. Too much will throw off your metabolism."

I sank back down and closed my eyes. "Where did you get the blood?"

"Does it matter?"

"I like to know."

Kennichi cleared his throat. "A car accident a week ago. I was first on the scene being the neighborhood doctor here. We moved one of the victims in here and there was a great deal of blood loss. I simply stored some of it in preparation for your visit."

I opened my eyes. "You knew I'd be coming?"

Kennichi suddenly seemed a lot older than I knew he was. "Lawson, there is nothing so mystical about it. One only needs to pay attention to the innate abilities we all possess to see how the universe flows. It is like a wheel, after all. We keep going around again and again. Your wheel has simply come around again and here you are. Here I am."

"I think I got a flat tire, friend."

Kennichi laughed. "Regardless of how you choose to interpret it, the fact is I knew you would be coming and I prepared myself for your arrival. Lucky for you, I should say."

"Lucky for me, indeed." I pointed at the cup. "What else is in that drink of yours?"

"Some special ingredients. Family secrets, really. But you should know that they have helped others before you."

"I believe it."

"And at the very least, the drink will make you feel better in the event we don't discover the true nature of what ails you."

"You mean in case I die?"

"Yes."

The clock on the wall read just after six in the evening. Darkness would come in a few hours. That would provide Talya with the cover she'd need to infiltrate the crime scene and steal a sample of what those punks might have laced their blades with. Kennichi began humming to himself. I cleared my throat again. "I don't suppose there's any way to tell what is in me from doing a blood workup, huh?"

He turned to look at me. "You know that your blood doesn't hold traces of what it contains. It metamorphosises what is ingested almost immediately. Any trace of that toxin is gone, but interestingly, the effects are still rampant. It leads me to believe that this toxin was precisely engineered for use against other vampires."

"Swell."

Kennichi nodded at the table. "Your best course of action is to take it easy. Try to relax and wait for your friend to return with the answers we need to make you better."

I suddenly wanted to get up and move. "I'm not much for relaxing when someone's trying to kill me."

Kennichi came closer. "Lawson, if you do not relax, then all you will do is aid that person in killing you."

"Yeah."

Kennichi looked at me with sad eyes. "It's been many years."

"Too long."

"I've missed you, my friend."

I clasped his hand with my somewhat good paw and squeezed it. "Likewise. I wish this wasn't how it had to be right now. I'd rather go out and have a good dinner and reminisce about the last time I was here than have to be here again."

"We can't always choose how our destinies unfold. All we can do is ride them as best we are able."

I looked away. "I've never been much of a fan of my own destiny."

"You toss it aside too casually. What you do is vital to the survival of your race. There is much honor in that."

"I suppose."

Kennichi frowned. "Your attitude wears on me."

"Huh?"

"Rest now, Lawson."

"Hang on, I don't want to rest. I—"

Kennichi turned back and placed his hand under my ear. I felt a slight bit of pressure and then the room faded into blackness again. My last thought as I drifted off was how I'd somehow forgotten the guy was a master of vital points manipulation.

I hoped Talya was having better luck than me.

CHAPTER TWENTY

The state I was in lying on Kennichi's examination room table didn't lead me off into some gentle slumber. Instead, I was treated to a maelstrom of my own past. I saw my fallen enemies rise up against me again and again, coming back when all the bullets in my gun wouldn't stop them or even slow them down.

I woke up screaming.

Kennichi rushed in with more of his family recipe, poured it down my gullet, and then snuck back out of the room. He'd mixed in something else this time and it left me totally relaxed.

But unable to sleep.

The dream that had woken me reminded me of the one I'd had back before I'd gone to New York. I had plenty of demons in my past. I hoped I didn't have a whole lot of them in my future.

That desire, of course, supposed I even had a future. If Talya didn't come back with the goods, I was a goner.

Warmth spread throughout my body. Kennichi's home brew probably would have made me feel like a million bucks if I hadn't been poisoned somehow. Even still, I was glad he'd gotten it into me.

Talya.

Japan.

They were both an oasis in my turbulent life. So why were they now part of the Hell that sought to engulf me?

I thought back to when I'd first met Talya in Boston during Cosgrove's last murder spree. He'd made a big mistake taking Simbik out. Simbik was good friend of mine. But worse for Cosgrove, Simbik had also been Talya's fiancé. Hell hath no fury like a professional assassin named Talya.

I smiled in spite of my wounds and the toxin running through my body. Talya's obstinacy back in Boston had been part of what made me fall in love with her. Her determination and professionalism even in the face of overwhelming odds had endeared her all the more.

And how she'd handled learning all about the vampire race—taken it in stride—had completed me falling head over heels for her. Well, that and how utterly magnificent she looked naked.

"He looks happy."

"Maybe he dreams about you."

"You think?"

"Well, perhaps not. He certainly is far too stubborn to ever admit it, of course."

I opened my eyes. "How the hell am I supposed to convalesce if you two jabber on every time I nod off?"

Talya turned to Kennichi. "You see how ungrateful he is? What I have to put up with? The attitude, I tell you."

Kennichi's eyes crinkled at the corners. "If I read your relationship correctly, there is also a fair amount of up-putting on his side."

Talya frowned. "I should have known you'd take his side."

"Uh . . ."

They turned back to me. I raised my better hand. "I hate to break up the repartee, but did you happen to find anything?"

Talya held up a black cloth bag. "One sample of the blade that bit you right here."

I glanced at Kennichi. "Can you run tests on that?"

Kennichi took the bag and peered into it. He nodded after a moment. "I have a gas chromatograph that should be able to make some sense out of this. It will take a little while to get the results."

"I'm not going anywhere."

Kennichi nodded and left with the bag. Talya slid onto the edge of the examination table and kissed me on the forehead. I could feel the heat bleeding off of her. She must have been running the entire way.

She looked at me, brushed her hand along the side of my cheek. "How are you feeling?"

"Been better, but I'm happy you're back." I pointed at my bandaged body. "I feel a little helpless without you around."

"Well, I'm back and I'm not going anywhere without you now. As soon as Kennichi tells us what you've got rummaging around your insides, we'll get you fixed up and then go have ourselves a sit-down with the Kensei."

I smirked. "Persuade him to give up his errant ways?"

She smiled. "Something like that."

"I usually let my gun do the talking for me. He's a far better negotiator than I am."

"I'm not much of a conversationalist myself."

I tried to lift myself up but my muscles failed me. Talya saw my effort and leaned down some more. Our lips met and we held the kiss for a lot longer than we needed to. But not as long as I wanted to.

Kennichi cleared his throat coming through the curtain and we broke apart. I could see he was torn between being Japanese and not mentioning the fact we'd been making out on his examination table and giving into his Western proclivities and chastising us for acting like horny teenagers.

The battle lasted two seconds. "The machine is set up and running the sample right now. We should know something within a few minutes." He turned to go back outside, but stopped and turned back with a wry grin. "You keep that up and I'll demand you name the child after me."

Talya actually giggled, something I'd heard her do maybe twice in the years I'd known her. Kennichi's body disappeared through the curtain and I hugged Talya close again.

"I love you." It felt good saying it.

She peered into my eyes. "You know, as bad as this whole lousy trip has been, the very best part has been being able to be with you for longer than twelve hours."

"Hey, we've packed a lot of loving into our twelve-hour smooch-fests."

Her face grew serious. "I want more than twelve hours, Lawson."

"I don't know how much more I have to give. I'm already pretty spent here."

"You know what I'm talking about."

I sighed and pulled away from her. "We need to talk about this now? Being that I'm somewhat close to death and all? Can't we maybe put this off for right now?"

Talya got off the table and walked over to one of the shelves where Kennichi had various bottles and containers of medicine. The labels were mostly in Japanese, but a few were in English. Talya pretended to study one of them and then faced me again.

"If you died right now—"

"Wow, spoil the mood, why don't you?"

"The mood was already spoiled. And I'm being serious. I need an answer from you."

I took a breath. "Go ahead."

She came closer to me. "If you died right now, what would your biggest regret be?"

A thousand possible responses flew from my brain. I thought about the deaths I'd left unavenged. I thought about the shadowy enemies still left lurking. I thought about my friends back home—

the few I had. I thought about the lingering doubts I had about how my mother had died all those years ago.

But as fast as they all came at me, only one bulldozed the rest out of the way. Only one juggernauted its way to the forefront of whatever tiny amount of gray matter I still possessed. And I spoke the words before I even realized I was going to.

"Not being with you."

Talya's eyes misted over. Maybe if I'd been feeling 100 percent I would have had some tears of my own. But as it was, the emotion of the exchange had taken a toll on me. I felt exhausted and tired. I could feel my eyes closing even though I wanted them to stay open. Even though I wanted to stay awake so I could make sure Talya was crying because she was happy and not because she was sad.

But I couldn't.

I felt her lips brush mine. A tiny kiss planted itself on me and I heard her whisper something in her native tongue of Kazak. It sounded nice, even if Kazak was one of the few languages I didn't speak.

It didn't sound like she was saying good-bye.

My dreams this time were a lot nicer.

But the wake-up call sucked.

"Lawson!"

Talya's voice was a harsh whisper. I could feel the energy of the room change. That and the fact that I didn't feel like a bag of shit anymore were the two things that dawned on me immediately.

I opened my eyes. "What is it?"

Kennichi was nowhere to be seen. Talya was furiously trying to help me off the table. "We have to get out of here."

"Why?"

"That cop, the Japanese guy you called Moko."

"What about him?"

"He's here!"

Shit. How the hell had he managed that?

Talya got my jacket on my shoulders. "I took all precautions. I triple-backed on myself to make sure I wasn't being followed. But I also had to hurry and get the sample back to Kennichi. He must have been there waiting for me or something, I don't know. My God, Lawson, I'm so sorry. I led him right to you."

"We don't know it was you." I slid my jacket on some more. "Did Kennichi find something?"

"He identified the toxin and gave you an antidote. But it's still going to take some time before you feel entirely better. You need to rest still. What you most definitely do not need is an annoying cop poking his nose around us."

I grinned. "Moko's definitely good at that."

Talya stopped. "I could kill him and be done with it."

I put a hand on her shoulder. "No."

"You sure?"

"We might need him." And I didn't want to have to kill him. At least not yet.

Talya shook her head. "I can't imagine why."

"It's better that we don't burn this bridge. If he becomes a problem later on, we'll take him out, trust me. The toxin didn't damage my sense of judgment about issues like that."

She smiled. "All right. Let's go."

"Where's Kennichi?"

"Stalling, I think."

I'd promised myself I wouldn't leave him without saying good-bye. Not again. Not like the last time. I sighed. So much for being a man of my word.

Talya got the back window open. "Can you climb?"

"I'll have to, I guess."

She gave me a hand up and I squirmed through the window. My hands throbbed, but a lot less than they had before. I got my body through the opening and dropped to the alley running behind the building. Darkness enveloped me as I waited in the shadows. I caught a whiff of soy sauce from somewhere close by.

Talya dropped silently a second later. She used hand gestures to communicate with me. I gave thanks for vampires having great eyesight in the darkness.

She dropped her hand to her side and waved me on.

Follow.

Together, we scampered down the alley, being careful not to disturb the trash cans or debris that littered the area. Kennichi deliberately kept the area around his office dirty and filled with all sorts of natural burglar alarms. It made sense, but it also made our progression a lot slower than I would have liked. If we got tripped up now, it would be our asses.

Talya stopped cold.

I did, too.

Her left hand formed a fist and the thumb pointed straight down.

Enemy seen.

I squirmed up next to her. I could make out two police cars with their lights off waiting at the end of the street. Why weren't they in front of Kennichi's house? Were they on patrol? Or were they attached to Moko?

I nodded for us to go back the way we'd come.

I heard the sound then that I knew well enough. I caught the scent of sulfur a moment later. A match being struck. A small wisp of flame lit up the other end of the alleyway.

The tip of a cigarette glowed bright red and there was a rush of smoke being exhaled into the air. Moko's face came into view a moment later. He held a nasty-looking gun in one hand and smoked with the other.

"I think, Lawson-san, that you and I need to have another talk."

CHAPTER
TWENTY-ONE

We sat surrounded by diners at a fugu restaurant on the back-side of nowhere. I had flashbacks to an earlier trip to Japan when I'd saved the life of what turned out to be a master sword maker and he treated me to dinner at such a place. Some of the very best restaurants in Japan are at family-owned hole-in-the-wall joints you'd never notice unless someone told you about them.

Fugu is blowfish and it contains a serious neurotoxin that can render you dead in a short time. First your breathing slows and then stops as respiratory arrest sets in. From there, cardiac arrest is a spit away from claiming you.

Fun stuff.

Chefs need to be licensed in order to even prepare the dish. Now and then, throughout Japan, there are still isolated cases where someone dies if the poison sac isn't handled just so and a little bit of the toxin spills into the fish meat itself. The adrenaline of even ordering such a thing combines with the pleasurable experience of seeing it masterfully prepared and placed in front of you. The final choice to bite into it and enjoy the culinary experience of your life is then in your hands.

Moko ordered three dishes. One for me. One for Talya. And one for himself.

Russian roulette, Japanese-style.

Talya sat with her back to the wall appraising the restaurant, which was a dimly lit wood-paneled hideaway with dangling scrolls in recessed parts of the wall called *tokonoma*. Ikebana flower arrangements dotted the expanse of walls. The conversation was hushed, possibly out of respect for the serious nature of the dining here.

I had a Sapporo draft in front of me. Moko had two. Talya drank green tea.

"We're not at the police station," I said after taking a nice long drag on my beer. Probably wasn't a good move on my part, what with the gallons of medicine swimming through my veins, but what the hell. Moko's appearance at Kennichi's clinic could mean that things were getting even more serious than they already were. A little alcohol might even help me adapt to the situation.

Moko eyed the package of cigarettes sitting in front of him. I could see the longing in his eyes, the need to take a smoke. But he wouldn't. Not here. No chance he'd wish to interfere with the smell and tastes of what was being served.

"Obviously," he said. He consoled himself with an equally long sip of his own beer. He had a backup if he drained the first one, after all.

"So, we're not in trouble?"

Moko sniffed the air. I couldn't tell if he was being derisive or genuinely wanted to catch a whiff from the kitchen. "I haven't decided exactly what you two are just yet, Lawson-san. And much depends on how you both answer some questions. If I'm satisfied you're telling the truth, well, then the night just might improve for you."

"And you're buying us dinner to bribe us into talking?"

"I never said I was buying. I merely took you here because I'm hungry. As far as I'm concerned right now, you can both wash dishes to pay off your tab."

"Wish I'd known that before you ordered for us," said Talya around a frown.

"There's no fun in that," said Moko.

Talya sipped her tea, set the cup down, and leaned closer to Moko. "I don't like skirting around issues. I know it's the Japanese way, but I'm not Japanese so forgive me for being blunt, but what the hell?"

Moko smiled. "You are most definitely not Japanese. In fact, you are a combination of Kazak and Chinese, if your file isn't mistaken."

I'd seen Talya blanch maybe once before. But even she leaned back for a second. "How'd you get my file?"

Moko smiled some more. "You'd be amazed what your countrymen are willing to sell these days. I could invade a small country if I wanted to and had enough disposable income."

Talya clammed up. Moko turned to me. "Interestingly enough though, there is no file to be found on my good friend Lawson-san here. You are truly what I would call an enigma."

I toasted him with my beer. "I suppose that's better than an enema."

"And with such a sarcastic bent to you, you'd think someone would know a little something about you. But no, no trace of you anywhere."

"I'm a mystery wrapped up in another mystery."

Moko took another drink. He didn't seem too fazed by anything. That worried me.

"As I said, there's no mention of you in conventional circles." He grinned and eyed the cigarettes again. "But I don't run exclusively in conventional circles."

I set my beer back down. "Which means what?"

"Which means I know you aren't human."

Uh-oh.

Moko held up his hand. "Now please, before you start sputtering all sorts of excuses and attempts to mislead me, bear in mind what I said earlier. Much of whether you enjoy your evening or not depends on how you answer my questions."

"I'm not agreeing with you."

"I wouldn't expect you to. At least not yet." Moko paused as the miso soup arrived. He took several deep gulps and wiped his mouth before continuing. "I know that you have stumbled onto something very serious here in my country. I know it involves someone called the Kensei."

Talya said nothing. I thought about letting Moko know there was a piece of tofu stuck to one side of his chin but decided not to.

"You," said Moko, pointing at me with his index finger, "were involved in a planned assassination attempt on a subway train the day you arrived in Japan."

"You have witnesses?"

Moko shook his head. "Not a one. But I have video."

"There's no video surveillance at that station."

Moko nodded. "Absolutely correct. Some of the neighborhood activists have stonewalled our attempts to install latest generation vid links down there. Jimbocho and Kanda are in a historic section of town after all. Despite our assurances to the contrary, they are convinced our installation will mar the stonework."

"But you say you have video."

"I do. I most definitely do. Because while there is no video in the station, there is across the street. The McDonald's there allowed us to install several cameras. And I have a fabulous shot of someone who bears an amazing resemblance to you emerging from Jimbocho the day of the killing."

"I didn't kill that guy. His target did. I guess I kept the assassin busy while his mark got into position behind him and gave him the good news."

Moko bowed his head slightly. "I appreciate your candor on that subject. And for what it's worth, you don't strike me as the type to stab someone in the back."

"I appreciate that."

Our dishes arrived. The fugu rested in a small puddle of sauce, its meat splayed open to reveal the juicy interior. We all took a moment to appreciate the care with which the chef had prepared our food. I offered a silent prayer to the gods about eating it. I wasn't sure what a neurotoxin would do to my system, but I also was pretty sure I didn't want to find out. Not after having been poisoned already once today.

"This is the safest place to eat fugu in all Japan," said Moko. "I would not have taken you here otherwise."

Talya poked at her fish. "I've heard this stuff can kill you."

"It can."

I broke my chopsticks. They split evenly down the middle. Moko nodded at them. "A good day to do battle tomorrow."

I said nothing but took a piece of the meat and chewed it. The vague taste of chicken was replaced by a slight tingling of my lips. The chef had been careful to leave just enough of the toxin to produce a slight sense of paralysis near my mouth. And the experience of eating it continued to flood my brain with memories of the sword maker and the time we'd spent in conversation in a restaurant like this years and years before.

For a moment, Talya and Moko disappeared and I felt transported back in time. Where had the years gone? I was the better part of a hundred and fifty years old and in many ways it felt like time was creeping up on me. I saw young people enjoying life and I felt jealous. That they'd made choices I could never make. That they'd do things I could never do. That they could love whom they wanted without fear of absolute reprisal.

Their destiny was their own to make what they wanted of.

My destiny had been handed to me. And I'd been living it without freedom of choice ever since.

I glanced back at Talya. I loved her but I couldn't love her. We lived a secret relationship. Forbidden because humans and vampires aren't supposed to fall in love. I'd be killed for it. And I'd killed others in the past for doing what I was doing right now.

Where the hell did I get the right?

From a cheap set of pewter scales I'd chosen at my centennial birthday in front of the Council. Born into a Fixer. An elite chosen one who could hand down punishments with one helluva lot of autonomy.

"Lawson."

I blinked my eyes and realized I hadn't even swallowed the food in my mouth. I did so and took a breath. Talya was looking at me intently.

"You okay?"

I took a drag on my beer and nodded. "Just seeing some ghosts from the past is all."

Moko eyed me as well. "You are a man haunted by shadows."

"Right now I'm being haunted by you. And I'm not sure exactly what it is that you want from me."

Moko's dish was half done. He rested his elbows on the low table and leaned toward me. "I want what you want. The Kensei."

My eyebrows must have jumped, because he leaned back and laughed some. "You're surprised?"

"Very."

Moko nodded. "That means my ruse has worked."

"Ruse?" said Talya.

Moko nodded. "You think I am an inspector with the Tokyo Metropolitan Police. Correct?"

"Yes."

"And I am. But I am also much more than that." His face wrinkled. "Or much less depending on how you look at things."

"Which means what?" Moko's games were getting old on me.

Moko aimed a finger at Talya now. "You came to Japan a few days before Lawson."

"Yes."

"To do what exactly?"

Talya glanced at me but I could only shrug. Things were being revealed all over the place and I wasn't sure how to answer anyone's questions anymore.

"To stop the flow of illegal organ trafficking."

"You came upon this how?"

Talya glanced at me as if weighing her options and then frowned. "I sponsor a small village in Africa. I give them money so the kids have a chance to get an education and actually be kids. Someone came to the village and slaughtered them, stole their organs. I followed the trail here."

"Do you know the reason those organs were taken?"

Talya shrugged. "Not really. I've heard things, of course."

"Like what?"

"Like they're sold to Chinese medicine merchants who turn them into aphrodisiacs and other elixirs used for a wide variety of things. I've also heard they're used by wealthy transplant recipients who don't want to wait for their turn to be called on a long list."

Moko took another sip of his beer. "Those are what most people believe stolen organs are used for."

"Is what Talya said wrong?"

Moko shook his head. "No. Not wrong. Just not all right."

"That doesn't make sense," said Talya.

"It makes as much sense as me saying Lawson-san here isn't human. I'm not wrong, but I'm not all right, either."

"So that leaves us where?"

Moko took a few more bites of his fugu and helped himself to the tightly packed dish of white rice. With several deft swipes from his chopsticks, the rice vanished. Moko chewed and then drank and then wiped his mouth before settling himself back with a sigh.

"Nothing like a good meal."

"Nothing like getting some answers, too," I said. I could tell Talya was ready to leap over the table and make Moko talk whether he wanted to or not. I'd seen Talya in action before and knew she could be quite persuasive if she wanted to be.

Moko sucked at his teeth. "The truth is this: the organs being harvested by the Kensei are being used to create a race of hybrid beings."

I shook my head. "What?"

"A hybrid race. The organs are combined in such a way that they are compatible to both types of species being brought together."

"What—like aliens?"

"Nothing extraterrestrial, I assure you. But it may well seem so to the uninitiated. Fortunately none of us fall into that category."

I cleared my throat. "What species are being combined?"

"Humans for one," said Moko. "And vampires for the other."

"Vampires?" Talya wore a grin on her face.

Moko stopped her. "Remember what I said. I know for a fact that you are both well aware of the existence of vampires on this planet."

I said nothing. Moko smiled and kept talking.

"You, Lawson-san, are a vampire. As was Matsuda-san. You are what's known as a Fixer—a special operationsesque commando, secret agent, judge, jury, and executioner all rolled into one heavy package."

He tuned to Talya. "You are a human. But your past involves wet work for the Soviets, espionage for them as well. In recent years you have done work all over the globe, vetting yourself in almost every large and small conflict known. You've been praised for your incredible competency by governments and individuals alike."

"You're making me blush," said Talya.

Moko ignored her. "You two met several years ago and developed, well—shall I call it a special relationship?"

"Friendship," I said. "Nothing more."

Moko smiled. "Your secret is safe with me, Lawson-san."

Talya frowned. "And what about you? You said you were a cop but were more than that. Since we're all letting the secrets out, how about you do us the same favor?"

Moko took a deep breath and let it fall out of him all at once. "I am like the both of you."

"Doesn't tell us much," said Talya.

"Doesn't it?" asked Moko. "All right then."

I frowned. "You're a vampire, too?"

Moko shook his head. "No." He polished off his second beer and slapped the can back down on the table. "I am both vampire and human. I am a hybrid."

CHAPTER TWENTY-TWO

Talya's words came out slow and measured. "How . . . exactly . . . is that possible?" She glanced at me. "I mean, from what I've been told, it's not physiologically a good idea to combine both species in a fashion like you. The results and all . . ."

"She's right." I shook my head. "There have been experiments over the course of our time but none of them have ever proven successful. Eventually, testing was banned due to the failure rates."

Moko's face was hard to read. Part of him seemed to be both sad and proud at the same time. "The testing continued in the underground. The Council, despite its powers and eyes on the ground in the Fixer ranks, does not catch everything."

I smirked. He had a definite point there. "Tell me something I don't know."

Moko gestured to the waitress and asked for sake to be brought over. We waited until she brought the hot container and three small cups and set it down on our table. Talya poured for us. Moko stopped her.

"That's not necessary."

Talya smiled. "I'm not sacrificing my independence by being polite."

Moko looked at me. "I think I'm starting to understand why you are so attracted to her."

I didn't say anything. Talya served Moko his cup first and then gave me one. I poured for her and the three of us held our cups up. Moko gave a curt bow and then we all tipped the cups to our lips.

Sake is best served hot—98.6 degrees to be exact. Drinking cold sake has gained some ground in recent years but I find it disgusting. Hot sake has a smooth bite to it that creeps over your body like a dull fog. I'm not a big sake drinker, but I do appreciate the lulling effect it has, especially when it comes from one of the master makers.

Moko put his cup down. I refilled it for him. Therein lay the problem with drinking sake. Japanese custom demands that cups be kept filled. Allowing someone's cup to be empty was considered rude. It meant by the end of the evening, you've had a helluva lot more sake than might be evident.

"We were designed some years back."

I took a sip of my drink. "We?"

"There were many of us. At least fifty."

Talya's frown crept into my peripheral vision. "The Kensei made you?"

Moko nodded. "Yes. There were supposed to be more of us. Many more."

"An army," I said then before even realizing I'd let the words jump out of my mouth.

Moko wasn't the least bit perturbed by my statement. "Exactly. He wanted us to help him take over. First the vampire world and then later on we would begin our systematic domination of humans and other races."

"So what happened?"

"The problem with creating a sentient race is just that—sentience. We were created in his image, to be adept fighters and skilled in a variety of methods for use as his private army."

"But?"

Moko shrugged. "But we didn't want to spend our lives killing for him. Being sentient and capable of reason and thought like any other living being, we knew what we were supposed to do. And it didn't sit well with the majority of us."

"That must not have gone over so well."

"It didn't. When he learned of our plans to stop him from carrying out his scheme for domination, he had many of us killed. Those who could, fled."

"You've been in hiding?" asked Talya.

"For many years." Moko drained his cup again. I signaled the waitress for another serving of sake. We were going to need a lot of it, apparently.

"The Kensei began hunting down those of us he could find. It has taken him a long time to do so, but he has been almost entirely successful."

"Almost?"

Moko smiled at me. "The hit on the train? You saved one of my brothers by stopping the assassination."

"That kid was a hybrid?"

"Yes."

"And the hitter?"

Moko shrugged. "One of the latest generation hybrids the Kensei is working on. He's gone to great lengths to ensure they don't malfunction like we did. The Kensei's specialty is genetics and he somehow isolated several genes he thinks will give him better control over his drones. But he still needs human and vampire organs to make them function."

"What sorts of attributes do these hybrids possess?" said Talya. "Are they some kind of, I don't know, supervampire?"

"No," said Moko. "But they do combine the best of what humans and vampires share—namely, extra strength combined with superlative regeneration abilities as derived through the ingestion of the life-force energy contained in blood." Moko sighed. "They're cunning, but not overly so. That's the price the Kensei paid when he altered their genetic sequencing. In order to be extremely devious, they need to be more sentient than they are now."

"I suppose that's one thing we can hopefully use to our advantage," said Talya. "I'm not crazy about facing an army of these guys, though. Our run-in on the train was almost enough to finish us off."

I looked at Moko's hands, wondering if he had the same claws that the other hybrids had almost finished me off with on the train. He must have noticed my interest, because he grinned.

"I do not have the additional weaponry the Kensei has since installed on the latest generation hybrids, if you're wondering, Lawson-san."

"I was." I took a sip of my drink. "The thought of facing an army of those guys . . ."

"He doesn't have an army yet," said Moko. "Perhaps ten all told. Supported by ranks of younger *teppo*—aspiring thugs who have been promised they will be transformed into hybrids in exchange for their service."

"The pseudopromise of immortality?"

"Something like that," said Moko. "I haven't been on the inside for a while now. Just what I hear from the few of us that are left."

"How many of you are left?"

Moko reached for his sake cup. "Two. Myself and my brother you saved on the train a few days back."

"Oh." I reached for my own cup. There didn't seem much point in saying anything else.

Moko put his cup down. "The Kensei is gearing up to build a huge new wave of latest generation hybrids. To do so, he needs a massive amount of organs. And there is supposedly a shipment of those organs coming into Tokyo very soon."

That got Talya's attention. She leaned forward. "Where and when?"

Moko shook his head. "That much I do not know. At least, not yet."

"But you can find out?"

Moko looked at her. "You want revenge?"

"I want justice for the children he slaughtered."

I looked at Moko. He seemed to have found some respect for Talya. I cleared my throat. "Forgive me for saying so, but wouldn't it be better for you and the other guy to just duck out of sight? Go somewhere else and survive? If the Kensei finds out who you are, you're dead."

Moko leaned back. "I've spent years concealing myself but remaining close enough so I can monitor him as much as possible. In that way, I will eventually see him dead."

"Might make better sense to stay alive for another day."

Moko nodded. "It might indeed. But what good is living life only for yourself? It's a selfish way to journey through the universe."

"Maybe by living you get the best revenge of all. The Kensei never got to exterminate all of you."

Moko shrugged. "It's a fair point. But one I don't agree with. The true glory in life comes from giving yourself up for others. By being selfless in all that you pursue so that the true rewards are revealed."

I took a deep breath and let it out slowly. "You'd sacrifice yourself for this cause even though your death might mean the extinction of your race?"

Moko smiled. "You compliment me by calling us a race."

"Damn straight. If you're a hybrid and have lived long enough to accomplish everything you have, then you're as much a race as what I'm a part of or what Talya is a part of. That's not something to be tossed aside so easily."

"Life is only worth living if you treat it as the greatest opportunity for doing good in the world."

"Even if it means your death."

Moko bowed his head. "We all die sometime, Lawson-san."

"But there's no reason to head off so soon."

Moko took another sip of his sake. "I'm not expecting to die anytime soon. I fully intend to make it as difficult as possible for the Kensei to kill me. I'm not treating myself as a sacrificial lamb."

Talya nudged me. "We need to find out where and when that shipment is coming in. I've got some things to discuss with the Kensei myself."

I nodded. "I've met his brother. Megalomania must run in that family. I'm sure we'll find him easily enough."

"You met his brother?" Moko's eyes crinkled. "I wasn't aware he even had one."

"Yeah, I met him." Images ran through my head of the Syndicate and all the crap they brought into my life. "Name was Cho. He ran an organized crime syndicate in New York City."

Moko frowned. "Perhaps they will be looking to synchronize their efforts? Extend their reach overseas?"

I shook my head. "Doubtful. Cho won't be synchronizing anything anymore."

Moko eyed me.

I nodded. "I killed him last month."

Moko let his breath out. "That certainly explains the Kensei's interest in you."

"There are a lot of people looking for revenge in this city right now." I lifted my cup to my lips again. "Here's hoping the good guys—that'd be us—get the chance to exact some first."

We drank deep and Moko took a sheaf of bills out of his pocket and put them on the table. "Dinner is on me."

I bowed quickly. "I take it we're all even?"

"You answered my questions honestly," said Moko. "In exchange, I was honest with you. It's a good start to a friendship, wouldn't you say?"

"Yes. But you lied."

Moko looked shocked. "Did I?"

"You said the night would get better if we told you the truth. Doesn't look like going after the Kensei is exactly a recipe for a good night."

Moko smiled. "That depends on your perspective. To my mind, killing a bad man such as he is is not only good, it is excellent." He stood and walked out of the restaurant.

Talya followed behind him. "Sounds like a damned good time to me, too, lover."

Was I the only one who didn't want to go at this head-on? Had my experiences with the Syndicate given me such pause that I was losing my edge? Was I shying away from danger now instead of running at it headlong like I used to?

Maybe it was time to get out of this racket.

I stood and walked outside. Moko was smoking a cigarette and looking very happy to be reacquainted with his tobacco. I put an arm around Talya. No sense hiding the fact from Moko. He knew all about us anyway.

"So, what now?" asked Talya.

"We get the time and location of the shipment," said Moko. "Then we go there and kill the Kensei."

"Where do we get that information?" I said. "Talya and I were on our way to meet someone Matsuda-san put us on to shortly before she was killed. But our plans were cut short by the attempted hit on us on the train."

"When you were wounded." Moko pointed at my hand. "How does it feel?"

"Better, actually."

"And the poison?"

Talya frowned. "How'd you know about that?"

"I told you, I get bits of information about what the Kensei is doing and how he's attempting to make this latest generation better than what he did with us."

"I think the poison is just about gone from my system."

"No doubt helped by the sake and beer."

"I guess."

Moko crushed his cigarette under foot. "It's time we got going."

"Where?"

Moko sniffed the night air as if looking to catch the scent of his prey. "Rappongi."

"The club scene?"

He eyed me. "That is where you and Talya were heading, isn't it?"

"Well, yeah, but—"

"Then we'll go there as well."

I held up my left hand. "We don't even know if the guy Matsuda-san told us about is still working."

"He is."

Talya stopped him. "You know him?"

Moko nodded. "Lawson-san does, too." He glanced at me. "It is the man you saved the other day on the train—my brother."

"That's Mao?"

"Yes," said Moko. "He's been feeding Matsuda-san information for some time. And now, at last, my wishes have been realized and answered by the gods. I finally have a Fixer here who can help me take down the Kensei."

I really hate coincidence. "Lucky for Mao I happened to be on that train."

Moko shrugged. "There are those who believe that everything in life is predetermined. The gods put you where you needed to be. You are, after all, a tool for good."

Talya laughed lightly. "He's definitely a tool."

"I don't like the idea of preordained actions," I said. "It takes the concept of free will out of the equation. And I'm a big fan of free will."

"We all have a destiny," said Moko. "Whether we choose to accept that notion or not is your free will."

I sighed. "Great, now this is my destiny. On top of my other destiny. Swell."

Moko smiled and laid a hand on my shoulder. "Sometimes, if you listen hard enough, you can hear the gods laughing, my new friend."

CHAPTER
TWENTY-THREE

Moko drove a small black Mitsubishi sedan that fit the three of us and not much else. Talya didn't look too excited about riding in it. Moko saw her concern and smiled.

"I think this is safer than taking the subway. As your experiences this afternoon have shown, the Kensei is apparently able to monitor you with ease."

"I've been thinking about that, too," said Talya. "And I've been wondering exactly how he's able to do so."

I slid into the passenger seat and waited for Moko to climb behind the wheel. He started the engine up, popped the car into gear, and we shot down the narrow wet streets. Moko lit a fresh cigarette. "The thing about Rappongi is the absolute lack of parking anywhere. Of course, I could go in there with the siren on and make it all official, but then that might also alert our quarry that we're in the neighborhood."

"The Kensei doesn't know about you though, does he?"

"No," said Moko. "He thinks I'm dead. And if luck holds out, it will stay that way long enough for me to get close to him and kill him."

"I'll fight you for that," said Talya from the backseat. "I've got the lives of a bunch of kids on my shoulders."

Moko frowned. "And I have my own fallen brethren to avenge."

"Maybe you two can split him," I said. "Cut him right down the middle and each of you can take half home to mount on your wall."

"Don't be bitter," said Talya with a smile. "I'm sure there'll be enough left over for you."

The streets flashed by us as Moko's windshield wipers flicked the drizzle from the glass. Their timing was soothing and I wondered if perhaps I'd had too much sake. Even though alcohol doesn't affect me as fast or in quantities near what it world take to disrupt a human, I could tell the day's events were catching up with me.

I bit back a cough that had welled up due to Moko's cigarette smoke. "How long until we get to Rappongi?"

Moko pointed at the digital clock on his dashboard bleeding green into the darkness. "Maybe thirty minutes. We're going to hit traffic soon. I'll have to use some back roads to avoid it. Plus, I want to make sure we don't have anyone on our tail."

I felt Talya's hands on my shoulders. "You okay?"

"Tired. Been a lousy day for this vampire."

"Try to rest. We've still got a lot to do tonight." Talya's hands worked into my muscles, kneading them into a gooey mass. I timed my breathing with her massage technique and gave another thanks to the gods for bringing us together.

It took two minutes for me to slip into a light sleep. I could hear the windshield wipers marking time as we drove. Moko seemed to be doing his best to avoid potholes that littered the back streets he was taking. Talya's hands kept working on my muscles. I could smell the rain-tinged air being drawn into the car.

I thought about home.

I wondered what Niles was doing now. He was supposed to be

covering for me while I was away. I thought about Wirek and how he might be handling his recent appointment to the Council. And then I thought about Arthur and how he'd probably be keeping Wirek in line when he was at the Council building on Beacon Hill.

My thoughts went to Jack as well, studying at the Invoker school in the Canadian Rockies. A few years back, a case of mistaken identity had led me to wrongfully execute Jack's father so a traitor on the Council could get access to Jack. Jack had the ability to conjure the spirits of dead vampires. I'd protected him and we'd grown close ever since. He was turning into quite a young man. He had a girlfriend, of all things. He'd handled himself well when I saw him briefly last month.

Some family you've got for yourself, Lawson, I thought with a smile. They were all fine people. But even with the friendship, something more was missing.

And that something sat behind me in the car, working on relaxing me. Talya didn't have to be asked to do anything. She just did it. She'd done her best to support an entire village of children and in return the Kensei slaughtered them. Where was the justice in that? How was it that good could be so terribly upset by evil?

My role as a Fixer has given me ample time to muse about the role of universal justice and how it works. Or rather, doesn't work. I've wondered for years if universal justice is a fallacy or not. How does the Balance exist when evil is allowed to run rampant without consequence for its actions? How does the universe tolerate the murder of innocent children?

It delivers schmoes like me. And Talya. And even Moko. We're the ones who have to stand in evil's way. We're the ones—and others like us—who are willing to put their lives on the line when everyone else would prefer to be a sheep being led to the slaughter.

Standing for good isn't easy. It sucks most times. Even the people you're supposed to protect will yell at you and tell you to not put up a fight at all. They'll accuse you of upsetting the natural balance because conflict is something we're supposed to be evolving beyond.

What bullshit.

Evil exists in many forms. I've seen plenty of all types. The violent psychopaths are out there, sure. But so are the subtle egomaniacs who hide their tactics under a cloak of supposed intelligent bullying. While everyone is busy being impressed, they quietly work their plans into fruition. Sociopaths come in many forms.

Who's to say which type is the more dangerous?

The Kensei was building a private army of human-vampire assassins. How he planned on dominating the world would make for interesting reading. I wondered if he was tied in somehow with the conspiracy I'd uncovered while battling the Syndicate.

Probably.

Cho had been a smart opponent. But even he had had his failings. And I'd come away from that encounter thinking there was probably someone higher up pulling his strings.

Someone on the Council?

I felt tension creep back into my body and then felt Talya's hands redouble their efforts. I sighed and allowed myself to relax some more.

The Kensei had an awful big tab to pay off. And he owed me for killing Yuki.

Behind my closed eyes, I could sense a change in the light. Things got a lot brighter. Neon probably. I opened my eyes and saw a million signs for bars and clubs and restaurants and a hundred other venues.

Rappongi.

Home to the nightlife of Tokyo for the young and the young at heart. Tourists flocked here to soak in the club scene. Japanese girls flocked here to find foreign guys to shack up with. You couldn't spit without hitting a business either controlled or protected by the Japanese mafia.

The yakuza.

In some ways they used to be viewed as a sort of Robin Hood entity. In reality, they were as cutthroat as any other criminal enterprise. They had their hooks into every aspect of the entertainment world in Japan. They also used their power to exert control over real estate, construction, and even politics. In the late twentieth century, it wasn't uncommon to find yakuza thugs roughing up political opponents of a chosen faction. They'd stage protests, hurt others rallying in support, and generally cause mayhem.

In recent years, the Japanese government had started a covert program of using yakuza families to supply raw intelligence on the happenings in Tokyo. Standing at the crossroads of technology in the Far East, Tokyo was a stomping ground for intelligence operatives from China, North Korea, the United States, Russia, and every other nation on the planet. Everyone wanted to be the first to sidle up to the latest generation technology. The government had their hands full trying to keep tabs on it all. So they used the yakuza families to monitor one segment of their intelligence-gathering—primarily anything involving real estate and shipping—while they handled the other segments.

It worked out pretty well. In exchange for turning a blind eye to certain yakuza activities, the government got some decent intel. But it's always risky bedding down with an enemy.

"We're here."

Moko's voice sounded gravelly and tired. I didn't know if he'd gotten any sleep lately himself or if trying to figure out who the hell Talya and I were had made his life a little hellish.

Or maybe I was just giving us way too much credit. Moko probably only needed a cigarette.

Sure enough, he stepped out of the car and yanked a butt out of the pack, rolled it over his bottom lip, and then lit a match to it.

"You don't like lighters?"

"Matches are more reliable."

"Yeah?"

He winked at me. "They can't be bugged."

I frowned. "You've had experience with bugged lighters?"

Moko took a deep drag, exhaled the grayish white smoke into the air, and laughed. "We're in Japan. Anything can be bugged here."

He'd parked his car near a Dumpster off the main drag. A hundred feet away, thousands of people jammed the streets and sidewalks as they tried to elbow their way inside the top-rated venues for the evening.

"The place where Mao spins . . . it's called Tony Tony's?"

Moko nodded. "That's right. Mao's been working here for a few months."

"How is it," said Talya, "that you and Mao could blend in so easily with the rest of society and make it difficult for the Kensei to find you? Surely he's had people looking for you all over the place."

Moko shrugged. "Well, he does think I'm dead, so that's been half the battle. I joined the police force. I had doctored papers and my expertise was well-founded. I moved into homicide and I've been there ever since. Plus, the job allows me to remain armed at all times. Mao chose an opposite extreme, but one just as interesting. He immersed himself in the entertainment world, which as you probably know is controlled by the yakuza."

"And isn't the Kensei considered a yakuza gumi as well?"

"Sure, but this club is owned by the Kagemaru gumi. They're the most powerful clan in Japan. No one messes with them unless they're willing to risk all-out war. And the Kensei is currently rather absorbed in other endeavors trying to build up his hybrid army to risk such a battle. It's one he would lose."

I sighed. "Maybe we should tip off the Kagemaru about the Kensei."

"They would never believe you, Lawson-san," said Moko. He waved that idea away and continued. "Mao found himself a cushy job. He's actually quite the DJ, and he can come here knowing that there won't be any trouble. Plus, he doesn't exactly look like an awesome powerhouse assassin. Kid's long and lean. Thin enough to put people at ease. And he dresses weird. His hair's bright red—just dyed it the other day."

"In other words, he does everything to stand out because it's his best way of staying invisible. Hiding in plain sight."

Moko nodded. "Exactly."

"He was targeted the other day, though," I said.

Moko nodded. "Even the best disguises aren't immune all the time. Knowing the Kensei, he's probably known of Mao for some time, but wouldn't risk moving on him until he could guarantee he was unprotected. Mao's not the best when it comes to detecting surveillance. He could have had a tail and not known about it. Once the tail identified him as vulnerable, the Kensei gave the assassin the okay."

"That's a lot of effort to go through to get to one person."

"He's patient," said Moko.

I pointed at the crowd. "Line's a mile long to get in here."

Moko shrugged. "They know me here. And you two won't have any problem getting in if you're with me."

We sidled our way to the front of the line and Moko nodded once at the cue ball juggernaut manning the door. He gave Moko a quick bow and stepped back to let us get through. The yakuza would respect Moko's badge to a point. We just had to be careful not to press our luck too much.

As soon as we cleared the entrance, the darkness exploded with a throbbing bass line and more neon lights and lasers than I'd ever seen in my life.

I've been to nightclubs back in Boston, but that was like comparing a kid's party at McDonald's to Disney World. In Japan, nightclub culture was huge. Jostling bodies swayed and dipped and grooved to a strange cacophony of techno, house, rap, reggae, and alternative rock. Somehow it all worked and the clubgoers were in a frenzy to dance to it.

Moko moved easily through the crowd. No one paid any attention to him. Talya and I registered a few interested glances but not much more. Maybe I was losing my looks.

I felt Talya's hand on my elbow and she smiled at me. Back in Boston, we'd been in a nightclub together hunting for Cosgrove after one of his murders. We'd only just started working together and as weird as it was for two solo operators to team up—a vampire and a human at that—it had felt good also. Back then I hadn't realized how much I was falling for her. Or maybe it was that I did realize it and I was just trying to pretend she meant nothing to me.

I smiled back, remembering that night and how she'd looked and how she'd smiled.

Moko led us to the front of the club to the VIP area. Another thick-necked club worker held a velvet rope back for us to enter. We sat at a small circular table surrounded by a high-backed purple velvet booth.

I sank into the cushions and felt like sleeping some more. Talya leaned forward, tapping her feet in time to the music. Moko lit a fresh cigarette and smoked.

I nudged him. "Well?"

"Well what?"

"Is he here?"

Moko tapped the end of his butt to the ashtray and nodded. "Of course he's here. This is his job."

"He know we're here to see him?"

"Probably."

"What's that supposed to mean?"

Moko pointed. "There."

I looked and saw the same guy I'd saved on the train standing on a raised stage behind a Plexiglas screen. A rack of expensive CD turntables and iPod hookups surrounded him while brilliant flashes of red, green, and yellow lights lit him up at intervals of two seconds. He had a different hairstyle now but it was him.

Mao.

"When he finishes this set, he'll be over to see us."

"How can you be so sure? He hasn't even looked over here."

Moko nodded at the waitress who brought us drinks. "As soon as we walked in, someone told him about us. This is probably one of the safest places to be in all of Japan, Lawson-san. Believe it or not."

I looked out across the sea of faces and bodies and wondered how that could possibly be the case. With all those unknowns, all those variables of personality embodying every facet of human emotion. Any one of them could be servants in the Kensei's army of hybrids.

How could we be safe anywhere?

CHAPTER TWENTY-FOUR

Mao took a break twenty minutes later and joined us at the table. As he approached, his eyes went from Moko to me and widened slightly. Moko held up a single hand and Mao seemed to calm down.

I bowed quickly and introduced myself and Talya. Mao returned our greetings and sat down. "You're the guy from the train."

"Guilty as charged."

He smiled. "I never got the chance to thank you for saving my life."

"You're welcome." I sipped my drink. "You were pretty good at handling that knife."

Mao glanced at Moko. "He knows everything?"

"Yes."

Mao looked back at me. "We were trained well. The knife was not a problem for me."

I glanced around the club. "The girl you were with, is she—?"

"Nah, just a fan I was taking home. She disappeared right after that incident, probably scared shitless by what she saw." He frowned. "That asshole ruined what should have been a very nice afternoon interlude for me."

Talya excused herself to use the restroom at that point. Moko leaned toward Mao. "Did you find out what we need?"

Mao nodded. "Sure. Freighter comes in tonight. About two in the morning down by pier sixteen."

Moko smiled. "Good."

"There's one thing, though," said Mao.

"What?"

"It's not just a shipment coming in. There's a shipment going out, too."

I frowned. "Of organs?"

Mao leaned back. "Not the way I hear it. Supposedly there are twenty of the latest generation hybrids going out. I don't know where they're headed. The ship is to be refueled during the off-load and then to set out immediately after for parts unknown."

"Where is it bound for next?" asked Moko.

"I hear it makes stops in Manila, Honolulu, and then San Diego. Beyond that, I don't know."

"You mind me asking how it is that you're able to come by such top-grade intelligence?" I sloshed my drink in my glass and took a sip. "I'd love to know how you manage it."

Mao smiled like he was talking to an idiot. Maybe he was. "I'm not just a DJ, pal. I'm what you might call a social engineer."

"What the hell does that mean?"

Mao spread his arms as if he was embracing the entire club. "You see these people? They love me. I spin tunes and take them away from this world. I transport them to a new level of ecstasy—a rhythmic paradise so intense they're grateful for a chance to escape. I give them that escape. They give me their loyalty in return."

I nudged Moko. "He feeling okay?"

Moko smiled. "Mao takes his job very seriously. He's a smart kid, so I forgive the momentary lapses in reality."

I looked back at Mao who was now bobbing his head in time to the music. Without looking at me, he said, "Guy I know comes in here a couple times each week. He feeds me the intel. Doesn't know a thing about why I want to know. I just have him feeding me pieces of info on a certain thing. A certain freighter named *Kagemaru*."

"And he—?"

"Works the docks," said Mao. He glanced at me. "That good enough an explanation for you?"

"Sure." I frowned. "Any possibility that this guy is a plant simply feeding you disinformation, though?"

Mao frowned. "You never know, I guess. But he seems legit to me."

That wasn't much of a recommendation, but we didn't have a whole lot to fall back on. If Mao's contact had intel about the Kensei, odds were we were going to use it, regardless.

Mao nodded. "My break's almost up. Gotta get back to work."

"Thanks for the tip," said Moko. "I'll be in touch."

Mao shook my hand once and then left. I watched him dissolve into the crowd. It parted to allow him to pass. He danced his way back to the stage, slid a pair of headphones on, and then went back to it, all the while never missing a beat.

I looked at Moko. "He's not coming with us, is he?"

Moko shook his head. "He would if I asked him to. Truth be told, I think he's a little scared what with the attempt on his life and all. Probably better if we take care of this ourselves."

"We're going to need some gear."

"That's not a problem." Moko stabbed his cigarette into the ashtray.

"You can get automatic weapons?" I was a little hesitant about Moko's pull with the police.

Moko sighed. "Lawson-san, I did not work my way up into homicide solely for the purpose of concealing myself. I have access to whatever we need. But it's not even necessary to go to police headquarters to get it."

"No?"

"We have everything we need right here."

"At this club?" I finished my drink. "I didn't know this was a Kmart, too."

"Excuse me?"

"Nothing."

"The yakuza who control this club will have what we need in the back rooms. Like any other crime-controlled business, they need to have weapons to fend off an attack if one should come. It's highly unlikely a turf war would erupt here, but they still take precautions."

I smiled. "And all we have to do is convince them that they should part willingly with those weapons because we'll do a much better job of using them than they will?"

Moko's eyes crinkled. "'Willingly' might be a stretch. But they will let us have them. Mao will have already paved the way for us."

"They like him that much?"

"You see the crowds that follow him? Mao is a legend in the dance circuit. People come to see him, to hear him, to dance him. This club is packed beyond capacity every time Mao spins. Even the bribes to the building inspectors who would ordinarily shut this place down for exceeding maximum head count have to be increased to address the sheer volume that Mao can bring in." Moko grinned. "His bosses are very pleased with his work."

"Amazing. I guess I never thought all that much about the night-club industry before."

"To say it's a lucrative business for the yakuza to be involved with is an understatement. What they make on markups for drinks is outrageous. There are door fees for people to get in, exclusive membership levels sold like to a golf club that ensure even more revenue. And then there is the illegal side trade in drugs and prostitution that help set places like this on a pedestal not seen elsewhere. Mao is the god who makes all that money possible."

"If you say so."

Talya rejoined us. "Well, that was fun."

"Took you long enough."

She smiled. "I had to wait in line and then I got propositioned three times."

"What?"

She patted my thigh. "Relax, lover. They weren't guys."

I raised my eyebrows. "And you turned them down?"

She smiled. "I didn't think you'd like any of them." She looked at Moko. "Mao left already?"

"His break was over. His adoring public won't stand to let him rest for too long."

I looked at my empty glass. "Moko was just telling me that we can find all the weapons we need here."

Talya nodded. "I believe it. On the way to the bathroom there's a heavily barricaded door with reinforced bolts. Two goons are on watch outside of it."

"The money room," said Moko. "It's almost self-contained. And branching off of it will be the armory."

"We're going to walk right in there?"

Moko shrugged. "Unless you have a better idea."

Talya looked at me. "Am I the only one who think it sounds crazy that the yakuza will just give us their guns?"

"I must be crazy, too."

Moko stood. "Come with me and we'll find out—"

The explosion was a brilliant boom of white light and noise. I figured they must have added a lot of magnesium to make it burn that bright. The effect on the club was instantaneous. The music died and the screaming began.

Without realizing it, I'd already moved to shield Talya with my body in the instant prior to the blast. I felt her underneath me.

"You okay?"

"Yeah."

Moko was already pulling me off of her. "Let's go!"

We got to our feet. Chaos was rampant. There was a major fire raging in the center of the floor, threatening to send the entire club up in flames. The sprinklers came on a second later, drenching everything. I could see about two dozen bodies sprinkled about, limbs blown off, the blood and water making the floor slippery. It was such a stark contrast to what had been there a moment earlier.

I couldn't see Mao anywhere.

Moko tugged on my arm. "We have to go now!"

"What about Mao?"

Moko shook his head. "He might be dead."

We moved as one toward the back of the club. Yakuza goons rushed past me. Some of them were armed. Maybe they thought this was an attack of the kind Moko had just assured me would never happen.

We pushed through the crowd of people looking for a rear exit. Moko led the way until we came to the reinforced door. Talya was right, it looked formidable. Only one goon was guarding it now, however.

Moko walked up to him and said something in Japanese I couldn't hear because of the screaming around me. The goon eyed Moko and shook his head.

Moko turned back to me. "He won't let us in."

I frowned. "You see?"

Talya shook her head. "Now what?"

Moko turned back to the goon and hit him so fast at the base of his chest with his finger, I could scarcely see it. The goon's face turned ashen and he dropped to the floor. Moko knocked on the door and waited a second. When it opened enough, Moko stepped through and I heard a momentary gasp.

The door swung open and Moko allowed us to enter. "Never take no for an answer."

We ducked past the tables piled high with money. There were

three workers packing it all up, too terrified to be concerned about us, especially since we didn't seem interested in the money.

Moko led us into another room. The walls were lined with weaponry of all types. Moko scooped up a gear bag and began shoving guns and ammunition into it. Talya and I did the same. In five minutes we had everything we needed. I hefted the bag and it must have weighed close to a hundred pounds.

I looked at Talya, momentarily concerned the bag would weigh too much for her.

Silly me.

She had the bag already strapped on and was ready to go. "This is just like being home again. Let's get the hell out of here before they decide they want their toys back."

Moko nodded. "There's an emergency exit over here we can get out of. I just need to get the car and we can get down to the docks."

"Stop!"

We turned all at once.

Two men.

Guns.

And wearing the kind of expressions I normally see on hardened professionals. Whoever they were, they weren't going to tolerate much.

"Put the bags down."

We slid them off our shoulders. Each bag clanged as it made contact with the floor. It felt good to have the weight off my back. But I wasn't crazy about having two guns aimed at me.

One of the men smiled. "Now where were you planning to go with all that hardware?"

"No place special," said Talya.

The second man looked at Moko. "Mao is dead."

Moko's jaw tightened. "How do you know?"

"His body is out there, split apart like a melon. His guts are draped all over the stage."

Moko said nothing.

The first man smiled now. "You, Moko, are the last one of your kind alive."

"Pity," said the second man, "that it will be a moot point in another couple of seconds."

I guessed they weren't yakuza after all.

CHAPTER
TWENTY-FIVE

"So, where is he?" asked Talya. "Your boss, I mean."

The first man looked about thirty-five with cropped black hair bristling on his scalp. Peeking up from the collar of his shirt, I could see the tail of some sort of mythical creature tattooed on his skin. He was yakuza, but not for the gumi that ran Tony Tony's.

"He's attending to other things right now."

Talya sniffed. "And so we get the errand boys, huh? You guys must really rate high on his screen if he sent you along to deal with us."

The second man with the ponytail jutting out of his head like a samurai topknot glowered at Talya. "He trusts us alone to be able to handle the three of you. And when we kill you, you'll know why."

Useless posturing always annoys the crap out of me. "He give you any sort of message to pass on to us?"

Crop-top and Ponytail glanced at each other. Crop-top shook his head. "No."

"Interesting." I nodded at Crop-top. "Would you mind giving him a message for me?"

Crop-top's eyes narrowed even more. "I suppose—"

Talya kicked the gun out of his hand and I barreled into Pony-tail even before the last word was out of Crop-top's mouth. Talya followed her kick up with a vicious chop to the side of Crop-top's neck. I heard the impact and the grunt that followed, but Crop-top recovered too quickly for his reflexes to be natural.

Meanwhile Ponytail was thudding on my back with a rain of fists. I took a breath, lifted him up, and then dumped him on the ground. I landed on top of him and started working my way up his body using my elbows and knees to jab points as I worked higher. He tried to headbutt me, but I ducked back and then brought an elbow up into his eye.

There was a dull crack, but I didn't think his orbital bone had broken, maybe just a hairline fracture. Regardless, the whole region started to swell. His breathing was coming short and fast and I felt him growl once before he brought a knee up sharply into my abdomen. I rolled off and got to my feet.

I could feel sweat on my skin. The day's activities were definitely catching up with me. Between the poison and the attack on the train, the revelations about Moko and his kind, and a bomb blast in a crowded nightclub, I was going to need a real vacation when this one supposedly ended.

Talya and Moko had Crop-top pinned. Ponytail didn't look like he gave a rat's ass what happened to his partner. That kind of concerned me. The look in Ponytail's eyes also concerned me.

And when he charged me, I got even more worried.

Because he didn't come right at me. He feinted with a lead kick and then followed up with a rear punch that screamed toward my face. I managed to slip it just so and as it went by, I tried to bring my right hand up under his to punch him in the throat.

That was the trap. And I fell right into it as he used his other hand to snake under my own, lock my arm out, and then pivot his body to move into a forward throw. I'd end up breaking my face or neck when the ground came rushing up at me.

But I sank my hips and got lower than him to keep my balance. I slid one of my feet back to widen my stance and it broke his rhythm. He turned and tried to reapply the throw but I pivoted and shot the edge of my hand into his neck under his voice box.

He gagged and disengaged.

I wondered if Talya and Moko were enjoying the fight. I sure as hell wasn't. My energy was sapped. And Ponytail looked even more pissed off than before.

I could see him revving himself up for another attack. I took a breath.

"Guys?"

The gunshot rang out and Ponytail's chest exploded in a crimson splash. He glanced down at his chest as if surprised by the sudden turn of events. Then he sank to his knees, slumped, and fell forward onto his face.

I looked over and saw Moko holding a pistol. Smoke slithered out of the barrel and the smell of cordite hung in the air.

"Thanks."

He nodded. "I thought it best to end this."

"I would have been happier with a moment or two sooner."

"He was helping me," said Talya. "This guy's a lot tougher to handle than he looks."

I glanced at Crop-top and saw him squirming. But Talya had his shoulder pinned to the floor. Any squirming he was doing would only make the pain worse.

Crop-top looked incredibly pissed. I looked at Talya. "What do we do with sunshine?"

Talya looked down. "Can't let him go. He'll go scampering off to the Kensei and warn him that we want to spoil all his fun. And I so despise walking into an ambush if I can avoid it."

"Yeah."

"He *was* going to kill us."

"Yeah."

When the second gunshot rang out, both Talya and I jumped. Again, Moko stood there calmly holding the pistol and looking like he didn't have a care in the world. He shrugged.

"Had to be done."

I looked at the two corpses on the ground and then at Moko. "You've kind of crossed the line here, my friend."

"What do you mean?"

Talya smirked. "He means you're a cop and you just killed two men."

"Self-defense," said Moko. "My life was in danger. As was yours."

The bullet holes over their hearts were too perfect for it to have been an act in the midst of battle. Any forensic newbie would see that Moko had calmly taken aim and plugged them both. "You think the department will see it that way?"

Moko popped the clip out of his pistol, checked the rounds, and slapped it back home. "I'm not too concerned about that right now."

"Maybe you should be." In the distance, I could hear sirens approaching. I wondered why they hadn't gotten here already.

"I am a police officer, yes. But I am also a hybrid. That comes first in my book. If I am not a cop, I'll still be a hybrid. That's where my priorities are."

Talya stepped off of Crop-top. "Well, it was nice shooting anyway. Especially being how I was about two inches away from where you were aiming."

Moko bowed slightly. "I apologize if that concerned you."

Talya grinned. "I didn't exactly have much time to think about it, now did I?"

"We need to leave," said Moko. "Right now would be good."

I could tell the sirens had stopped out front. We grabbed the gear bags and found our way to the back exit. Moko took point and Talya and I followed. Behind us, I could still hear the screaming and wailing of the wounded who'd been marred by the bomb blast. Somewhere in the rubble, Mao's body lay ripped to shreds.

Another casualty in the war with the Kensei.

Another person who needed avenging.

Moko led us back to his car, hefted the bags into the trunk, and then slid in behind the steering wheel. Talya and I got in just as a fleet of cruisers raced past us heading for the club.

"Close," said Talya.

"Too close."

Moko started the engine. He glanced around and eased the car out of the space and down the street. At the end, we turned right, entered the highway traffic, and set a course for the harbor.

"He'll know we're coming anyway," said Moko.

"You think?"

Moko nodded. "He has not gotten to where he is now by being stupid. When his men fail to report in, he will assume we have gotten away. He will take appropriate measures to ensure we do not gain access to him without a fight."

"Then we'll fight,' said Talya.

"We've been fighting," I said. "Truth be told, I could use a nap and a drink."

Moko reached into the glove compartment and handed a small tumbler to me. "Here."

"What's this?"

"What you require, I think."

I took the lid off the tumbler and the familiar copper scent reached my nose and made my mouth water. Moko glanced at me across the front seat. "You aren't the only one who requires that to survive. Part of the price of being a hybrid."

"You don't need it now?"

"I had some earlier," said Moko. "That is all yours if you need it. And judging by the way you've exerted yourself today, I'd be inclined to suggest you finish it off. I won't need any until the day after tomorrow." He winked. "If I live that long."

"Such an optimist," said Talya.

I lifted the tumbler to my lips, tilted my head back, and let the thick syrupy blood spill into my mouth. I swallowed quickly, never really having gotten comfortable with the idea that I drink blood in order to survive.

Within thirty seconds, I felt the hit. My body absorbed the life-force energy from the blood and infused my own system with it. I felt terrific. Even in the wake of everything that had transpired today, I felt like I could go out and run several marathons.

Before this night was through, I might just have the opportunity to prove I could do that.

"Feel better?" Talya placed her hands on my back and gave me a quick squeeze.

"Much." I handed the tumbler back to Moko. "You're a life-saver."

"It's no problem." He glanced out the windshield and checked his bearings. "I've been in your situation before and know how tough it can be."

"But you won't need any more until two days from now?"

Moko shrugged. "Part human, part vampire. Guess we take a slower time to process the life-force energy than true vampires do."

"But you do need it. Just like a pure vampire would."

"Absolutely. Plus, it gives us that supercharge, so to speak."

More neon flashed by but it was intermittent now. We were on the outskirts of Rappongi, heading away from the nightlife mecca of Tokyo toward the harbor where countless ships would unload their wares in one of the busiest ports in the world.

Moko's police radio crackled now and again. Reports were scattered, but mostly focused on the bombing.

"Must have been a small bomb," I said. "They could have leveled that place, but chose not to."

"Mao was the target, I would think," said Moko. "But they could have easily gotten us, too. Perhaps they weren't aware we were there."

"Nah, they knew enough to send those two guys in after us. They knew."

"So, why spare us?"

Moko shrugged. "Perhaps the Kensei has more respect for us than we thought. Perhaps he didn't think we'd be foolish enough to allow ourselves to be killed by a bomb."

"Doesn't explain why he just didn't total the joint," said Talya. "I wouldn't think someone like the Kensei would give a damn if he killed thousands in his quest to get at us."

"Guess we'll have to wait until we get there to ask him," I said. "How much longer, Moko?"

He lit a cigarette and promptly filled the interior of the car with smoke. "Maybe twenty minutes."

I listened to some more of the police chatter. "No one seems to be looking for you."

"I'm off duty," said Moko. "But I'm sure I'll have a stack of messages waiting for me when I check in. And if they think it warrants my attention, they'll call me up tonight."

I tried to breathe in the thick smoke. Thank God I didn't have to worry about lung cancer. "You might be a little busy."

"I might be a lot busy," said Moko.

I looked over my shoulder at Talya. She looked entirely unfazed by the smoky interior, but then she always handled things like that better than I did. "You think those guns in the bags we scored are going to work all right?"

Talya shrugged. "Checked some of them as I was grabbing them. Some had been freshly oiled. Parts seemed to run together smooth enough to ensure adequate operation. Ammo's in good shape. All in all, I think they'll be fine. As long as it goes bang and a bullet comes out of the end, that's all I really care about."

Moko chuckled around the cigarette. "It would be unlike any yakuza gumi to have faulty weapons. It would be a tremendous loss of face for them if they were caught with guns that didn't fire when they squeezed the trigger."

"And they'd be dead," I said.

"Yes." He smiled. "There's that."

We sat in silence as the minutes crawled by. Traffic was light heading down to the sea. I cracked the window and could smell the salt in the air. The scent of brine hung heavy outside of the car. Now and again, I could hear the horns and bells of ships coming in or weighing anchor.

And then the superstructures of the freighters rose up in front of us like some seaborne city. Moko slowed the car to a stop behind a huge Dumpster.

"We're here."

Behind me, Talya gave me another squeeze and then slid her hands away. It was time to go to work.

CHAPTER TWENTY-SIX

The smell of brine and fish cloaked the air. We slipped out of the car and waited while Moko took stock of the area. We wouldn't do much talking from here on out. Hand signals would cue us as to how we'd proceed.

Moko took point and Talya brought up the rear. Despite the fact that I was feeling much better, the other two deemed it best if they kept me in the middle like some wounded lamb they had to protect. It grated on me a little bit, but at least they were going to include me in tonight's activities.

We moved along the outside of the corrugated tin warehouses that all seemed to be rusting at the same places. Bits of litter sprinkled the area and I could hear the rats foraging for whatever food they might find in a place like this. Every now and again, a breeze would rip through the small alleys and bring with it a fresh wave of briny air.

Moko moved like a ghost. Even his shadow seemed to slink along on its own accord. I knew Talya was behind me but I wouldn't have otherwise because she made absolutely no noise whatsoever.

I kept my own footing as small and balanced as I could. My

heart was racing but that was par for the course. We were going into combat, after all.

Moko stopped a few times to recon the area. I appreciated the fact that he seemed to be scouting for possible ambush sites. I'd been in a few too many lately and I wasn't at all eager to go blundering into another one.

We could see the superstructure of the *Kagemaru* rising above us like a floating skyscraper. We could also hear ambient noise now that betrayed the presence of dockworkers trying to unload and load the ship simultaneously.

Talya patted me once on the shoulder and it felt good to have her back there. Moko returned and waved us on to the next waypoint. We took cover behind a stack of crates all carefully stenciled with shipping destinations and customs tracking numbers. Moko pointed at the ship itself and we could see she was resting fairly high in the water. I took that to mean she hadn't been loaded up yet, otherwise her waterline would have been much lower.

Scores of workers directed the overhead cranes and transport trolleys. We saw a lot of crates coming off of the ship and many of them were long and metallic. I glanced at Talya who shrugged. Maybe the *Kagemaru* was shipping other items as well, concealing the true nature of what she was supposed to be doing under the cover of legitimate items.

Another breeze blew over us and I caught a new sound farther ahead. Judging from the way they were talking, they weren't dockworkers.

Next to me, Moko froze. We did, too.

And then we saw them.

Two pairs of men armed with Heckler & Koch MP5K-PDWs—collapsible submachine guns that were lethal at close range and pretty damned dangerous at longer distances as well.

But these guys didn't look like the security patrol for the docks. Those guys would have been outfitted with maybe revolvers or a semiauto pistol. Guys carrying weaponry like what we saw in front of us meant they were obviously someone's private force.

I was banking that they were the Kensei's men.

They split up and each patrol took an opposite end of the ship to watch over. No one stayed near the gangplank, however, and this struck me as odd. I looked at Talya again and saw the frown on her face. She leaned in close.

"I don't like it."

I nodded. "Like they left it open on purpose?"

"Sure. Let it look tough with the guys on patrol but leave the obvious choice open to encourage us to take it."

"And once we're on board?"

Talya frowned. "Another ambush."

"Great."

Moko leaned in. "I suggest you two take out the team at the far end of the dock."

"What are you going to do?"

Moko leaned back. "Overwatch. I'll wait here to see that reinforcements aren't a problem for you."

"All right. But you'd better keep them occupied if they hear us taking out their pals down there."

Talya and I turned and scooted back the way we'd come up to the docks. We circled the pier and got into position behind the patrol. There was too much open ground to sneak up on them directly. We'd be seen easily.

Talya gestured for me to follow her and we snaked our way back and farther down the pier. A heavy container truck blocked the line of sight with the *Kagemaru*. And a stack of crates sat nearby. On the other side, the pier dropped into the bay.

Talya nudged me and pointed. I followed her line of sight and saw what she wanted to do. Just below the lip of the pier was a small walkway the workers might have used to scrape barnacles off the sides of ships that came in close. It ran the entire length of the pier as far as we could tell. And it seemed to run right up next to where the patrol lounged around.

I glanced at Talya and whispered, "Risky."

She shrugged. "Not much choice unless you want to do the frontal thing. Which strikes me as suicidal."

"I'm not a fan of the frontal thing."

"We'll have to hit them at the same time," said Talya. "Are you feeling well enough to jump up from the walkway?"

"Do I have another choice? I can't let you handle it alone. You'd be mowed down by those PDWs." Given more time and resources, we would have created a far better plan than what we were about to do. But as is so often the case, operators need to improvise and hope for the best.

"All right then. Let's get going."

I took point and led the way down onto the catwalk. I would have much preferred a wooden walkway instead of the aluminum one that greeted our feet. I stood stock-still hoping the sound of my feet landing on the walkway hadn't alerted the patrol we were coming.

Talya waited to check on the patrol but shook her head and then came down with me. We doffed our shoes and tied them around our necks. Stocking feet would enable us to move quieter than if we'd kept our shoes on.

I eased myself forward, taking each step as slow as possible without taking too long. I wasn't sure how much time we had. Things might move out of our control at any time. The other patrol might get bored and join our targets. The Kensei might show up and ruin our plan to ambush him. Anything could happen. It had been one of those vacations.

We got to within ten feet and stopped. We had to jump up onto the pier and quickly disable two guards without either one of them getting off a shot or a scream.

Easier said than done.

I took a quick glance over the top of the walkway to confirm they still had their backs to us. Luckily, they did.

I gestured to Talya which one she should take. She nodded.

I did a couple of small plyometric squats to prepare my body. Talya did the same. She looked at me and I mouthed a three, two, one countdown.

And then it was time.

On the count of one we both squatted and then launched ourselves up and over the lip of the pier. We came down directly behind our targets. I brought my hands up fast, scissoring them over the exposed neck of my target, shutting off the blood and oxygen flow to his brain immediately.

His lights went out fast and he started to slump to the ground. I let go of him long enough to catch the PDW before it hit the ground and alerted everyone we were there.

Talya, meanwhile, had chopped the back of the other goon's neck with the side of her hand, knocking him out. She nodded at me and then we eased both the guards over the lip of the pier and down onto the catwalk where no one would see their bodies.

Talya came over. "Now what?"

I looked to our left. "Let's see if the Kensei is on board."

"Yeah."

If we'd wanted to, we could have entered the ship itself hopefully far enough away from the other patrol that they wouldn't see much beyond two shapes walking up the gangway. But that wasn't how we intended to get on the ship. A wide-open gangplank looked too inviting and therefore, too likely that a welcome party awaited us.

We put our shoes back on.

Talya picked up the PDW and hefted it. "Full clip," she whispered.

Mine felt about the same. And it felt real good to have such a dependable weapon in my hands. We were well armed now along with the firearms Moko had brought from Tony Tony's.

We moved casually along the pier, trying our best to look like the patrol we'd just taken out, guns aimed low to suggest everything was all right. I wondered if Moko was watching us right now. He'd have to figure out how to get on the ship for himself.

The gangway was surprisingly close now. None of the dock-workers paid us any attention. It didn't really surprise me. Japanese work ethic demanded the workers fairly concentrate on doing what they were being paid to do rather than look around and wonder about the appearance of a gaijin and a woman holding guns and going up into the ship.

Talya pointed and I nodded. The ropes that held the *Kagemaru* to the dock stretched out nearby, thick bundles that were maybe three inches in diameter.

Talya slid the PDW around her back and leaned over the edge, grasping the rope. She kicked her feet up and shimmied the entire length up to the lip of the ship. Once she'd gotten over the lip, she scanned the area, looked back, and waved me on.

I followed the same route and in two minutes we were both on the ship.

On deck.

Deserted.

I glanced over the side of the ship to where the stack of crates had concealed us along with Moko. I scoured the dark, trying to see if he was around.

Nothing.

I looked farther down the pier to where the second patrol was supposed to be stationed.

They were gone.

Behind me, Talya grunted.

I turned.

"Where'd they go?"

I shook my head. "I don't know."

"No sign of Moko, either?"

"None."

"You think?"

I frowned. "I don't know."

Talya's PDW came up higher. She had the butt in her shoulder ready to bring it up to ready position. I could feel my own heart beating faster. Something wasn't right. And I didn't know what to do.

Talya nudged me. "We need cover."

Ahead of us, a door led into the superstructure itself. But there was no telling what might lie inside. A team of well-armed guards who would mow us down in a second? The Kensei?

"No choice," said Talya. "We can't stay out here exposed like this."

I moved to the doorway and put my ear against the metal door. I couldn't hear anything on the other side, but there was no guarantee something wasn't there. The door could easily have been thick enough to prohibit me from hearing squat.

I grasped the handle and turned it ever so slowly.

It didn't squeak and I breathed a sigh of relief.

Talya stood to one side of the door, the muzzle of her PDW up and ready to fire as I cracked the door open. A musty smell from inside greeted us.

That and darkness.

Talya moved forward. I kept my back to hers, protecting our rear. She stepped over the lip of the entryway and I did the same. I closed the door behind us.

We stood in absolute darkness and waited.

I could hear us breathing hard. It sounded so much louder in the close confines of the room. Gradually, I could see some ambient light from up ahead. I nudged Talya and we began moving toward the light.

It took us three minutes to get to the next door. Talya squeezed the handle and turned it. The door hissed open this time and I took up the first slack on the trigger. My stomach was jumping all over the place and I was very close to unleashing a full magazine just on principle.

The light from the room hurt my eyes. We stepped in blinking. The door closed behind us.

The light vanished and we were both blind for a second.

The light came back but this time it was a deep red, like the main power had failed and the backup generators were working.

I blinked furiously.

"Welcome aboard, Lawson."

I brought the gun up but it was snatched out of my hand. Next to me, I heard Talya drop to the ground. Someone had clocked her on the back of the head and she was down.

"I told you it wouldn't be a problem."

That voice. I blinked more now, trying to get my eyes accustomed to the light.

"You did. And I thank you for keeping your end of the deal."

I looked up. Armed men surrounded Talya and me.

But they weren't the real concern. I was more upset by who stood in front of me.

The Kensei.

And next to him . . . Moko.

CHAPTER TWENTY-SEVEN

"This isn't exactly how I saw the rest of this day unfolding." I glanced at the crumpled body of Talya on the floor and my heart ached for her then. But I couldn't let it show. Knowing the Kensei, he'd use that against me for all it was worth, which, in truth, was plenty.

Moko eyed me and shrugged. "Sorry. But my own needs come before those of others."

"That's real Bushido of you."

The Kensei smiled. His pale skin seemed to almost glitter in the red lighted room. "I always enjoy the interplay between the traitor and those he's betrayed. It's so nice when reality hits." He clapped his hands. "But alas, we don't have such time this evening. I'm in the midst of some very extensive and expensive preparations and I need to make sure things are completed on time and in order."

I frowned. "Your organ shipments?"

He looked at me. "Yes."

"You're not surprised."

"That you found out? Why would I be? I know you're good at what you do."

"Is that the closest I'm going to get to a compliment from you?" I tried to grin again, but I'd noticed Talya moving ever so slightly. It was hard to not bend over and see if she needed help. I had to keep reminding myself she was a big girl playing in a big game and she could look after herself.

Tough as it was to do that.

"I could have just as easily insulted you, Lawson. Your reputation is apparently a house of lies."

"God, that's so cliché."

The Kensei ignored me. "You just don't live up to the hype."

I shrugged. "I've got good PR."

"Apparently." He shook his head. "I mean, I've spent the better part of ten minutes now debating whether I should be the one to kill you or just delegate it to one of my talented henchmen here."

"Thanks for the in-depth consideration."

He shrugged. "Well, there was nothing else to do. The lights were out and I was bored."

Talya had shifted but she was moving so slowly that they might not have noticed it in the dim light. I hoped they didn't. "You're really flattering me here."

"What I decided was that I should let my assistant Hana take care of you."

From behind the Kensei, a lithe man dressed entirely in black stepped forward. I couldn't see any weapons, but that didn't mean he didn't have a stockpile on his body somewhere. What drew my attention more than anything else about him, though, was his face.

"As you can see," said the Kensei, "he has no nose."

"And his name is a little joke you use to constantly remind him of that fact." I sighed. "Classy."

"Hana is the veteran of many scrapes and battles. He used to work for another yakuza gumi before he came to me. His specialty before I employed him was roughing up protesters for various political parties. He became quite good at it."

I pointed at the two small blowholes on his face. "Looks like someone gave him some trouble, though."

The Kensei shrugged. "His former gumi caught up with him and punished him for leaving their ranks."

"They cut off his nose?"

"And slashed his wrists and cut his neck open. When I found him, he was hovering between life and death. Most of his blood had spilled out into the alleyway. The rats were wading through it, eager to find the source. I believe he would have been eaten, clothes and all, had I not stumbled onto him."

"And you did what?"

The Kensei smiled. "I offered him a choice."

"I find that hard to believe."

"I needed a body to experiment on. He wasn't exactly in much of a condition to say otherwise. I took that as his consent."

I wondered how much longer it would take Talya to recover. "You experimented on him how?"

"He's a new generation hybrid. Part vampire and part human."

I could sense energy coming from Talya now. She was readying herself and I needed to keep this going as long as I could until she sprang into action.

"That's impossible. Our species were never meant to commingle."

The Kensei sniffed. "Hardly. In fact, I think you know it's not. You still bear the scars of your encounter with some of my earlier hybrid assassins on the train, don't you?"

"I do." My hands had healed up pretty well thanks to the juice I'd had from Kennichi and Moko. But I wasn't looking forward to going into battle against one so soon after my previous encounter.

Beggars can't be choosers and I've always been a bit of a beggar. Sucks to be me.

"A pity my children didn't finish you off when they had the chance," said the Kensei.

"They were too busy dying," I said. I nodded at Hana. "So this guy has those special fingernails?"

The Kensei nodded. "Nice touch, huh? I confess I've always been into comic books. I figured science would forgive me for a little hero worship."

"I don't think the Council will forgive you for toying with evolution."

"Vampire evolution is a joke anyway," said the Kensei. "We're not evolving fast enough. Don't you know that every few thousand years nature does something remarkable? It mutates a certain species. In the span of only a few generations, significant changes take place that can alter the entire path of a species."

"Yeah, nature does that." I shook my head. "Not some cuckoo albino freak in the bowels of a ship."

The Kensei's jaw tightened. "I'm going to enjoy watching Hana take you apart piece by piece."

"I've heard that before."

The Kensei smiled. "Really, though, enough of this silly bravado. You won't be having an open casket funeral, Lawson."

"No one would come anyway. What difference does it make?" I took a small step backward. I at least wanted to make sure I could control the space if Hana suddenly rushed at me. I hoped Talya was almost ready to do whatever she was planning. The situation in the compartment was going to get hairy pretty fast.

"We're not fighting here," said the Kensei.

I felt the energy suddenly dissipate. "Why not?"

"Because I enjoy watching a good fight." He closed his eyes and took a breath of air. "I love being a spectator to greatness."

"Another compliment?"

His eyes narrowed. "Not directed at you, Lawson. Hana is a supreme master of several old martial *ryuha*. I believe this will fall into the category of 'toying with' rather than a fast decimation. And it will be a treasure to behold." He nodded at the other henchmen with the rifles. "Get them all on deck."

I stood fast. "I'm not going anywhere."

The Kensei nodded. "Shoot the girl."

I put my hands up. "You know, some fresh air would actually do me some good. Let's go to the deck."

The Kensei smiled again. "I've heard your wit is something else. I do enjoy the commentary that comes out of your mouth."

"You should see me vomit. I'm a riot."

Hana grabbed Talya off the floor far too easily. How strong was that guy? I was thankful Moko had given me the juice back in the car. I wasn't thankful that he'd sold us out, though. I wondered what he was getting out of the deal.

The two henchmen nudged me out of the compartment, back the way Talya and I had made our entry. I stepped back on the deck and we turned left toward the front of the ship.

A cool sea breeze swept over the hull and lashed my face with salty air. I sucked in a few lungfuls. Always good to flush the blood with oxygen before a fight. And I had the feeling Hana wasn't going to be the easiest guy to put away.

Moko came up behind me. "Sorry it worked out this way, Lawson."

"Are you?"

"I'm not into betrayal. It's something I've never done before."

I grinned. "Well, glad to see those New Year's resolutions are working so well for you."

Ahead of me, I could make out a raised deck. There was a high chain-link fence all around the perimeter. Outside the fence were two dozen seats.

I stopped and looked at the Kensei who was cloaked now. "You broadcasting this on pay-per-view?"

"I told you I enjoy a good fight. And Hana will ensure that I have something to cheer for."

"I hate being the visiting team."

The Kensei smiled. "Shall we wake your girlfriend up? Maybe she can cheer you on."

"No need."

Talya's head snapped back and up into Hana's face with a dull thud. If Hana had had a nose, the effect would have been tremendous. Blood would have sprayed everywhere and Talya could have probably gotten out of his clutches, reversed the situation, and we could have taken the lot of them out.

But since the Kensei had chosen some freak without a nose for me to fight, Talya's effort went pretty much unnoticed by him. He simply grunted and then clamped his hands around Talya even more. I could see his fingers pressing deep into her skin. Talya's teeth were showing and she inhaled sharply. The pain must have been intense. I'd never seen her react that way before.

It pissed me off.

I looked at the Kensei. "So after you rescued freak boy over there, and turned him into a hybrid, did you run out of money or something?"

The Kensei stopped and considered me for a moment. "Why do you ask?"

"You couldn't give him a new nose?"

He smiled. "I did, but he wasn't happy with the one I picked out."

Another henchman appeared closer to the cage and opened the rudimentary door that would grant Hana and me access. I could see the perimeter measured maybe twenty by twenty.

More than enough space to die in.

"Lawson."

I looked at Talya. Her head was up again and she was trying hard to smile at me. "Kick his ass."

I smiled and tried to look all tough, but it was a show. She knew it and I knew it. Hana was going to be a tough nut to crack. And I was nowhere near a nutcracker.

"It's time." The Kensei patted me on the shoulder. "It's been delightful knowing you, Lawson. I believe my brother would have enjoyed this greatly. Seeing you dismembered and all."

"Your brother was more of a warrior than you'll ever be."

The Kensei stopped and came back over to me. "What did you say?"

"You heard me. Cho at least had the guts to fight me himself."

"I fought you before. We were so rudely interrupted by your girlfriend there, if you don't recall."

I tried my best to glare at him with contempt. "But Cho would have insisted I fight him to the death. He wouldn't have handed it off to some underling the way you've done it. He would have been proud to face me in battle. He would have—"

"Cho is dead. You killed him." The Kensei leaned in close to me. "And no amount of baiting is going to get me into that ring with you. I have far more important things to concern myself with than the destiny of some pathetic Fixer. You will die in there, Lawson, mark my words. And Hana will not be gentle. He will not give you any quarter or show you any mercy when the deed is about to be done. You're going to suffer and suffer greatly."

He stepped away. "Put them in the cage."

I felt myself herded toward the door. I turned back and saw the Kensei walking toward his seat. He had a radio up to his mouth, speaking into it. I heard the ship's horn sound.

We were pulling out of port.

Swell.

I stepped into the cage and got myself over to the far side. I knew Hana wouldn't come at me until his master was seated and ready.

But I wanted some time to ready myself. I did a few knee bends to get some blood flowing to my legs.

Hana stood at the other side of the cage not moving at all.

Just watching me.

I couldn't tell the ship was moving aside from the slow progression of buildings and the rest of the wharf as we passed it. The freighter was almost too large to actually feel the sea beneath us.

I figured the Kensei would wait until we'd cleared port before he gave the command to fight. After all, he wouldn't want the port authorities to be able to swarm the ship in the event they were astute enough to hear my death screams.

Bummer.

I did a few more knee bends and jogged some in place.

I looked up and saw the Kensei still turned and talking into his radio.

So I launched myself at Hana, hoping against hope that my surprise move would be enough to give me the upper hand.

CHAPTER TWENTY-EIGHT

I covered the distance with a leaping punch aimed right at the spot between Hana's eyebrows, hoping to knock his brain so hard that he just dropped unconscious to the floor.

That was the plan anyway.

Hana merely lifted one hand and swatted me away like a fly. My momentum carried me beyond range of him pretty fast, but I crashed into the chain-link fence and thought I might have the impression left on my skin, like the time I feel asleep on a pair of corduroys and woke up with vertical lines on my face.

Hana turned and regarded me as I rose up and assumed a fighting posture. I could hear the Kensei yelling something, but I wasn't about to stop and pay attention. Not when I'd already started things off. If the Kensei wasn't seated properly or hadn't ordered his favorite salty nuts, then too bad.

I brought my right leg up, feigning a kick at Hana's crotch, and then threw another punch at his throat. Hana shifted to the inside of my kick and used his own knee to knock it off its path. As I came down, my momentum carrying me past him, I chopped at the side of his neck with my left hand.

He gritted his teeth, latched on to my arm, and then pivoted, throwing me across the cage. I rolled and felt his energy moving now, coming at me fast. As I got to my feet, Hana had thrown his lead leg at my head.

I ducked and rolled at him, lashing out toward his crotch.

Hana jumped and dove out of the way, his own roll carrying him far away again.

Both of us got to our feet and circled.

Real combat's a bitch. It never looks as pretty as the movies. It's never about a thousand blocks and punches that people can miraculously avoid and counter time and time again. Real fighting takes your breath away. It floods you with adrenaline and makes you want to puke and shit at the same time.

And there's very little time to do anything fancy.

Hana rushed me now, going low for a tackle. I brought my knee up, but his shoulder jammed it and then he was wrapping himself around me, lifting to toss me onto my back. I clapped my hands down on his ears, hoping the air pressure would cause his eardrums to rupture.

I heard him grunt again, or maybe it was me as my back hit the deck and the wind rushed out of my lungs.

Hana started maneuvering his way up my body, keeping himself low to maintain the ability to use his own body weight against me. I felt his elbows dig into the insides of my thighs and cried out. If you've never had someone elbow you on the inside of your knees and thighs, you're missing a real treat.

Yeah.

I brought my elbows up and used them against Hana's face. It looked completely bizarre using them against some guy with no nose. But I scored a hit on the outside of Hana's orbital bone. I saw his vision blur with tears and then the swelling started.

Good, that would keep him—

I screamed and felt Hana slicing me with his nails. He'd dug them into my stomach like he was going to reach in and simply yank my guts out all willy-nilly.

I rolled and dislodged him. I had five shallow stabs into my stomach, but the bleeding wasn't bad. It wouldn't kill me, but it hurt like a bastard.

Hana's hands were bloody and now I heard the Kensei cheering him on.

Hana swiped at my neck, hoping to tear the muscle up there and flay open my trachea. I ducked under the swipe and then came up behind his arm, moving with him as he tried to draw it back. As he did, I got my body behind it and jerked his arm back across my chest.

I heard the snap and knew I'd scored on his elbow. Hana screeched and dove away from me clutching his useless limb. As he did so, he backhand-slashed me with his free arm. I felt the nails slice across my left cheek.

Copper stained the air. We could smell each other's blood now. The deck was getting wet from sea spray and sweat and blood.

Footing was a problem.

Here's a simple fact for you: most fights go to the ground.

And if you're not comfortable fighting there, you're going to be done as soon as you fall. You can go from an upright scenario to a ground one pretty fast and if you aren't careful, you'll die quickly. Especially if the other guy gets desperate.

Hana turned his diving roll into a backward roll and knocked my legs out from under me. I went down again and tried to immediately get up on all fours to greet him.

Instead, he somehow managed to wrap my legs up and as I turned, I felt him clamber onto my back.

Not good.

His hands wrapped around my neck and I could feel him trying to yank my head back and break my neck. With his legs wrapped underneath my own, I didn't have much purchase. I could feel him pulling but he could only do it well with one arm, since I'd broken his other.

The pressure was uneven and turned me slightly. I could feel my body rise up on one side and his foot came free, allowing me to go with the pressure and reverse my position.

I rolled and as I did, my right arm came all the way around, chopping down onto the front of Hana's neck right by his voice box. He gagged. I chopped to the side of his neck with my left and then grabbed his bad arm. As I did, I got my left leg up and put the edge of my shoe against the side of his neck.

Then I pulled with everything I had left.

My body flew back as I straightened my leg and my arms.

Hana's neck snapped.

And time stopped.

I rolled to my feet and checked him over. How the hell do you kill a hybrid anyway? Was it enough to kill them as you would a human or was I going to have to find a toothpick on this ship and do him that way?

Hana didn't move.

I became aware of the fact that everything was quiet.

Except the sound of the wind.

And my own labored breathing.

I ran a hand over my face. It came away slick with sweat and blood, but not much else. I wouldn't be entering any beauty contests for a while, but otherwise things were cool.

My stomach hurt like hell, though. The Kensei had obviously outfitted his hybrids with some nasty toys. And Hana knew how to fight.

The chain-link fence door opened. Two of the Kensei's henchmen ratcheted their rifles and aimed them at me. I glanced at the Kensei sitting on his chair farther up than the other spectators or crew or whoever the hell they were.

He didn't look happy.

I eyed the two guys with guns and looked back at the Kensei. "So, this is it? I kill your beloved creation and you just shoot me?"

The Kensei paused. I could see Talya. She smiled at me, but I could see her concern etched on her face. Moko just stood there not saying anything.

"Bring him to me."

He hadn't even shouted it. But somehow, I could hear the harsh whisper as it floated down from the seating area. The two henchmen grunted at me.

I smiled at them in return.

At least I was alive for a few more minutes.

I walked back onto the deck and felt the adrenaline dump make me go woozy. In the wake of combat, you still feel like shit. I gulped down some air and swallowed hard, forcing myself to focus on what might be coming next.

I climbed the steps to where the Kensei sat.

He was wrapped in some sort of silk robe that made him look positively ridiculous. I didn't think this was the right time to insult his fashion sense, however.

He eyed me as I came abreast of him. "You were not supposed to kill him."

I chuckled. "Yeah, I know. I was supposed to die. Funny thing about that is, despite the fact that my life tends to suck with one very small exception, I still have this unearthly attachment to living."

The Kensei looked back into the cage at Hana's corpse. "Hana was a mighty warrior."

"Well, he knew how to fight."

The Kensei eyed me. "I wasn't looking for your agreement."

"Ah." I glanced at Talya and waggled my eyebrows. I've found it's the little things that help keep morale up when things look mighty bleak otherwise. Talya smiled back at me and raised her own eyebrows as if to say, "What's next?"

I shrugged. In truth, I didn't know.

The Kensei seemed to be concentrating on something. I watched his lips move and then saw his hands fold into some sort of strange mudra finger positioning. I frowned. I'd seen a lot of strange crap in my time. My martial art has its own mystical side to it, one that uses finger-entwining mudra and spoken mantra to aid in the visualization of a better future.

Somehow I didn't think the Kensei was doing anything like that.

He turned to me then. "I have said my prayers for Hana's spirit."

I kept silent.

"You, Lawson, are also a mighty warrior."

Wow. Another compliment. "Thanks."

"It occurs to me that I may have been mistaken about you."

"Yeah?"

"Perhaps you were right to suggest that we battle each other. If I had agreed, then perhaps Hana would still be alive now."

I shrugged. "He might not be."

"How do you figure that?"

"Because after I killed you, he'd be so crazy for revenge that I'd kill him, too."

The Kensei sniffed like he'd stepped in dog crap. "You must be delusional. Hana was a great fighter but I am even better."

"We've tussled briefly. But I don't know that I'd agree with your assessment of your skills."

He smirked and I found I was really getting tired of watching him grin at me. "You have rested?"

"Not really." I needed a lot more time than what I'd had.

Another breeze blew over the deck. My eyes watered in the night air. The farther we got away from port, the more concerned I got about being thrown over the side and having to deal with sharks.

The Kensei looked at me and then spoke to the henchmen behind me. "Take him below and lock him in one of the spare compartments. Put the girl in with him."

He looked at me. "You will be allowed to rest for four hours."

"Wow, generous of you."

The Kensei ignored me. "After four hours have passed, we will meet out here on deck."

I sighed. "Not that silly cage thing again."

"We will face each other as samurai faced each other hundreds of years ago."

"A sake drinking contest?"

"With drawn swords." The Kensei frowned. "I hope your *kenjutsu* skills are as good as your unarmed abilities. You will need every ounce of talent you possess if you wish to defeat me."

Somehow I didn't feel like tossing another wisecrack out there. Something about the look in the Kensei's eyes set my blood cold. And even though I'd just fought for my life and won, I knew the coming battle would be even worse.

My arms were pinned behind me and a rifle barrel poked me in the spine. "Move."

I allowed myself to be prodded along toward the interior of the ship.

Talya came with us. We walked in single file and it was nice to know that we'd at least have some time together before the showdown.

I'd have to figure out something that would enable me to even the odds. I didn't exactly feel like I was on my best footing right then.

"Lawson."

I turned. The Kensei stood in the doorway.

"Yeah?"

"Enjoy your last time with your woman. Then prepare yourself for death."

Oh yeah, like I was going to have sex when I knew that I was going to have to have an exhausting sword fight later on. I frowned.

"Thanks."

"I will see Hana's death avenged by your own demise."

"Swell."

He turned and disappeared from view, his silly robes swirling in his wake. The guard barked a command to move and I did so. The sooner I got my head down and slept, the better.

Four hours was going to be over before I knew it.

And I wasn't looking forward to what was coming next.

CHAPTER
TWENTY-NINE

If you've never been in the bowels of a freighter, you're not missing a damned thing. Talya and I were herded into a dank compartment that smelled of rust and stale water. It was cold and we huddled in the corner. In the darkness, Talya probed my wounds.

"The cuts were deep, but I don't think—" She stopped herself and smiled at me in the gloom. "Guess it's not really going to affect you much. Is it?"

"Nope. Would have been worse if he reached in and grabbed a fistful of entrails. Luckily, he didn't."

"He was good, though, wasn't he?"

"Seasoned." I grunted. "Yeah."

"The Kensei will be even better."

"No doubt."

"Do you know what style he fights with when he has a sword?"

Even though we were whispering, the sound seemed to echo off the metal walls. "I don't have a clue. And most of my sword-fighting skill comes from a fairly old tradition. I don't know how they match up. And I won't know until I get out there and face him."

Talya's hand was firm on my shoulder. "Is there anything I can do to help?"

I put my head on her shoulder and nuzzled her neck. "How 'bout a drink?"

She nudged me away. "Even now, you're trying to be funny?"

"I'll bet some fancy-pants shrink would tell you I use my humor to mask my fear."

"Is that it?"

I sighed. "No, I think I'm just a wiseass. Always have been. Always will be."

"Some day, that cavalier attitude is going to get you into trouble."

I glanced at her and laughed. "Yeah, because we're having ourselves such a nice little vacation right now."

Talya smiled. "You're not the only one who can be funny."

I kissed her. When we broke for air, her hand stroked my face. "I don't think I've ever loved someone as much as I love you."

I thought about all the women I'd ever been with in my life. All but two were just for sex. Convenient relationships that guaranteed me a steady supply of fun in the sack. I didn't see anything wrong with that, personally.

I'd only loved two women in my life. Robin was my first girlfriend almost one hundred years ago. That crazy psychopath Cosgrove had slaughtered her. When he came back to Boston, I finally managed to kill him.

But not before I met Talya.

And fell in love with her.

"We're quite the couple," I said.

"How do you mean?"

"Look at the two of us: trained killers locked in some freezing cargo hold of a decrepit freighter that is bound for exotic ports carrying all sorts of human and vampire organs. We're prisoners and I'm supposed to be fighting some albino freak in a few hours."

"Just imagine all the stories we'll tell our children."

I looked at Talya. "I don't know that that's possible, babe. Vampires and humans don't mix all that well."

"Well, it can't be impossible. How else would you explain the fact that the Kensei has been able to produce hybrids?"

I shrugged. "Maybe he knows something that the rest of the vampire race doesn't."

Talya slumped back. "Just would be nice."

"What?"

She smiled. "Having kids with you."

"Sure, we could have family fun time. Sniper hour, close-quarter pillow fights, nighttime recon, we'd be the hallmark of a family utopia."

Talya laughed and I realized how much I enjoyed listening to her when she did. "We would have quite the family life, wouldn't we?"

I leaned into her again. "You ready to give up your life? I thought you enjoyed what you do too much for that."

"I do love what I do. I'm addicted to the excitement. I won't pretend I'm not. I was chosen at a young age to become what I became because they could see that. The KGB knew what I was before I even knew it. They could look into my skull and see what made my blood race."

"At least you had people examining you. I picked up a set of rusty scales and the next thing I knew, I was on a bus headed for Vermont. They called it destiny. I called it a pain in the ass."

"Doesn't change what we are."

I sighed. "Kids would sure change that."

"Yes, they would."

"I don't know if I'm the father type, Talya."

"And I don't know that I'd ever make a good mother." She looked at me. "But we can dream, can't we? We can imagine a life that is a far cry from the life we have now."

"Better than considering the alternative, I guess."

"Which is what?"

"Me dying in a few hours."

Talya sighed. "I was trying to keep you focused on something else."

"Kind of hard to forget it, you know?"

She stayed quiet for a minute. "Did I ever tell you about the time I was in Berlin?"

"I never knew you were in Berlin."

She elbowed me. "Lawson, I've been in just about every hellhole and city in the world. I think it might be easier to list the places I haven't operated in rather than the ones I have."

"Okay."

"It was '83. We got word that a CIA special projects team was shepherding a group of Russian and East German scientists out of the country through a tunnel built under the wall."

"What made the scientists so special that they had to get them out?"

"They were experts in the field of paranormal research."

"Ah, that explains it then."

"I think a lot of U.S. schools were still conducting secret research for the U.S. government into remote viewing and other phenomena. The Warsaw Pact was far ahead. You guys needed a break and a boost and it was deemed this was the best way to do so. Recruit and convince a group of them to defect to the West."

I thought about the logistics of trying to break the scientists out. "Must have been some op."

"The tunnel entrance was under a toilet in the basement of an apartment building that sat almost two thousand feet away from the wall. They'd cleared the other buildings way back because so many tunnels were being dug."

"I don't like to think about crawling through a tunnel under a wall like that. Must have been awful."

Talya ignored me. "I was assigned to kill them as they emerged from the tunnel on the other side. Not in East Germany you understand, but in West Berlin. I was told that those three scientists must never be allowed to speak with the Americans about their research."

"And what about the Americans protecting them?"

Talya paused. "I was told to kill them, too. It was supposed to be a warning shot to the Americans that they were not to use their special projects teams in Berlin ever again."

"So, what did you do?"

"I flew into West Berlin a week ahead of time and started making my arrangements. I got myself an apartment in the building where the tunnel exited. I was able to recon it fairly well without attracting much notice. At that time, I don't think the West even knew who I was yet. I wasn't on the map, so to speak."

I nodded. Surprise was always a plus in covert ops. "Best time for you to pull something off like that."

"Exactly." She paused. "It felt very strange to me and I don't think I'll ever forget it, that way you get when you know that in a short time you have to go into combat and you might not come back."

"I know the feeling."

"You know you've got the advantage—surprise and superior weapons. You've got the skill or else you wouldn't be in the place you're in. But it doesn't comfort you. You see all these other impossible scenarios running through your head. All the what-if's that you think because you're a human being and that's what humans do."

I knew exactly what she was saying. I'd had the same experience enough times. "Vampires, too."

"And you can't really sleep. You can't eat much. Hell, you can't even move your bowels even though it feels like that's exactly what you want to do every second of the day."

"Maybe it's the way we prepare ourselves for the coming stresses."

"I stayed awake almost two straight days before the mission. I couldn't do anything but check and recheck my weapons. I'd already done it countless times but I did it again because that's what I was trained to do. And that's all I could do. And in the end, when that clock finally ticked down and I made my way down to the basement to do what I was supposed to do, it was like this giant weight being lifted off my shoulders. Like I could finally move again."

I looked at her. "You killed them?"

She smirked. "Nope. Not a one."

"Why not?"

"Don't think it was a matter of conscience."

My turn to smile now. "I know you too well for that."

"It was a ruse."

"What?"

"The escape. It was a ruse the Americans had pulled on us. They knew the Russians would never let them take their best experts. They knew Moscow would dispatch an expert at problem removal. And it might be someone they didn't know. So they rigged the entire place with video cameras and as I came down into the basement, my mug shot was captured and blasted to Langley."

"Creative. What about the three experts?"

"They escaped. While we were focused on the tunnel, they simply caught a car and drove across the border with forged papers. It was a brilliant plan."

I frowned. "Seems like it would have been easier to just pick the scientists up and make sure they couldn't go anywhere than let them run on a leash."

"That's what I thought, too. And then I knew why."

"Enlighten me."

"It was one of those times when things were done a little tit for tat. Honor among thieves? The United States and the Soviets used to give each other little bits of stuff from time to time. And I found out that the Americans had relinquished plans for a new weapon system only a few months before."

"Why the hell would they do that?"

Talya smiled. "Weren't you operational during the cold war?"

"Yes." I had more than a few memories of my own. Vienna. Malta. Madagascar. The countries and cities swirled past in my mind.

"It was never about superiority. Surely you know that."

"What was it about then?"

"Détente."

"You saying that if the Americans had a weapons system that was better than the Soviets, it would have tipped the power too much?"

"Sure. And if the Soviets freaked about the United States having something better, then the temptation to just go nuclear in the event of a crisis would have been too great. So the Americans let us get the same thing to keep the sides even."

"So you owed them, in other words."

"Yes."

"And you and the scientists were the tidbits given up."

"I wasn't pleased," said Talya. "I was furious. It was the first time I'd felt like I was really expendable. That I could be given up if it suited someone higher up than me."

Again, I knew what that felt like. "Not a good feeling."

"No."

"So, what's your point?"

Talya smiled. "Does there have to be a point?"

"Uh . . ."

"You haven't been thinking about the Kensei for the last few minutes, have you?"

"No."

She smiled. "Okay, then."

"What?"

"There's your rest."

"My rest? That was my rest?"

"Yes."

"I don't feel rested."

"It was just an expression."

I leaned into her. "I don't understand you sometimes."

She whispered into my ear. "That's what makes us so good for each other."

"Any other words of advice?"

"Yes. Don't die."

"Yes, ma'am."

I got to my feet and shuffled around the room. I've never liked waiting for someone else to call the shots. It's not my way. I'm aggressive and I like dictating the flow of battle.

But Talya's story had sparked something in me.

Now all I had to do was make sure I could make it work.

CHAPTER THIRTY

We waited another hour. And then I banged on the door. Loud. And constant. I knew sooner or later someone would come down and see what the hell I was doing causing such a ruckus.

I heard someone's boots outside the door. "What do you want?"

"Water. I'm dehydrating in here."

There was a pause. "You don't get any water."

"I don't think the Kensei will be happy if I pass out before he has a chance to slit me through with his sword."

I could hear the guard talking to his pal in the corridor. I shook my head. You see these plans work all the times in the movies, but they never do in real life. I figured I had nothing to lose by trying it out, however.

After thirty seconds, I heard the latch unlock. I steeled myself for the battle. It felt good knowing that Talya would have my back.

The muzzle of a rifle came through the door first. "Step back."

I stepped back.

The first guard came through, followed by another. The way they moved told me they'd been well trained. The first guard didn't step in front of the other guard's field of fire. Smart.

The first guard held a big bowl of water. "Here."

I took it and brought it to my lips and drank. "Thanks."

He frowned. "Where'd she go?"

I shook my head and turned.

Talya had vanished.

I almost dropped the bowl of water. The first guard started flapping and called for his friend to come in. As soon as the second guard cleared the door, I sensed something drop from above. Whatever it was crashed into him with such force that his rifle clattered to the ground.

That left the first guard and me to deal with each other.

He didn't go for his gun but launched a punch right at my face. I dipped to the inside and used my own punch to knock the inside of his arm back and away, shifted forward, and caught him with a hard chop to the side of his neck. He dropped back but I followed and wound my arm over his, entangling him. I grabbed the back of his neck, twisted, and spun him around violently. I heard the crack and he slumped to the floor dead.

Talya got up off the floor. She smiled at me in the dim light.

I looked up. "How'd you do that?"

"Saw it on an old episode of *Miami Vice*. Works pretty well, huh?"

"I'd say."

She got the guns and handed me one of them. "Ready to take the battle to the enemy?"

"Yeah."

"You want point or what?"

I nodded. We nosed our way into the hallway. I kept the AR-15 in the low ready, able to snap it up and fire if need be. Talya kept herself turned sideways so she could cover me and cover our rear in case they came at us from that way.

It was still dark outside, which worked in our favor. I knew somewhere the Kensei would be preparing himself for battle. Probably deep in meditation about how he intended to slice me open, I thought.

Instead, he was going to get a great big surprise.

And then I'd have time to deal with Moko and show him why I despise traitors so much.

We stepped onto the deck and tasted the salty air again. The waves were surging and we seemed to be sailing straight into a storm. Great. Probably the Kensei wanted to use the storm to mask the ship's path in case they were being tracked.

But it also made fighting that much tougher. And I don't like being on boat in the middle of a storm. It always reminded me of the time I went whale watching off the coast of Cape Cod. We hit rough seas and at one point the boat was taking them broadside so with each wave, the damn ship would loll until you could almost reach out and touch the water. I stayed inside the cabin and put my head down, trying to will the ocean back into a peaceful state. We saw some amazing whales later on, but when I got my pictures back, there was a bob of red hair in each one from the woman who kept jutting her huge noggin into the camera frame, effectively blocking my superb photography.

But Cape Cod was a world away. And while I could feel the freighter moving in relation to the ocean, it wasn't nearly as bad as the whale-watching trip. Lucky for me.

Talya was still braced by the door leading inside. "We need to move."

She was right, of course. The problem was, I wasn't sure which way to go. We had two things to consider: speed and stealth. If we had more time, we'd opt for more stealth. That meant moving a lot quieter and slower than we were. But with daylight potentially around the corner and my supposed prom date with the Kensei, we had to move quicker.

Moving faster means there's a greater chance of making noise. But I weighed it against the ambient noise from the surging surf and decided we could risk it.

I pointed up and Talya swung out, crouched down by the

stairwell as I went up. I stayed low, trying to minimize exposure. If anyone poked their head over and saw me coming, he'd take rounds from Talya and then we'd be up and moving at light speed.

But no one looked over the edge and I crested the stairs in short order. I could see the wheelhouse now. Two people were inside, but the Kensei was not one of them. I figured he'd have his quarters somewhere close by, though, rather than in the bowels of the ship where we'd been located.

Talya came up and crouched four feet away from me. You never bunch up when doing stuff like we were. Tactically, it made no sense. Someone could stitch you in a single burst. You stay close enough to convey information but far away enough to ensure your safety as a group. If one of the team gets dropped, the other keeps going.

I motioned what I'd seen and Talya nodded. We'd make our approach on the wheelhouse, incapacitate anyone inside, and stop the ship. From that point on, we'd work down from the top, clearing as we went.

It wasn't going to be easy, but then again, when was my life ever easy?

Yeah, I couldn't remember a time, either.

We moved in synch. One of us would move while the other provided cover. It's almost impossible to run and shoot at the same time in combat. Your rounds go off target and you end up wasting ammunition. So you run, drop, and then fire. And while you're running, your teammates provide cover.

Talya and I moved like we were a practiced team. I almost enjoyed it.

We got to within twenty feet of the wheelhouse and I could make out who was inside.

Moko.

And the captain.

I grinned. Looks like I wasn't going to have to wait so long to deal with him, after all. And that suited me just fine.

I hand-signaled Talya again, letting her know how we'd hit it. We got to the outside of the door. I checked the handle and hinges. It opened to the inside, which worked in our favor.

We stacked and had another look around. We'd climbed up almost forty feet over the height of the deck. Somehow, looking down from where we were made me feel a lot higher than we actually were. Combined with the angry swells and whitecaps I could make out, it was shaping up to be a nasty night at sea.

Or morning.

Talya squeezed my shoulder to let me know she was ready. On my count, I'd shove the door open and we'd both rush in, breaking the room into quadrants that we would be able to immediately cover.

Talya and I were a duo where in an optimal situation you'd have four team members. But we'd make it work. For close confines like this, I would have actually preferred using pistols, but the AR-15 wasn't too big and we could bring it to bear fast.

I held up three fingers.

Then I placed my left hand on the door handle, keeping my right index finger along the trigger guard of the AR-15. I took several deep breaths.

Squeezed and turned the handle.

And shoved.

Behind me, Talya added some pressure to keep us going.

The door shot open.

I went right, with the door, bringing the AR-15 up, ready to shoot if I needed to.

Talya went left, also bringing her gun up to bear.

Moko's eyes went wide.

The captain stammered.

I stepped in and used the butt of my gun on Moko's jaw. He went down fast and I took his weapon from him.

Talya moved closer to the captain but he put his hands up and shook his head like he was trying out for *The Exorcist* remake.

Moko moaned and I flipped him over on to his stomach. I kept frisking him and found a hidden knife in a sheath on the small of his back. I glanced at Talya but she was still aiming at the captain.

She wouldn't shoot him. Not unless she had to. And we still needed him.

I rolled Moko over onto his back and nudged his mouth open with the barrel of the AR-15. "I should probably just shoot you now and save us all some trouble."

"They'll hear the shot."

I frowned. But he was right. I backed off, keeping the barrel aimed right at him. If he tried something, I'd stitch him and worry about the noise factor when I had to.

He rubbed his jaw. "That wasn't necessary."

I cocked an eyebrow. "Yeah, I should probably have just shot you."

"No, you shouldn't have."

Talya moved closer to the captain. "Lawson."

"Yeah?"

"What about this guy?"

I glanced at the captain. "Turn this thing around and head back to Tokyo."

He started to shake his head. "I can't do that. He will kill me if I do."

Talya stepped closer. "And I will kill you if you don't do exactly as he said. Now turn the ship around and get us back to Tokyo. Now."

He frowned but got behind the wheel and spun it. It was tough feeling the boat move with the strong seas, but gradually we moved.

I watched the compass heading and saw we'd reversed direction, heading north instead of south.

Talya looked at me. "He'll know something's wrong now."

I nodded. Our surprise was going to be short-lived. "Yeah. No time to spare."

"Good," said Moko. "Now we can go and kill him together."

I looked back at him. "You're not going anywhere. Except maybe straight to hell."

Moko held up his hands. "You've got me all wrong, Lawson."

"Doubt it."

He looked like he was dying for a cigarette. "You really think I'd sell you out after all this time?"

"You did."

"No. I did what I had to do in order to make sure we all got on the ship successfully."

"What the hell does that mean?" asked Talya.

Moko sat up on his haunches. I moved myself out of range of his kicks, just in case. "It means while you and Lawson made your approach from the other end of the ship, I was discovered by a guard team we hadn't seen before. They brought me in and when I was face-to-face with the Kensei, I had to come up with something."

"So you told him what?"

"That you were coming."

"What about you? I thought he wanted you dead, as well."

Moko nodded. "Yes, he did. But I convinced him that I was a little boy gone astray who comes back to his father in the end. He wants to believe that, so he did."

I shook my head. "I don't think he'd be that easy to fool."

"Would he let me walk around here with a gun if he didn't trust me?"

I frowned and took his rifle from the floor. "Well, let's see."

I hit the magazine ejector and then popped a round off the top of the stack. It felt heavy enough to be live. But something looked strange. I slid the magazine back into the rifle and ratcheted a round.

"Looks real enough," I said.

"I told you," said Moko.

I nodded.

And then shot Moko with his gun.

CHAPTER
THIRTY-ONE

The look on Moko's face was one for the ages. Disbelief, amazement, anger, embarrassment.

He looked down, probing with his fingers. He took them away and brought them up to his eyes, staring and studying.

"There's no blood," he said finally.

"There was no bullet." I let him have the gun back. "The Kensei never trusted you. He gave you blanks instead of live ammo."

"Bastard."

I shrugged. "In his place, I would have done the same thing." I glanced at Talya. "He knew Moko was bullshitting him."

"Imagine that." But Talya knew that if the Kensei had suspected Moko, there was no way this was going to get any easier.

Talya eased herself back some so she could cover one of the entrances to the wheelhouse, just in case we had some unexpected company show up. I was expecting an appearance any minute.

Moko got to his feet. "Lawson-san, you've got to believe me when I tell you it was the only way I could have gotten us all on this ship."

"You could have disabled the patrol," I said. "Talya and I did it despite the difficulty."

"I was careless," said Moko. "I made noise and the patrol had me covered. Too far away for me to do anything. I had to surrender."

"And now what? You want me to give you a real gun and risk getting another knife between my shoulder blades?" I shook my head. "Ain't happening, pal. Not today, anyway."

"Lawson."

I turned. Talya was closer to the hatchway. She nodded out into the darkness. Her voice was a whisper I somehow heard over the roar of wind. "Shadows. Movement."

I nodded. I turned to Moko. "You and happy over there are going to resume your watch on the bridge here." I nudged the captain with the barrel of my gun. "Any crap and I put the first three rounds into your head."

He grabbed the wheel and stared straight ahead. I tossed Moko's gun back to him. "Here. Make sure you look like you're in character."

"Lawson . . ."

Talya was already situated behind the door, out of sight of anyone who would come through. There was no chance of them seeing her and shooting through the thick metal. By the time they knew she was there, we'd be on them.

I needed a place to hide. I glanced around and saw a small stack of boxes in the corner. Too small to hide behind, but I was out of time. I crouched down and tried to snuggle as much of my frame as I could behind the boxes. I imagined my ass was probably hanging out, but what can you do?

Just as I finished squirming, I heard the footsteps approaching. I counted two pairs of feet. They stopped just outside the hatchway.

"Moko! We heard a gunshot in here."

I imagined Moko turning with that great disdainful look on his face. "Stop being ridiculous. Why would there be a gunshot in here?"

There was a pause. I didn't like this. We needed them inside. If they stayed out of the wheelhouse, we couldn't be sure we could take them down without one of them sounding an alarm.

Not good.

I heard one of the goons say to the other. "Check his gun."

Damn.

We had one inside and one out. I heard the goon step over the lip of the hatch.

"Give it to me."

Moko unholstered his weapon and handed it to the goon. The goon now had to sling his weapon in order to examine Moko's.

Now . . .

I came up, already aiming. I got my sights on the guy outside and squeezed off a single round. It smacked him in the middle of his forehead and he went toppling back over the railing, falling into the ocean some forty feet below. The rainstorm had helped mask the sound.

I hoped.

Talya came out from behind the door even as the second goon was fumbling for his weapon. She used the stock against the back of his skull and he went down with a thud.

Talya looked at me. "Close."

"Yeah."

Moko reached down for the goon's weapon. I trained my gun on him. Talya put her hand on my arm. "Wait."

I looked at her. "Are you kidding me? We trusted him before and he got us ambushed on this damn boat."

She nodded. "Yeah, and if he wanted us dead—really dead—then he had plenty of opportunities to do it earlier on when we weren't armed. He could have killed us a million times before this and he didn't. I find it doubtful he would have gone through the trouble to set us up here when he could have done it so much sooner."

I took a breath. "You sure?"

"Nope. But I'm almost sure."

I lowered my gun. Moko came up and slung the rifle over his shoulder. He nodded toward Talya. "That's some woman you've got there."

"Yeah." I pointed at his gun. "You even look at me funny and I'll waste you. Talya makes good points about you, but I'm still not convinced. You're overdrawn on the trust account. Make a deposit to cover the overdraft and I'll think about being friends again."

"We should go."

Moko and I looked at Talya. She shrugged. "You guys are just going to wax macho at each other for another few minutes of time that we don't actually have. I thought I'd save you the trouble. Can we go and find the Kensei and then finish this?"

"What about him?" I pointed at the captain who suddenly looked a lot more scared than he had previously.

"Easily solved," said Talya. She chopped him on the side of the neck and the captain slumped to the ground. I looked at him and his skin seemed much paler than before.

"Is he dead?"

Talya frowned. "Probably not. But who cares? He took a job working for the Kensei. Guilt by association and all that jazz."

"Helluva woman," muttered Moko. He took up a low-ready stance with his gun and looked at me. "Who's on point?"

I eyed him and he finally sighed. "This isn't necessary, Lawson. I assure you I'm trustworthy."

"Your willingness to take point might just go a long way toward restoring my faith in you." I pointed to the exit on the opposite side of the wheelhouse. "We'll exit that way."

"We're not going to wait for the Kensei here?" Talya looked at me. "Doesn't that make the most sense?"

"Not anymore. If he knew Moko wasn't reliable, there's no way he'd let him stay in here with only the captain. He must have something else cooking and right now, this is the most dangerous spot for us to be in. We need to keep moving."

She nodded. "All right then."

Moko popped the door and looked back at us. "Are we ready?"

Talya took up the middle position and I stayed back to guard our rear. I glanced at Moko. "Slow and quiet but keep moving. If we get bunched up we'll be killed easily."

Moko grinned. "I've already been shot once tonight. I don't wish to repeat that anytime soon."

"Especially with real bullets," said Talya.

I followed them out of the wheelhouse and back into the windy rain and darkness.

I wondered what was waiting out there for us.

CHAPTER
THIRTY-TWO

I halfway expected Moko to turn on us as soon as he cleared the doorway. I pictured him spinning and hosing his way through Talya, the bullets tearing through Talya's body and into my flesh. I kept my gun ready to shoot him just in case.

But Moko seemed immediately preoccupied with getting us under cover as soon as possible. He led the way out of the wheelhouse and toward the entrance to the lower decks.

We'd be working our way down into the bowels of the ship, which is where Talya and I had come from. Moko showed his skill at clearing areas bit by bit. He went by the book as he approached corners and any place that would expose us. He moved slow and made almost no noise.

Talya glanced back at me a few times and raised her eyebrows to show she approved of his skill. I approved, too. Moko knew what he was doing. I just hoped he wasn't leading us into another trap.

We moved down another flight of stairs and the finished rooms of the upper decks gave way to more steel walkways and twisting winding networks of pipes . Steam issued up from somewhere far below us. It hissed and curled like a snake, enveloping us in its coils until we passed. It was hot enough to make me wince as my hand touched it.

Moko's hand went up on the third level down.

We froze.

I could see him scanning the area ahead. I hadn't heard anything yet, but his vantage point was different than ours. That's what it meant to be on point. You were the eyes and ears of the team. And hard as it was, Talya and I had to trust Moko if he thought he saw something dangerous up ahead of us.

I saw shadows shift.

Guards.

They weren't moving though. That concerned me. I eased forward until I was close enough to cup my hand and put it over Moko's ear.

"Ambush?"

He nodded. Talya frowned and gave me the signal for "How many?"

Moko held up two fingers and spread them apart to indicate they were separate from each other. I scanned below us and could see one shadow shift again.

They were tired.

Being a sentry is always a hard thing to do. When you first assume the post, a natural level of adrenaline keeps you alert and ready for anything. Gradually, time wears you down. No one shows up so you start to get less concerned. You start thinking about other things you'd like to be doing. Your weapon gets heavy. Your eyelids droop.

And that's usually what an invader or saboteur will wait for: that moment when your reflexes sag. When they can get in there, finish you off, and continue on with whatever mission they have to accomplish.

We didn't have the luxury of time, unfortunately. We needed to get to the Kensei before he realized we were coming for him.

I was trying not to fool myself. There was a strong possibility that the Kensei already knew we were coming for him. That might have been why there were two concealed sentries waiting down below.

We'd have to take them at the same time, much the way Talya and I had had to take out the guards on the dock. If we were late, the other one might get a warning shot off and spoil the little party we had planned for the Kensei.

And that wouldn't be fun at all.

Moko slid his gun off and handed it to me, making sure to keep his hand on the swivel joint the strap attached to. That's the problem with slings for guns. If it moves, it will make noise and alert your enemies. Moko had the experience to understand that would happen, though, and made sure he didn't make any noise. I was careful to take the gun and place it on the ground.

Before I could take my own gun off, Talya slid past me and moved off with Moko.

Great.

I had the spectator seat to this. I wasn't crazy about Talya doing it herself, because I didn't want her to get hurt.

Even as that thought crossed my mind, I almost laughed. I didn't have much to worry about. But those guards down there sure did.

Talya and Moko disappeared in the gloom. I watched them separate and then vanish. Shadows shifted. I heard one of the guards attempt to quietly clear his throat, but the sound of it echoed up to me.

I wondered how Moko and Talya would take them out. I hoped they'd arranged some kind of countdown to do it. Otherwise, things would get hairy. I glanced around and wondered about how bad the ricochets would be in the mazelike grid work that we were in. You wouldn't have to be a crack shot to do damage in here.

After what seemed like an interminable wait, I thought I heard a single dull thud. But it didn't come from one side or the other;

it almost sounded like it was in stereo. I realized they'd done it at exactly the same time.

Talya reappeared first followed by Moko. She smiled at me. Moko took his gun and gave me the thumbs-up.

We moved on.

As we descended, I saw the vague outline of two bodies. They'd been concealed, but not as much as Moko and Talya would have liked. There wasn't much of any place to stow them, so they'd done their best with what they had. Still, if any other of the Kensei's men came down here, we'd be found out for sure.

Moko kept leading us down. More steam clogged the air. Dings and whirls and hisses sounded in the air. Each one made my heart tick a bit faster. The environment seemed to close in around us, but it was only in my mind. We were well below the waterline now, so I figured that had something to do with it.

It didn't make me feel any better.

Moko stepped down on to the next flight of steps. I could see we were almost at the bottom of the ship. I assumed the engine room would be down here. Along with, I hoped, the Kensei.

I could make out stacks of crates ahead of us. They were huge, almost as big as what I'd seen cars transported in. But I knew there weren't any cars in those crates.

There were organs—vampire and human—stored in them. Probably masked with something else in case the ship was stopped and searched.

But the grisly nature of the cargo made me feel sick. I wanted to put the Kensei out of business. People had died in his wake. For his sick experiments. And now it was time to end it once and for all.

I was especially eager to put him out of business just because he was Cho's brother. I didn't think the genes in that family had any goodness in them at all. Better to just wipe them all out and start over some other time.

Moko gestured ahead of us as if to point out the crates. I

nodded. Talya frowned. She was personally invested in this, too. I wondered what was going through her head now.

Moko took another step.

And then he exploded.

CHAPTER THIRTY-THREE

The explosion took Moko off his feet and threw his body across the room. The concussion wave rocketed into Talya and me as well, slamming us back onto the stairs. I heard Moko's gun go clattering away. His body lay amid the crates, twisted unnaturally.

There was a good deal of smoke playing with the steam from the pipes. Talya and I got to our feet and rushed down to Moko's body. His eyes were closed and there was a lot of blood pooling around his body. It didn't look good.

Talya felt for the pulse in his neck, but stopped and then pivoted, squeezing off three rounds even as the first sounds of approaching guards reached my ears.

I ducked behind one of the crates and got down some rounds of my own. Two goons took them across the throat and head. They went down fast.

Talya was picking her targets carefully. On semiauto. I chose full and let a stream of rounds fly. I stitched three more guards while Talya got her share.

And then I heard the click.

Dead man's click.

We were both out of bullets.

The air stunk with cordite and the pressure on my ears from firing in the relatively close confines of the room was immense. I swallowed a few times to try to clear them. It didn't do much good, but being deaf was looking like the least of my worries.

Talya glanced at me. "We're screwed."

"Not a bad way to phrase it."

I poked out from behind the crates and saw the Kensei striding down the stairs flanked by more guards.

"Being out of ammunition is never the prescription for success in battle."

He was wearing a black kimono tucked into a black split-skirt hakama that had been tucked into his split-toed tabi socks.

"You're looking every bit the samurai tonight."

He dismissed my comment with a wave of his hand. "Samurai. Ninja. Makes no difference."

"Looks can be deceiving anyway."

He eyed me. "And what does that mean?"

"You don't have the honor to claim either samurai or ninja as your title. You're just another thug who thinks they're above the law."

He smiled. "Well, one thing's for sure, Lawson: I'm above you."

I nodded. "You go right on thinking that."

"Are you going to come out or do I have to shoot you instead? I'd much rather we had our fight now. Hana's death must be avenged. The circle of honor must be closed."

I frowned. "There you go again with that word. It's always those with the least amount of honor and integrity that think they have the most and choose to preach to others rather than figure out their own flaws. Easier, I suppose, to mock others than face your own demons."

The Kensei rested his right hand on the pommel of his sword. "Whatever you think of me makes little difference. In the end, all that matters is your death."

"Swell."

Talya put a hand on my arm. "Don't go, Lawson."

"I've got a choice?" I tried to smile but it was a bit in vain. Talya shook her head and then I stepped out from behind the crates, looking up at the Kensei. "I've got a request."

The Kensei smirked. "You don't have the right to a request."

"See? You talk a good game about honor, but you'd deny your opponent one last wish? Rather pathetic of you."

He frowned. "What is your request?"

This wouldn't go over well with her, but I had to say it. "I want Talya put on one of the smaller boats and set free. There's no need for her to be involved."

"Lawson!"

I turned. "Talya, what the hell else can I do?"

"You can let me fend for myself, by god." The expression on her face wasn't exactly the heartwarming tearful farewell I was naïvely hoping for. But her safety meant more to me than how she might react to my request.

The Kensei pursed his lips. "Seems to me as though she's involved herself in this pretty deeply. I may not be able to excuse her from her obligation to die by my sword as well."

I shrugged. "You don't let her go and I'll rush you right now. Your boys there will shoot me dead before your blade has a chance to split me in two."

"They won't fire unless I command them to." But even as he said it, I knew he didn't believe it.

I smirked. "You think? Seems to me they're pretty trigger-happy. And I don't think they'll be crazy about letting me get too close. They saw what I did to Hana, after all."

The Kensei considered his options. "The woman goes free and you and I battle. Is that it?"

"That's it."

I felt something smack into my back. It hurt like hell and I turned to find that Talya had thrown her weapon at me. "You bastard."

"You'd do the same thing if our places were switched."

Two of the Kensei's men rushed past me and grabbed Talya, dragging her from her place behind the crates. As she struggled past me she looked at me. "You don't have the right to deny me this."

"I'm trying to do this the best way I know how. I love you."

Her eyes misted over but there was anger on her face. She turned her head away from me and stomped forward up the stairs. As she passed the Kensei, she spat in his face. "I hope he kills you."

The Kensei wiped his face with a tiny swatch of cloth from inside his kimono. The he gestured to me. "Come up on deck and see that I am true to my word. We shall release her into one of the craft with a motor. We are not too far away from Tokyo yet. With luck and a good current, she should be able to make it back."

I nodded and followed him up the stairs. Behind me, three guards had the guns trained on me just in case I tried something. But I wasn't going to try anything right now. I needed to make sure Talya was safe before I tried to turn the tables on this thing.

I looked over my shoulder. Moko's body still lay amid the crates, blood already turning a darker shade of maroon. I thought I smelled something and shook my head quickly. Moko was gone.

And death never smells good.

Topside, the wind had increased. The seas frothed over and slammed into the sides of the ship. Miraculously, the freighter was handling it very well. I looked up at the wheelhouse and saw one of the Kensei's guards manning it. He waved at me.

So much for leaving us adrift.

Another of the Kensei's guards was speaking into a radio. I heard the industrial whine of gears and saw a crane positioning a small motorboat above the deck. The boat came lower and I watched Talya clamber aboard. She didn't look back at me.

I wondered if this would be the last time I saw her.

The crane lifted the boat off the deck and I watched it swing over the side. The crane operator had to be careful now about putting the boat into the water. If he did it at the wrong time, the boat would get swamped.

But he timed it perfectly and Talya's boat caught the top of a swell, resting there for a moment before falling away from view.

"Bye, babe."

I swallowed hard and faced the Kensei. "Thank you."

He eyed me. "She means that much to you?"

"Yes."

"She's human."

"Yes."

"What you do is illegal." He wore a smug look of self-righteousness on his face that I dearly wanted to cut off of him. As if he was anyone to give me a lecture on abiding by the law.

I smiled. "Takes one to know one, doesn't it?"

The Kensei shrugged. "I have no moral problems with my lot in life. You, however, are a tormented soul. The mighty Fixer . . . bound by laws, which even he cannot uphold. I find the irony delicious. The quandary must keep you up at night."

"What keeps me up at night is knowing the world is still full of delusional assholes like you."

The Kensei shook his head. "Is that any way to talk to me? After all, I didn't have to grant your request. And I could easily have us turn around and run over your lover's boat back there. The engines in it don't have near the amount of horsepower needed to outrun us."

"Forget about her. You want me. So let's get on with it already."

The Kensei nodded at one of his guards. The guard spoke into a radio and I heard another sound in the predawn air. Like a chain being unleashed. I thought I heard a big splash.

"We're dropping anchor," said the Kensei. "The latest weather reports indicate this storm is fading quickly. Rather than continue on our way, we'll simply drop anchor here, do battle, and then once you're dead, we'll be on our way."

"So I'm like a rest stop on the highway of life, huh?"

The Kensei sighed. "Does your sense of humor ever abandon you?"

"Not so far."

"Even in the presence of death you somehow manage to maintain it. I must say I'm somewhat impressed."

"Only somewhat?"

"It's always tough to ascertain whether it's bravery or outright stupidity that gives a man the ability to mock his situation."

"A friend of mine once told me there was no situation so bad it couldn't be made fun of."

"Is he alive still?"

I thought about him. He'd been a friend once. A timid and weak man who gave up his dreams too young. He allowed his life to be dictated by the imaginary constraints of society. In doing so, he pretty much died.

"No."

The Kensei nodded. "So his grand philosophy didn't carry him through. That's a pity."

"We're beyond that stuff now."

"Indeed."

I pointed at his waist. "You are going to give me a sword?"

The Kensei clapped his hands and I saw another guard bearing a long case. He stopped short of me and presented me with it. I bowed as I accepted it and then opened the case.

Inside, I saw the black scabbard and the braided handle of the katana. I removed the sword and handed the case back to the guard, who bowed and then left.

The Kensei had a degree of reverence in his eyes as he ran them along the length of polished steel. "That sword belonged to my brother."

I frowned. "You're kidding me."

"He never used it. His lack of height made it unwise for him to try to wield it. But it is a fine weapon, nonetheless. And one I somehow find fitting for your use here today."

I hefted it and it felt like a good sword. I slid the blade out a few inches and saw the hamon temper line. There were kanji characters near the tsuba hilt guard. I recognized a few of them.

"This sword is old."

"It is indeed."

"Amazing how they can stand the test of time."

"But we cannot," said the Kensei. "And now, it is time to see which one of us stands the test of time and steel better than the other."

I slid the blade back into the scabbard and nodded. "I'm ready."

CHAPTER THIRTY-FOUR

We were at the darkest time of night, just before the predawn light broke. When our natural circadian rhythms were at their lowest ebb. Classically, it was a great time to attack an unsuspecting enemy.

But I was feeling ready at long last. I never look forward to going into battle. It's just not something that makes me feel good. But on the other hand, I was tired of what I'd gone through to get to this point and now wanted it all over and done with.

Closure.

Maybe that's what I was looking for.

There were scores of bodies in my wake and not all of them deserved to be there. In New York City, I'd started unraveling a thread of some greater conspiracy. I'd hoped to take a vacation before I came back and chased it down to its source.

Had I found it here with the Kensei?

I didn't know.

We squared off on the deck where I'd fought Hana only a few hours before. The cage was gone now. The Kensei knew I wouldn't look to escape or get away. He knew I'd stick by my word. He'd let Talya go. The least I could do was take him on.

Sometimes my sense of honor can get me into real trouble.

I could hear the waves sloshing against the side of the ship. The Kensei had been right; the storm had seemingly dissipated into thin air. Overhead, puffy clouds still embraced the horizon, but I could sense their movement to the east. We'd be clear in a little bit and the day would most likely be sunny.

The Kensei stood about twenty feet from me. Real sword fights aren't like the way you see them in movies and TV. First of all, the distance is totally wrong. In reality, by the time you get as close as fights are staged in Hollywood, the game's already over. It's a three-foot razor blade, after all.

Nor do real sword fighters bash their carefully crafted blades together. Real *kenjutsu* is determined in the space of a few cuts, acute distancing, and a strong spirit.

I just hoped I had all three.

The Kensei bowed toward me, but he kept his head up. He didn't trust me, after all. I smiled at the thought.

And I bowed.

The air was still except for a small breeze. I heard the faintest sounds. And one that sounded louder and more ominous than all the others: the sound of the Kensei unsheathing his katana.

The blade gleamed in the dim light, catching some rays from the floodlights over the deck.

I slid my katana out of the scabbard. I was right about it being a good sword. Well-balanced. I raised it high overhead, feeling it move with my arms. A good weapon is always an extension of your body, rather than some tool you just stick in your hands.

My breathing had shallowed somewhat. I took a deep breath to flush my blood with oxygen. It had been a while since I'd had any juice, but I hoped I had enough left in me to see me through this.

The Kensei was pure vampire. I was lucky on that count. Facing another hybrid might be too much for me.

272 / JON F. MERZ

I imagined the Kensei's goal would be to decapitate me with a single stroke and then stake my heart to make sure I was dead.

Sounded like a plan to me.

"You might be wondering why we're using steel blades."

His voice almost caught me off guard. I'd have to watch that. It was the little stuff that could knock your focus out of whack and give your opponent the briefest of openings. And with a killer like the Kensei, a little opportunity was all he would need to cut me down.

"I assume they have some type of coating on them? More pine resin or something that we'll find toxic?"

He grinned at me. "Nothing so rudimentary as that. No, I've had them treated with the same toxin I've endowed my latest generation hybrids with on their claws." His eyes gleamed. "Perhaps you had a taste of that already?"

Yeah, I had back on the train. Luckily for me Kennichi knew how to neutralize it. But I wasn't kidding myself. If I got cut out here seriously, I'd die at sea.

"Let's get on with this."

He nodded and I could see him muttering something under his breath. Perhaps some type of sutra. Maybe some kind of incantation. I'd been around enough to know those things existed and could do some damage if I let them.

I said a small mantra I keep in mind for myself during times like this. "Don't fuck this up, Lawson."

He came at me in so fluid a motion I hardly had a chance to register it. I felt my body jerk out of the way as the blade hissed through the air where I'd been standing a split second earlier. How he'd managed to cover the distance in so short a period of time confused the hell out of me.

But there was nothing I could do except go with the energy and try my best to thwart his efforts.

I opened the distance up again. I didn't want him coming back with another strike and catching me across the middle. I waited with the sword held vertically by the right side of my head. The tradition I study calls it *hasso no kamae*. I called it "lop my ear off position."

The Kensei regarded me for a second. He held his sword low, pointing toward my lead foot. We circled slowly, using our feet to try to position us for the most advantageous strike.

He stabbed up at me, going straight in for a heart thrust. I stepped left and let my sword drop toward his hands. He'd been expecting that and changed his cut to arc back toward my middle. I had to change direction, step right, and let my arms fly up to avoid his blade. I whipped my left leg around and cut down diagonally at his neck.

But he spun out of the way and opened the distance back up again.

I was panting.

My heart hammered in my chest.

And we hadn't even done all that much.

"You're good."

I cocked an eyebrow. "I didn't expect a compliment from the likes of you."

He shrugged. "I can admit when I'm facing a skilled opponent. Your skills won't save you, but you should know that I respect what you're capable of."

"Uh . . . thanks. I think."

He nodded as if about to lecture a classroom on the subject. "Your Nine Demons School is an old one. Almost five hundred years, isn't it?"

I shrugged. "Kuki Shinden-ryu is old. But it's also broken into a couple of different families now. I'm not sure which one is the oldest."

"They all spawned from one point. But even the most powerful of nine demons can't protect you against my tradition."

"If you say so—"

He came at me again, raising his sword up from the ground. But this time he was aiming for my throat.

I had to vault and roll out of the way, careful of the live blade I had in my hands. Rolling with a sword is a bitch. I was lucky not to take my hands off as I did.

I got to my feet again and hesitated. The Kensei hadn't moved.

He was frowning.

Problem? I sure hoped so. I hoped he had seen something that told him I was too much for him to handle and he was going to just surrender and let me kill him and be done with it.

Yeah.

Instead he held his hand up. "We need to stop."

"Excuse me?" There was no way I was going to stop now. Not with the battle already joined. The Kensei might have been able to work himself back up after this, but I wasn't sure I was going to be able to. I needed to finish this now.

Then I heard a deep rumble from somewhere in the ship.

An explosion?

But who? What?

Before I could say anything, one of the doors leading to the deck blew open and black smoke streamed out. The ship suddenly listed.

We were sinking.

CHAPTER THIRTY-FIVE

The Kensei turned to walk away.

"We're not done here."

He looked back. "Are you mad? If we don't do something, we'll both die."

"I'm ready for that."

He frowned and then with a wave of his hand, sent two shuriken throwing stars zipping toward me. I used the sword to deflect them. They clattered away harmlessly. The Kensei sighed.

And then charged.

His sword came raining down at me. I dove out of the way. The Kensei's blade embedded itself into the deck. Splinters flew everywhere. He wrenched it free and then turned to face me again. "You're insolent. You don't deserve the honor of a proper battle."

"And just a second ago you were complimenting me. Boy, the honeymoon really ended fast, huh?"

The Kensei leapt forward to my left side and slashed horizontally. I could tell he was putting more strength into his attacks. It was almost as if he'd been toying with me before and now that his ship and cargo were in jeopardy, he was really trying to kill me.

The realization didn't make me feel any better, but I didn't have any time to dwell on it. The Kensei redoubled his attack and brought his sword high over head. I had no time to move and used the blade to block his attack, canceling out my lecture on proper *kenjutsu* I spoke of earlier.

The clang sounded like a sharp bell in the dark of predawn. I let the Kensei's energy slide down and away and then sliced horizontally at him, but he concaved his body and my blade went arcing through empty space.

I got to my feet. The deck was tilting more now and footing was difficult. I sank my knees more to compensate for the loss of balance. I noticed the Kensei was in a lower stance as well.

His eyes were black but his skin seemed to glow almost translucent. He was a freakish warp of nature, just like his brother.

But he moved much faster.

He launched another attack: a high overhead downward cut followed by a stab and then a horizontal slash. He drove me back, closer to the rail of the deck. The sea below us lurched. The waves might have sensed the ship was sinking, because they seemed frothier than they had been. Like they could taste the future and knew they'd be claiming us in a few more minutes.

I heard a deep groan from the belly of the ship.

"The engine room is taking on water," said the Kensei. "My cargo will be lost. All because of you!"

He rained another series of attacks down on me. I could feel my strength going with each successive attack. If I didn't end this soon, I'd never be able to withstand his offensive.

But how? He kept coming at me. There was no break I could discern. No moment when I could penetrate his defenses and use my blade on him. He left no opening for attack.

He came at me again. I deflected the first two attacks but only just managed to get out of the way of the third attack. I felt the sharpest sensation of pain as he cut across my rib cage on my left side. The air went copper. My mouth salivated even though it was my own juice spilling out of me.

More explosions sounded from below us. I caught sight of something out of the corner of my eye. Movement on the deck.

Gunfire.

Screams.

The Kensei didn't seem to notice, however. He was far too intent on finishing me off.

He wouldn't rest until I was dead.

My ears went hollow. Sound seemed to disappear then. I had the most unusual image in my head, one I couldn't even describe. And I heard the grandmaster's words come back to me then in that split second of time and space.

Give up to succeed.

My head swam. What did those words mean? What had I failed to interpret about them? Where was the secret in them that would enable me to survive?

The Kensei drove me back, slashing and cutting at my body. My sword moved but it wasn't going to be fast enough to keep up. I deflected his attack and my arms felt like lead. They hung almost useless at my sides.

I tasted blood in my mouth. Sweat ran down my face. My breath was shallow. Hoarse.

I was defeated.

The Kensei leaped at me again. I saw his sword arcing down toward my head as if he was prepared to split me in two. Probably he was. I don't know.

Because in that moment, my body took over. And all the words left me. I sank down on my left knee, stepped forward and in with my right leg, and shot my own sword straight up.

The Kensei's sword arced over me and beyond my body, harmlessly cutting air.

My own sword sank deep into the Kensei's chest beneath his heart.

A jet of blood erupted from the Kensei's mouth, splashing the deck behind me. I saw his kimono go darker still as more blood rushed out of his chest cavity. His body weight and energy propelled him closer to me until most of my sword was sticking out of his back.

His eyes were coal black.

I slid the blade out of him. "I hope you and your brother enjoy Hell."

I cut horizontally and the Kensei's head flopped off, rolling a short distance away on the deck. I cut a piece of wooden deck railing off and then used it to stake the Kensei's body. I felt sure the combination of the Kensei's own toxin and decapitation had done the job, but I wasn't taking any chances.

Not anymore.

The wood into his bloodstream would seal the deal.

There was a release of air or gas or something from his lungs. Then the body sank and caved in.

I dropped the sword to the deck and sank on my knees. I was trying to get some oxygen into my lungs. I needed juice. I needed to drink and replenish myself. Otherwise I was going to die.

I felt along my rib cage, knowing that the Kensei's blade had cut me and that I had the toxin in my body as well. But how much of it had gotten into me? I lifted my shirt and there was barely a red line where he'd cut me. Interestingly enough, I didn't feel bad at all.

Sound had vanished again. No more gunshots. No more screams. No more explosions.

Quiet enveloped the ship except for the occasional groan from somewhere below.

I felt a hand on my shoulder but I couldn't do a thing about it. One of the Kensei's men must have returned to finish me off. I resigned myself to my fate.

"Be quick about it."

"Lawson."

I looked up.

Talya.

I smirked. "What took you so long?"

She smiled. "You ever try climbing up the side of a freighter with only slimy rope to help you along?"

"Nope. And remind me never to try."

She helped me to my feet. "The explosion almost knocked me back into the drink."

"What caused it?"

Her eyes seemed a little sad. "Moko? Maybe he wasn't dead after all. Just unconscious."

"He sure looked dead to me."

She nodded. "Slumped over the crates down below he would have looked like a goner to anyone. But I guess he wasn't quite done yet. Seems like he got his vengeance. There's no way the Kensei will ever traffic organs again."

"I hope not."

The ship listed more. Talya grabbed me. "Time to go."

We eased our way down to the boat that was bobbing in the water. Talya helped me swim for it and we hauled ourselves aboard. I heard one final blast and the freighter went over on its side.

We watched it for a few more minutes until the water sucked it beneath its waves. The Kensei and his hybrid henchmen vanished along with Moko and all those organs.

Talya cranked the engine to life. "You know how to plot a course?"

I smiled but my eyes drooped. I tried to answer but blackness claimed me instead.

CHAPTER THIRTY-SIX

It took us just over twelve hours to get back to Tokyo. A fishing trawler plucked us out of the swirling ocean. The deckhands supplied us with enough blankets and hot tea to warm my bones through, and speeded up our trip. I still needed juice, though, so when I finally stumbled back to my hotel in Kashiwa after the four-hundred-dollar taxi ride, the first thing I did was chug a vial of the thick syrupy stuff.

Then I fell asleep.

Strangely enough, the toxin that the Kensei had managed to get into my system with that one cut didn't hurt me. Maybe I had some type of immunity to it now that I'd been close to death and fought back before. I hated to think about it, but at least if I ever ran into it again, it wouldn't be such a problem.

Sunday dawned gray and flecks of drizzle dotted the sidewalks and streets of Kashiwa as I made my way back to the subway station for the twenty-minute ride to Noda.

Fewer people were in attendance at the grandmaster's dojo this time. I met up with Henry and we trained together. I was feeling pretty crusty, but Kennichi-san had done a good job making me slightly less craptastic—at least I got to say good-bye to him this time. Plus we were wearing black uniforms so even if I bled, it wouldn't necessarily show. And I thought I'd be the only one who could smell it.

The ninety-minute class seemed to speed by. The clock on the wall kept gonging out in fifteen-minute increments, but I was almost beyond caring about it. My body felt tired but good. The techniques came easily to me this morning and Henry and I enjoyed the class.

But all good things come to an end. And with the final gong of the clock, the grandmaster clapped his hands. We lined up and bowed out. Then he turned and smiled at the room.

"Godan test."

My stomach hurt.

I grinned. After everything I'd been through. After all the pain and suffering and the friends I'd seen lost, after all of that, my stomach ached at the thought of going through the test again.

I thought about Yuki. She'd been loyal and brave and insightful. I would have enjoyed talking to her more.

I thought about Moko and how he'd been something. Not quite an ally but not quite an enemy, either. I had respect for him and how he'd chosen to die.

I saw Henry scurry up to the front of the class. The grandmaster smiled and held the bokken on his head.

"Start!"

He brought the sword up and held it there with his eyes closed, deep in intense thought. I saw creases around his eyes. The energy changed in the room and in the split second that he brought the sword down, Henry rolled out of the way. The bokken slammed into the mat where Henry's body had been just a split second previously.

Everyone clapped. I clapped. Henry looked like he was in shell shock.

"Next."

No one moved.

The grandmaster cocked an eyebrow at me. I couldn't quite tell if there was a mischievous twinkle in his eye or not. "Next?"

I took a breath and moved up to take my place. Why was I doing this? What was I trying to achieve? There'd be no shame in not taking it, would there? After everything that I'd been through since the last time, no one would look down on me if I refused the test. I could always come back and try again, couldn't I?

No.

There was a time and place for everything. Zero had taught me that a long time ago. And those lessons kept coming back to me.

It was my time.

Do or die.

Give up to succeed.

Those words again. I sat down and closed my eyes. I was determined not to move until my body took over and moved me by itself. I wasn't going to jump the gun this time. No way.

I thought about Talya.

I saw her smiling face. I saw the way the wind blew her hair and made her laugh. I felt her warmth when we touched. I smelled the delicate perfume of her hair and skin.

And then I thought about the words.

I'd give it up for her.

Everything.

No reservations.

No ego. No looking like the hero. No pride. She was the person in my life I'd give everything up for. She meant more to me than anyone else.

I'd gladly die for her.

In that second, I understood the grandmaster's words. Maybe they meant something different to someone else, but that's what they meant to me.

I smiled—

And in that miniscule moment of time and space, the world lurched as my body rolled out of the way of the descending sword.

And then I opened my eyes.

I was sitting about twelve feet away from where I'd sat down. There was tremendous applause echoing in my ears. I was facing the grandmaster. I bowed from my sitting position and he smiled, his voice solemn and proud.

"Yes."

I felt Henry's hand on my shoulder. I turned, grinning like some silly happy fool. And we shook hands.

And now I knew why Henry looked like he was in shell shock.

I was in it, too.

CHAPTER THIRTY-SEVEN

"I'd hoped we'd be able to spend some more time together."

We were sitting in a pizza joint in Kashiwa. It wasn't actually a real pizza joint, at least not the way they are back in the States, but it would have to do. I made peace with the fact that they served the pizzas on pita bread with corn kernels on them and sucked down some of my beer.

Talya laced her fingers through mine. "I would, but I've still got some loose threads to tie up on the organ trafficking thing."

I frowned. "The Kensei's dead, y'know."

She nodded. "Yeah. But he had contacts and affiliates scattered across the world. All of them eager clients awaiting their shipments."

"And you're going to pay them all a visit?" She was leaving the relative safety of where we were and striding directly into more danger.

She smiled some more. "A lady's work is never done."

"I almost pity those guys."

She frowned. "No chance. They deserve the justice they're going to get. I don't pretend to be anything other than what I am. I've got regrets in my life but I don't want to add any more on top of the pile I've already got."

I looked deeply into her eyes. "Am I one of the regrets?"

"What?" Talya looked at me. "Lawson, you're the best thing that's happened in my life in forever."

I took another drag on my beer. "I'd give it all up, you know."

"Give what up?"

I spread my arms. "This. What I am. Everything. All you have to do is name it and it's yours."

She laughed. "You're crazy."

"Not even close."

Talya bit into her second slice of bizarre pizza. "Lawson, we don't have that luxury. It's not who we are."

"Why not?"

"You're divinely chosen to be what you are. I don't know if I was, but I know I'm a good fit at what I do. I don't know if either one of us could ever have a normal life. What the hell would we do? Be accountants?"

"Ugh." I shook my head. "I hate numbers."

"Yeah, me, too. But you get my drift. How could we walk away from doing what we've done all our life?"

"I'm not saying it would be easy."

"It'd be damned near impossible and you know it. Plus, I don't know about you, but I'm not crazy about running around with a marker on my head from the vampire-governing body. I've got enough people already who want to see my imitation of a corpse."

I sighed. "Marry me."

Talya choked on her pizza. I gave her some of my beer. When she was done stuttering and coughing she looked at me with tears running down her face. I couldn't tell if it was from what I said or the choking.

"Lawson . . ."

I held up my hand. "You don't have to answer now. I'm not asking you to. I just wanted to put it out there. Give it some thought. Mull it over."

She stopped moving for a moment. "You're serious."

"Yep."

She whistled. "That must have been some test you took."

I grinned. "Let's just say it made me think about a number of areas of my life."

"I guess so."

I went back to my beer and watched Talya try to navigate more pizza. "We could have some kids."

This time she managed to keep her mouth closed. She chewed quickly. "I thought you said that was impossible."

"I thought it was."

"It's not?"

I shrugged. "The Kensei was able to make a hybrid. Why not us?"

"Uh, because I don't feel like being experimented on."

I touched her hand again. "Maybe there's no real secret to it. Maybe we just have to try."

She smirked. "At the very least, it'd be fun trying."

"True enough."

We finished the pizza and I paid the bill. As we walked out of the restaurant, Talya snuggled in close to me. "I have to tell you, you sure know how to steal a woman's breath away."

"It was the least I could do after you went to so much trouble planning this vacation. I haven't felt this rested in years."

She punched my arm. "Always the wiseass."

We stood on the walkway by the subway station. I knew what was coming but I didn't want it to.

Talya kissed me on the lips. I held her for as long as I knew I could. When we parted there were more tears in her eyes.

"It's time for me to go."

My heart hurt. "I know it." I hugged her close. "I wish I could go with you."

Her voice tickled my ear. "I used to think I worked best alone.

But I think we made a pretty awesome team this time, don't you?"

"We're awesome every time we're together, baby."

She hugged me tighter. "You know how to find me, right?"

"You gave me the new cell phone and the backup. I won't spend my nights wondering about where you are now."

She tried to smile, but it came out lopsided. "Just know I'll be bringing a little justice to my world."

"Likewise."

She kissed me again and I tasted the salt of her tears on her lips. I kissed her harder and we broke apart but hugged one last time.

"I love you."

"I love you, too, Lawson."

And then she was gone. Sucked into the swirling mass of commuters who raced around us like water around a rock in a stream. I wanted to call after her. I wanted to race after her and help her.

But that wasn't our way.

A dull purr from my jacket pocket broke the aftermath of my sudden loneliness. I plucked my cell phone out and punched the button.

"Yeah?"

"Lawson."

The trans-Pacific call came though loud and clear. "Hello, Niles."

"Just about done over there?"

"Just about. Why?"

"Because we've got trouble back here in River City, pal. Bodies. Lots of bodies. It's bad. And I can't keep the Council off our backs much longer. I need you in Boston. Pronto."

"I'm on my way."

I disconnected and took one final look at Kashiwa. The maelstrom of millions of humans completely unaware of the lone vampire in their midst suddenly reached out for me. I felt the surging pull and gave up resisting. In a moment, the crowd swallowed me up.

On my way back to Boston.

Home.

AUTHOR'S NOTE

During a trip to Japan in February 2003, I was honored and privileged to undergo the same test Lawson takes during *The Kensei*. The fifth degree black belt examination in Bujinkan Budo Taijutsu is a strange and moving experience ill-described with even the best of words. I have, however, endeavored to convey my own experiences as best I am able, so that you, too, might experience even a fraction of the wonder that Lawson and I both felt when we passed the test successfully.

Jon F. Merz, 2011

ACKNOWLEDGMENTS

I owe a big ol' debt of gratitude to those who have helped make this book a reality:

To my agent, Joe Monti, for his excellent insight and love of reading, 'riting, and publishing (third time's the charm, pal, and I couldn't be happier!); thanks for making me a better published writer.

To my editor, Daniela Rapp, for being the editor I've always dreamed of having and forcing me to bump my game up to the next level, for understanding the true nature of this project, and for making sure Lawson had a new home.

To my teacher, Mark Davis of the Boston Martial Arts Center in Allston, Massachusetts, for his guidance, support, and friendship over the last two decades. None of this would have been possible without you lighting the way along a very challenging, humbling, and winding path.

To my wife, Joyce, and my sons, Jack and Will, for their smiles, love, support, and faith through all the good times and the bad. I love you all dearly.

To my friends and brothers-in-arms for the bond forged in training and tested in the crucible of real life. Those who know, understand.

To the cast and crew of *The Fixer* television series for their hard work, dedication, and belief that Lawson should be on TV screens all over the world.

And finally . . .

To Dr. Masaaki Hatsumi, Thirty-fourth Grandmaster of Togakure-ryu Ninjutsu and head of the International Bujinkan Dojo, my sincerest and most humble thanks for nearly cleaving me in two on that drizzly cold day in February 2003. *Hontoo ni domo arigato gozaimashita!*

GLOSSARY

Aikido: Martial art of blending with an opponent's energy in order to off-balance and throw them—without causing harm to the attacker. A supposedly more "refined" derivative of aikijutsu, Morihei Ueshiba started aikido back in the 1920s based on his affiliation with the rather cultish Omoto-kyo religion.

Bokken: Wooden sword used in *kenjutsu* practice.

Bushido: "Way of the Warrior"—the code of conduct that samurai warriors traditionally followed.

Chappatsu: Hair dye used by Japanese youth that stains it a brownish tea color.

Ema: Prayer boards.

Fugu: Blowfish; a delicacy in Japan provided the chef is good enough to remove the entire poison sack containing a lethal dose of neurotoxin.

Gaijin: "Outside person," a non-Japanese person

Gassho: An expression of respect.

Giri: A complex notion of debt or obligation within Japanese society. Refers to one's position within society, the obligation to perform, or the act of doing something for someone else who is then in your debt.

Godan: Fifth degree black belt.

Gumi: Gang; used when denoting yakuza affiliations.

Hai: Yes.

Hasso no kamae: A fighting posture in *kenjutsu*.

Jujutsu: "Way of harmony"—an ancient and comprehensive system of Japanese martial arts utilizing striking, joint locks, throws, and grappling. Unlike many modern definitions, jujutsu is not properly defined as the "way of yielding," but more as a means of harmonizing with an attacker so as to defeat them. Jujutsu comes from a much older term, "yawara," which more properly denotes the actual meaning of the word. Please note that jujutsu is not the same as the modern-day mixed martial arts style of jiujitsu or jujitsu.

Juppo Sessho: Ten-directional awareness; a principle in ninjutsu suggesting that the defender ought to have the awareness and ability to affect an attacker in ten different ways from ten different directions.

Kampai: Cheers.

Kanji: Japanese writing system based on Chinese characters.

Kendo: "Way of the sword"—a sport martial art where practitioners wear bamboo armor and takes turns beating the holy bejeezuz out of each other using *shinai*. Points are scored with blows to the head, body, and hands.

Kenjutsu: "Techniques of the sword"—a martial art using the Japanese katana sword and companion shorter wakizashi sword. Together the katana and wakizashi are referred to as "dai sho" (literally big and small, referring to the lengths of the two blades).

Komban wa: Good evening.

Koppojutsu: "Bone art"—an old system of Japanese martial arts that utilizes the manipulation of an opponent's skeletal structure to produce massive damage.

Kuki Shinden-ryu: One of the nine families of Japanese martial arts that Lawson studies; the name means "secrets handed down from nine demons."

Kuso yaro: Japanese equivalent of "motherfucker."

Namae: Name.

Noda-shi: Town of Noda in Chiba Prefecture where the Grandmaster of Ninjutsu lives.

Ohayo (gozaimasu): Good morning.

Omote: Outside, outer

Rappongi: Area of Tokyo home to dance clubs and bars

Ryu(ha): Family or lineage usually associated with martial arts.

Sake: Japanese rice wine; pronounced "sah-kay" not "sah-kee."

Sandan: Third degree black belt.

Sararimen: "Salarymen"—typical 9–5 office types.

Shikin haramitsu daikomyo: Opening proclamation for ninjutsu training, meaning, "In everything we go through there exists the possibility of finding something that will lead us to enlightenment."

Shinai: A split bamboo training sword used in kendo.

Shiro-maku: Wedding kimono, usually white.

Teppo: Literally, "bullet"—used to denote low-level yakuza thugs anxious to work their way up and so willing to do anything to get there.

Tokonoma: Recessed portion of wall traditionally reserved for scrolls inside homes and restaurants.

Torii: Gates.

Ura: Inside, inner.

Yakuza: Japanese mafia.